# The *LOST BOAT*

FIVE SHORT AND THREE LONGER SHORT STORIES by some of China's neglected contemporaries, edited with an introduction by Henry Y H Zhao.

FORGET EVERYTHING YOU KNOW about contemporary Chinese fiction. These stories will shock and compel. You will learn something new about life and literature, not just 'life and literature *in China*'. The world of these writers is not without its horror and violence, but its representation is one aspect of a sophisticated, maturing artistic vision which distinguishes a new generation of young Chinese writers who will demand recognition in the West.

HENRY Y H ZHAO lectures on modern and contemporary Chinese literature at the School of Oriental and African Studies, University of London. He writes extensively on comparative and contemporary Chinese literature. He is, himself, a fiction writer, and a member of the editorial board of one of the most famous Chinese literary magazines, *Today*, founded during the late-seventies in China but, since June 1989, published in exile from Stockholm.

# The *LOST BOAT*

AVANT-GARDE
FICTION
FROM CHINA

selected & edited
with an introduction by
HENRY Y H ZHAO

*wellsweep*

First published in 1993 by
WELLSWEEP PRESS
1 Grove End House
150 Highgate Road
London NW5 1PD

Reprinted with corrections April 1994

Represented & distributed in the UK & Europe by:
PASSWORD (BOOKS) LTD
*serving independent literary publishers in the United Kingdom*
23 New Mount Street
Manchester M4 4DE

0 948454 83 0   hardback
0 948454 13 X   paperback

Caroline Mason's translation of the 'The Lost Boat' by Ge Fei will appear in the American
journal of cultural studies, *Polygraph,* published by Duke University, Durham NC.

BRITISH LIBRARY CATALOGUING-IN-PUBLICATION DATA
A catalogue record for this book is available from the British Library.

The publisher gratefully acknowledges the financial assistance of the
ARTS COUNCIL OF GREAT BRITAIN.

Designed and typeset by *Wellsweep*
Printed and bound by E & E Plumridge on recycled paper

# CONTENTS

# The *LOST BOAT*

○

# INTRODUCTION

# THE NEW WAVES IN RECENT CHINESE FICTION

## HENRY Y H ZHAO

THE YEAR 1985 marked a great turning point in modern Chinese fiction — the beginning of what Chinese critics now call the 'New Wave'. The post-Cultural Revolution era had ended and an entirely new fiction was beginning to take shape. Critics recognised a trend and gave it this rather nondescript name. Looking back, we find that this period was unlike others in the development of modern Chinese fiction. New Writing was pushed to centre stage not by cataclysmic political events but by a gradual accumulation of cultural influences.

Firstly, there was the marked cultural stratification that was settling into place around 1985. Thanks to new policies implemented over several years, most of the publishing houses, though still part of the state apparatus, were no longer subsidised by the government. They were left to sink or swim in the market place. As far back as the beginning of the 1980's, the influx of translated Western detective novels was already irritating serious scholars and readers of literature. But it was reinforced by a flood of reprinted romance and martial arts novels from Taiwan and Hong Kong. Finally a upsurge of new home-produced popular literature — romance and crime fiction — deepened the inundation. By 1985 popular reading matter and pulp magazines had all but taken over the market place for fiction.

At the same time, reportage or 'faction' (*baogao wenxue*) rose to prominence in Chinese cultural life and began to attract great attention. Topics such as the reform campaigns in rural and urban areas, sensational current events and controversial social issues were soon being dealt with as literary reportage, combining factual discussion and lively description. While most of those pieces showed full support of the official reform programme, some were more impatient. The most notable work in this genre was the script for the highly controversial and extremely influential TV mini-series *River Elegy* (*He Shang*) in 1987, a work with barely disguised political intentions, a hybrid of literature, scholarship and politics.

The emergence of these two kinds of literature severely reduced the readership of Chinese fiction. This caused a financial crisis but it also enabled Chinese fiction to eschew all the non-literary functions it had previously been forced to take on, and to free itself from social and ideological pressures. The shrunken readership also became more elitist, consisting mainly of students. By distancing itself from the immediate social need of entertainment and edification, Chinese fiction had won the right to develop in its own direction.

In 1985 Chinese literary circles were excited and bewildered by a new fiction that would have been inconceivable in previous years. This work was written by hitherto unknown and sometimes previously unpublished young writers. The successful debut of a whole generation of new writers inspired the term 'New Wave Fiction' (*Xinchao Xiaoshuo*). Authors who had enjoyed a great reputation before 1985 suddenly found themselves unable to compete with the emerging younger talents, and minor writers who had managed to publish in the huge literature market now found themselves pushed relentlessly down-market into 'pop' literature. Some critics now argue that truly modern Chinese fiction — able to hold its own in 20th century world literature — did not emerge until 1985. Yet at that time no one had any idea of the tremendous changes which were taking place except for a few young men and women writing in the new manner.

The New Wave Fiction can be roughly divided into three actual 'waves': Stray Youth Fiction (*Shiluodai Xiaoshuo*), Roots-Seeking Fiction (*Xungen Xiaoshuo*), and Avant-Garde Fiction (*Xianfeng Xiaoshuo*). However, these are not to be seen as successive stages of recent Chinese writing. The earliest representative works appeared more or less simultaneously during 1984–85. Liu Suola's *You Have No Choice* (*Ni Biewu Xuanze*), Xu Xing's 'Variations Without a Theme' ('Wu Zhuti Bianzou'), and Chen Jiangong's 'Curly' ('Juanmao') marked the inception of Stray Youth Fiction in 1985. A Cheng's *The King of Chess* (*Qi Wang*), and Han Shaogong's *Da Da Da* appeared in 1984 and 1985 respectively, launching the Roots-Seeking genre. While a few stunning pieces, such as Ma Yuan's novel *The Temptation of the Gangdisi* (*Gangdisi de Youhuo*), and Can Xue's story 'Mountain Cabin' ('Shanshang de Xiaowu') appeared in 1985, and represent the beginnings of the Avant-Garde Fiction proper.

Though these three huge breakers of New Wave Fiction rolled in at almost the same time, their waters receded separately.

Frustrated but still rebellious urban youth features in works by such writers as Liu Suola, Xu Xing, Wu Bin, Duo Duo and in certain works by Hong Feng, Chen Cun, Wang Shuo, Chen Jiangong and others. On the surface, those works appear to develop the theme of individualism already seen in the fiction during the immediate post-Mao years, especially those on the life of 'rusticated youth' (educated urban youth sent to the countryside during the Cultural Revolution for re-education). However, the two treatments take opposing stands on the issue of individuality in Chinese society. In the fiction of the immediate post-Cultural Revolution period an affirmation of individual values was strongly contrasted with the absurd extremism of collective pressures brought to bear on them by cruel political campaigns. A kind of heroism is needed for this type of social protest. In Stray Youth Fiction what we find is not so much a protest against society but a nihilistic defiance of any value system.

In his discussion of these authors, Liu Zaifu, the eminent Chinese critic, suggests that the following is their central concern. 'They no longer appeal to society, nor do they try to prove their values. They are now their own masters, seeking their own positions. Thus literature has passed from the stage of reflection to the stage of pluralistic search.'

While fully agreeing with Liu's view that these works represent something entirely new in Chinese fiction, I doubt whether there is such an optimistic and confident note in the Stray Youth Fiction, or, for that matter, in New Wave Fiction generally. On the contrary, the force of their writing lies in their negation of everything, even the significance of their own existence.

Maybe I am a ne'er-do-well, maybe.
I'm not clear what I want apart from what I've got. What am I?
What's more annoying is that I'm not waiting for anything.

This is the beginning of Xu Xing's 'Variations Without a Theme', a shocking story about the impossibility of society's embodying any values. Hong Feng's *Going to the Funeral* (*Ben Sang*) is another typical case. Travelling to attend his father's funeral (in traditional Confucian ethics, the saddest and most solemn of events), the protagonist not only finds all kinds of hypocrisy surrounding him but also the signs of his own baseness. For instance, he makes love to a former girlfriend while his father is being cremated. This is a deliberate defiance of all values, even one's own personal values. The protagonist gives up any effort to search for anything as he sees clearly that the loneliness which surrounds him is impenetrable.

These authors are of the same generation as those who wrote about the lives of rusticated youth, but in the latter there is still anger after disillusion, after the betrayal of their passionately held idealism. For the stray youth now roaming in the city streets, there is no excitement or anger. The last shred of idealism has perished.

Stray Youth Fiction seems to have reached its apogee with Liu Xihong's charming short novel *You Can't Change Me* (*Ni Buke Gaibian Wo*), Hong Feng's *Going to the Funeral*, both published in 1986, and, during 1986–87, with Wu Bin's series of novellas *City Monologue* (*Chengshi Dubai*) in 1986-87. In these works a nihilistic negation of all values is pushed to its extreme. Afterwards, it was popularised as a melodramatic theme in the hands of a writer like Wang Shuo — *Leader of the Pack* (*Wan Zhu*, 1987), *Half Fire, Half Sea Water* (*Yiban shi Huoyan, Yiban shi Haishui*, 1988) *Playing Heartbeat* (*Wan de Jiushi Xintiao*, 1988) *Whatever You Do, Don't Take Me Seriously* (*Qianwan Bie Ba Wo Dang Ren*, 1990). Wang Shuo's popularised variation on Stray Youth Fiction, with his playful virtuosity in urban slang and his indulgence in newly found sexual freedom, became a marvel of the market place in 1988 when three of his novels were filmed.

Roots-Seeking Fiction marks a more dramatic episode in the development of contemporary Chinese fiction. Around 1984 the Chinese academic world began a heated discussion on whether Confucian cultural structures were to blame for the repeated, humiliating failure of Chinese modernisation during the previous hundred years. With vigorous promotion by many gifted young writers such as A Cheng, Han Shaogong, Zheng Wanlong, Li Hangyu, Zheng Yi and others, the years 1986–87 welcomed Roots-Seeking Fiction as a new, longed-for discovery. The new school of young writers went in a number of different directions to find their roots and revitalise Chinese culture. They went 'outside' the mainstream Confucian culture to isolated pockets of minority culture still untainted by civilisation; or 'sideways', towards Daoism and other religious cultures which were frowned upon by China's various orthodoxies; or 'down', to the peasants and mountain villagers who lived by instinct rather so-called civilised norms.

For most of the Roots-Seekers, the fictional search for a solution was an unconscious manifestation of their frustration with the apparent impotence or infertility of Chinese culture. Yet this search looks rather like an escape, an escape from the social problems literature is supposed to help to solve, and an escape from the culture it is too exhausted to deal with. Such 'roots', once found and assimilated, were supposed to serve as revivifying sources of energy badly needed by a senile Chinese civilisation. This intention is clear in such works as

Zheng Wanlong's series of stories about the shamanist Oroqen hunters; or Li Rui's sequence *Stolid Earth* (*Hou Tu*) about peasants deep in the Taihang mountains; or Hong Feng's story 'The Prairie Song' ('Bo'er Jinzhi Huangyuan Muge') about a journalist's romantic encounter with a Mongolian herdswoman whose boldness in love makes a miserable contrast with his civilised manners.

With this kind of escapism, romanticism is inevitable. Mo Yan was once asked where one might find the enviably brave and shame-free men and women of his *Red Sorghum* (*Hong Gaoliang*), and his answer was revealing. 'They are nowhere to be found in China today, but they once existed, and will live in this land again.'

Nevertheless, some Roots-Seeking writers were dissatisfied with this self-delusion, and found quite the opposite of what they were looking for — a process of deterioration that inevitably befalls any society, even imaginary ones. This can be seen in such Roots-Seeking works as Zheng Wanlong's 'Yellow Smoke' ('Huangyan') and Yang Zhengguang's 'The Dry Ravine ('Gangou'). But Han Shaogong's *Da Da Da* is the most surprisingly acute criticism of any process of civilisation. The novel is a devastating exposure of some of the inveterate traits of Chinese culture — the absolute dichotomy of good and evil, and the propensity for collective cruelty. It is in fundamental contradiction with the author's stated intention that 'literature should strike its roots deep into the soil of traditional culture'. What he had actually written is a sort of uprooting fiction.

As far as the fiction itself is concerned, any chaos of theory need not be regretted, since it provides critical readers with much food for thought. The best works of Roots-Seeking Fiction are as thorough in their criticism of traditional Chinese culture as much writing from the first radical, short-lived period of Chinese modernism which accompanied the May Fourth movement from its inception in 1919. What is significant and relatively novel is the exploration itself. Whether the work is entirely successful in its search for new, mysterious cultural roots is of secondary importance.

During 1987–89 the discussion of the nature of Chinese culture was taken up seriously by other circles — by philosophers, historians, sociologists and even political activists. There arose an intellectual movement dedicated to the re-examination of Chinese culture. Other art forms, most conspicuously cinema, began to achieve sensational successes by exploiting the Roots-Seeking themes, following the path paved by the earlier fiction. Paradoxically, the widespread socio-intellectual fervour dampened the enthusiasm for Roots-Seeking fiction. It ground to a halt by the end of 1987, and many of its authors took a definite turn in a new direction, toward avant-garde experimentalism.

The development of 'Avant-Garde Fiction' proper exhibits a different trajectory. The early authors of Avant-Garde Fiction, Mo Yan, Hong Feng, Ma Yuan and the Tibetan writer Trashi Dawa, were, at first, regarded as part of the Roots-Seeking trend. In 1986, however, the newer writing distinguished itself and showed full stature with Ma Yuan's *Fabrication* (*Xugou*), Hong Feng's *Not Far from the Pole* (*Jidi zhi Ce*), and Mo Yan's *Red Locust* (*Hong Huang*).

Alongside such terms as 'Stray Youth', 'Roots-Seeking', 'Wound' and 'Reform Fiction', 'Avant-Garde Fiction' seems out of place. The others are all named after their particular themes and subjects. In fact, the name is most appropriate. As Chinese fiction developed away from an emphasis on particular themes, the emergence of Avant-Garde Fiction as a distinct genre signalled a change in the rules of the game.

During its early development from 1984–87, most of the Avant-Garde writers came from, or were based in, the more remote, marginal regions of China. Can Xue was from Hunan, Hong Feng from the North-east, and Mo Yan from the countryside of Shandong. Trashi Dawa was from Tibet, and Ma Yuan was also based there. The subject matter and exotic place names in these texts made them appear to resemble the work of the Roots-Seeking authors. Some Chinese critics concluded that modernism in China avoided the cities — perhaps because of the enormous pressures of 'reality' in the latter. Instead, the new modernism sought out the backward and lethargic life of China's marginal towns which seemed to lend itself to the 'far-out' mentality of modernism. This supposition soon proved to be premature. By the end of 1987, another generation of avant-garde writers, all new names, made a spectacular appearance: Su Tong with *The Escape of 1934* (*Yijiusansi Nian de Taowang*), Ye Zhaoyan with *The Story of the Date Tree* (*Zaoshu de Gushi*), Ge Fei with *The Lost Boat* (*Mi Zhou*) and Yu Hua with *One Kind of Reality* (*Xianshi Yizhong*).

Strangely enough, most of these authors are based in the industrially advanced Yangtze river delta — Su Tong and Ye Zhaoyan in Nanjing, Sun Ganlu and Ge Fei in Shanghai, and Yu Hua in Zhejiang. Perhaps it is no accident either that the young critics most ardently defending the Avant-Garde Fiction are also based in this area, along with the three most important literary magazines — *Harvest* (*Shouhuo*), *The Purple Mountain* (*Zhongshan*) and *Shanghai Literature* (*Shanghai Wenxue*) — to have supported Avant-Garde Fiction.

Just as it proved dangerous to draw easy conclusions from the marginal-central and rural-urban dichotomies, we must take care in concluding that the capital, Beijing, has been slow to produce an avant-garde literature. Generally speaking, Beijing intellectuals have shown greater concern for immediate social issues. At the same time that the Avant-Garde Fiction arose, a New Realist Fiction (*Xin Shishi Xiaoshuo*), much more successful with the reading public, has been being vigorously developed by Liu Heng, Liu Zhenyun and others in and around Beijing, and also by the two women writers Chi Li and Fang Fang in Wuhan.

There is a very obvious difference between the writers who established themselves before 1987 and the younger writers who emerged since. The pre-1987 authors belong more or less to the generation of the 'rusticated youth' for whom the Cultural Revolution was a nightmare destined to haunt the rest of their lives. This is obvious from, for example, Can Xue's *The Muddy Street* (*Huangni Jie*), Ma Yuan's *On the Level Up or Down* (*Shangxia Dou Hen Pingtan*), or Mo Yan's *Five Dreams* (*Wu Meng Ji*). Born in the 1960's, the younger writers are too young to remember a great deal about the Cultural Revolution which started in 1966. Even on those occasions when they write directly about the Cultural Revolution, for instance, Yu Hua in his ghastly story '1986' ('Yijiubaliu Nian'), the events of the Cultural Revolution seem to be pointing to something beyond the horrifying experience of that particular national tragedy.

The term 'avant-garde' has, itself, a temporal aspect. The avant-garde of the past may be conventional today, and today's avant-garde is likely to be old hat some time in the future. However, this is where the name can mislead us. The term, particularly as it is used to describe this group of contemporary Chinese writers, indicates a sociocultural mode of literary discourse, and/or a particular author-reader relationship. Just as the popular fiction of one hundred years ago may still be characterised as 'popular' today, so avant-garde literature may be treated as 'avant-garde' for years to come.

The current Avant-Garde Fiction is representative of the first truly avant-garde movement in Chinese literary history. Although in the 1930's and 1940's there were small groups of avant-garde poets, Chinese fiction writing was never inclined towards avant-garde experimentalism. Until the rise of the recent so-called Avant-Garde Fiction, Chinese fiction had always centred on particular themes, and has tend towards the didactic, aiming to send a message by way of the text. The thematic intention might be utilitarian (Revolutionary Literature of the 1930's, Reform Fiction of the 1980's), propagandist (Praise Fiction of 1950–78), reflective (Wound Fiction of early 1980's), critical (Stray Youth Fiction), consolatory or reflective (Roots-Seeking Fiction). We might even say that all modern Chinese writers before the Avant-Garde Fiction, despite wide-ranging differences, used a variety of means to persuade the reader to accept a 'correct' interpretation of the literary text, and, consequently, of the world. The desire for the reader to share common assumptions is the aim of all these writers, although the degree of the exertion is different with different periods and groups. There is a prescriptive overkill in all high Communist Chinese literature (post-Yan'an when Mao Zedong in 1942 set out the guidelines for true revolutionary writing and also the subsequent Praise Literature) which categorically refuses the reader's right to individual interpretation, whilst the May Fourth and most New Wave Fiction allows the readers some room for alternative interpretative positions. We must remember that Chinese readers have long been taught to take note of the intentional context of any piece of writing. It has become natural for them to seek out and adopt the intended, prescribed or recommended interpretation.

In sharp contrast, Avant-Garde Fiction deliberately denies the reader any clue to a 'correct' interpretation. Part of its charm, especially for Chinese readers, lies in the play between the titillating possibility of intentional significance and the lack of reliable guidance as to a 'real' meaning. We may say that any 'real' meaning of these narrative texts lies not simply in their content but also in the formal features of their narrative structures and strategies.

With the inception of the New Wave, Chinese fiction has finally returned to the point where modern Chinese fiction set out, to the fiction of the May Fourth period. Once again Chinese literature is strongly influenced by the discourse of an elite, with a strong countercultural aspect, a sharp critique of mainstream culture which nonetheless refuses to provide solutions for political or social problems. This literature serves as a corrosive, attacking the hard crust of the dominant culture.

The New Wave Fiction has also returned enthusiastically to the formal experimentalism of the May Fourth movement. In the fifty years before the Avant-Garde Fiction arose, few Chinese authors made any further experiments in narrative form. This rediscovery of formal experimentation has highlighted the purely literary values of the New Wave Fiction and helped to make it worthy of the attention of students and general readers throughout the world.

There is as yet no let up in the flow of Avant-Garde Fiction works; it now seems to be widening into a flood and fanning out over a wide area. New authors such as Bei Cun, Yao Fei, Zhao Botao, Ye Shuming, Yue Ling, Yang Zhengguang and many others are joining in. Even the disastrous political tragedy of June 4th 1989 has done little to slow down the trend.

It is easy for western readers and critics to assume that the latest Chinese avant-gardism is yet another import from the West, like Coca-Cola and Discos. Some comments of this sort have already been made. I would urge western critics to take a fresh look at the evidence with an open mind. Certain influences must be acknowledged, such as that of Latin American fiction, especially Gabriel García Márquez, on Roots-Seeking Fiction; J. D. Salinger's *Catcher in the Rye* was widely read and admired by Stray Youth Fiction writers, and a number of Borges' short stories have been influential since their translation into Chinese. Yet none of these influences can fully account for Chinese New Wave Fiction which, as I have tried however briefly to show, is the product of recent developments in Chinese cultural life, and the uncomfortable attempt to accommodate long-lived Chinese literary traditions in a modern and rapidly changing world. I am sure that the translations in this collection will surprise readers in the West, who will realise that, far from being imitations of one kind or another, these stories and short novellas are quintessentially Chinese, and could only be Chinese.

The selection was made with a view to offering in English some of the best Chinese New Wave Fiction. For this reason, literary value has been our primary consideration. There have been a number of compilations of contemporary Chinese writings. Regrettably, most scholars of contemporary Chinese literature still regard the work of Chinese writers as interesting chiefly for their sociological or political content. The very titles of these books (*Mao's Harvest, Stubborn Weeds, Seeds of Fire*, amongst others) reveal the underlying intention of the selections. While it is clear that contemporary Chinese literature has a sociological significance, it would be a shame if it were only ever read in this light. It would be particularly inappropriate when, as I have tried to show in this introduction, a whole generation of Chinese writers have outgrown and set out to put behind them an overtly political or sociological mode of fictional discourse.

One purpose of this compilation is, then, to compensate for this tendency, to give readers a chance to see for themselves the literary qualities of some of the best recent New Wave Fiction. Examples of

Stray Youth and Roots-Seeking Fiction have already been translated elsewhere for their sociological content. This selection will provide two further stories which fall into my categorisation of Stray Youth Fiction, and three which I consider fine examples of Roots-Seeking. But the main part of the book will be devoted to three short novellas which are, in my view, landmarks of the nascent Avant-Garde Fiction. It is my hope that this book will give some indication of the great and important changes taking place in the world of contemporary Chinese literature. I hope that it will demonstrate the unique contribution which Chinese writers are now making to twentieth century world literature, and that it will convince western readers and critics that if they continue to ignore this new literature, it will be their loss.

# The
# *LOST*
# *BOAT*

o

# SHORT
# STORIES

# THE BRAKE-STONE

## LI RUI

HIS EYES WERE FIXED on the red flower-patterned scarf knotted at the back of the other man's head, staring, staring. The red flowers seemed to leap upwards — burning flames licking his heart — and a sharp pain made him gasp for air. A huge gong filled his head and somebody was pounding it, boom, boom. Golden stars danced. The large flowers blossomed into a red mist that filled the whole sky ...

'Fuck all your ten thousand ancestors!'

Moisture dropped from the red mist, trickling into the corner of his mouth. It was salty.

The brake rope he had wound around his wrist suddenly flexed. He staggered, and then, with a thump, fell onto the hard mountain track like a stuffed stack. Wrapped in a sheepskin coat turned inside out, he looked like a mass of dirty black wool writhing on the ground, like some dead animal being dragged along by the rope. In the cart, the woman, sitting on top of the lime heap, screamed, panic-stricken.

'My husband!'

Rocks and stones tore ruthlessly at his flesh like knives or saws.

'Screw your mother sideways. Drag me to my death? Fine! Death'll save everyone a lot of trouble!'

The thought of his imminent death flashed across his mind and tightened all his muscles. He braced his legs, and his body arched backwards. But the cart had been slipping too fast, there was no way he could stop it, his whole body was once more dragged forward. The black mass of wool, covered in dust, shuddered grotesquely. His two cloth shoes rolled onto the roadside, one in front, and one behind him.

In the midst of this turmoil, the driver, who was sitting in the front and wielding a whip, suddenly pulled on the hand brake and screaming hysterically, hauled back fiercely on the reins. With great difficulty, he stopped the cart half way down the steep slope. The shaft-mules spat white froth, and with hind legs bending up into their bellies, they fought with all their strength to resist the weight that came crushing down on them. The driver, overcome with rage, reined in furiously. He turned his head, and spat obscene curses at his helper,

'You motherfucking imbecile, have you never pulled a brake before? Do you think it's a joke to slide down on a narrow track like this? Aren't your wife and kid on this cart? Fuck you and your woman! What was the matter? Did you see the devil?'

The black mass of wool on the ground staggered to its feet and then walked back to put on its shoes. Without uttering a word the brake man returned to his seat and again wound the brake rope tightly around his wrist. The driver roared,

'Hold on to it!'

He relaxed the hand brake, eased off the reins, and cracking the tip of his whip in front of the shaft-mules, shouted in a more amiable voice,

'Walk on, red mule.'

The cart shook again, one of the rubber tyres pressed on the sharp angle of a protruding stone, and gave out a muffled groan. The cart crashed forward again with a loud thump, sending up a cloud of stifling, white dust. The driver's voice was pained, as if he had felt the wounding of the rubber wheel.

'Oh, no — my poor little wheel!'

The floral scarf tied behind the back of the head began to jog from side to side. From where the brakeman sat only the patch of red bobbing up and down and the dazzling white mountain track were visible.

Along the winding mountain track, they were accompanied by a dizzy precipice, sometimes on their right, sometimes on their left. White waves tumbled at the foot of the steep precipice, but their sound, as they travelled high above seemed very distant, as if from another world. The driver had been too greedy. His cart was completely overloaded with lime. After making good use of the running boards, he had still piled the goods high above its sides so that they formed a little hillock on top of the cart. A worn out shoulder bag covered the top of the hillock and on it sat the young wife in a coloured dress, swaying to and fro. A baby was sucking at her breast. As the cart swayed, one caught glimpses of soft, white belly under her closely fitting dress. Yet only the night before, this white belly had been caressed by a man other than her husband ...

'Fuck all your ten thousand ancestors! They're all useless, useless. Every one of them!'

The gong in his head was still booming. The mist in front of his eyes rose up again. No gun to hand. If only there had been a gun, that head bound up in flowers would have been blown to pieces long ago!

'Bloody useless! You and your ten thousand ancestors!'

Seeing the murder in her husband's grim eyes, the woman on the cart felt that the end of the world had come. A chill wind of despair gripped her. Not knowing what to do, she held the baby tighter and tighter in her arms — the son for whose life she had damned herself. Had she known her husband would feel this way, she would have preferred to die resisting the night before. Men were animals!

He felt himself shivering, the mist in front of his eyes had cleared, and the back of the head in the floral scarf appeared again. It was that very scarf that the bastard had worn last night, in that small room in the inn to the east of the town ...

After the drinking, both men's faces had turned the colour of raw liver. The liquor had been too strong for the brakeman, his head was spinning. His wife had stood on one side urging their benefactor to drink more.

'Elder brother, have another drink. If it were not for that eighty *yuan* of yours, they would have kept our baby in the hospital. We owed them the money. How can we thank you enough!'

'Well, maybe there is a way ...'

The man had taken the cup from her hand and sniggered. He had taken off the scarf and shoved it into her dress. The woman's soft breasts had felt his burning fist.

Some time before all this their son had fallen ill and had to be taken to the hospital. The brakeman's wife also had to stay in the hospital to keep the boy company. A month and a half later, when they failed to pay their bill, the hospital wouldn't let them go. The brakeman had been furious, stamping and bellowing at the gate. Then came the life-saving eighty *yuan*. Finally the driver had become bolder and more authoritarian in the way he ordered him around.

'Go and feed the mules. Go to the well and fetch more water for later. Then go into town and get me a packet of cigarettes.'

Dazed from drink, he had obeyed, but was able only to do the things slowly, one after the other. By the time he returned with the cigarettes, the door of the small room was bolted. That was the moment when the big copper gong started pounding in his head. He had been stupefied by the shock — wanted to smash the door in — but he was afraid of losing face. All of a sudden he remembered the smile on the man's face as he sent him away on the errands. It was the same smile as when he gave them the money. All year round he had to follow this bugger carrying goods in his cart. Every minute of the day he was under his control. Now they were even more indebted to him for the eighty *yuan*. The realisation of what was going on made his legs give way. He squatted down on his heels against the wall. Separated only by thin window paper, noises came from inside the room. It had not been hard to imagine all the details. The big copper gong in his head struck continuously. Boom! Boom!

He did not know how long it had lasted.

When the driver came out he was wearing this very same scarf on his head. Seeing the brakeman, the driver had looked momentarily taken aback, then he smiled and tossed a few words over his shoulder,

'I'll sleep somewhere else. You look after the animals tonight. As for the money, forget about it. It doesn't matter whether you pay it back or not.'

With that, he left.

The power of the drink was overwhelming; his head was more clouded than ever. He stumbled into the room, stripped his woman naked, and, after beating her, finally threw himself on her hungrily.

Under the blazing sun the road was steep and long and so white that it dazzled the eyes. He felt he was losing control of himself. All he wanted to do was to kill, to see blood — no gun, but there were stones!

'You and your ten thousand ancestors! A man must do what he has to do! If I don't butcher this bastard, I'll be the one who's useless!'

The road was too short. Soon only half of the sixty mile journey was left. He had no gun, no stones, no opportunity, and apparently, not enough courage. The huge head wrapped in the floral scarf, and the chin cut square as if by an axe — he could picture all of it without the head turning round. The broad frame of the man wrapped in his sheepskin vest, the red-tasselled whip flourished threateningly over the shoulders. Confident, majestic, arrogant, he had always been in full command — in command of the four mules, the cart and of the brakeman himself. He heard again the sounds that had come from the room while he squatted against the wall. That great copper gong sounded once more, boom! Water gushed out from the red mist, hot and salty.

'Screw your ten thousand ancestors!'

The whitish track led up to the sky. The rubber-tyred wheels reached the most dangerous slope on the whole sixty mile journey. The Leopard Ridge, like an insidious, whoring lecher, seemed to sneer down on him. The mules lowered their heads and arched their backs, their hooves struggled with difficulty. Lumps of sandstone, crushed by their hooves, flew off in all directions. The driver held the brake with one hand and with the other, he lashed the whip with sharp cracks.

The cruel tip struck closer and closer to those long swaying ears. The obscenities poured out.

'You bastard sons of fucking donkeys. Don't give up now! Greyhead, don't you dare play tricks on me now. Blackie, up, up! Up! Brakeman, look out! Oh, go to hell, you bastard!'

The woman, rocking from side to side on the top of the cart, glanced fearfully downward into the dark abyss, and all her muscles stiffened. With one hand she hung tightly onto a thick rope. The sound of the river water roaring at the bottom of the abyss drifted up to them as if to raise the spirits of the dead.

Climbing along the very edge of the precipice, the cart and the mules, the bodies and souls, all seemed to be hanging onto fragile reins that were ready to snap.

'Papa ...'

The woman called out in a helpless moan. No answer. Her words were like gossamer floating from her lips.

An eagle flew overhead. In the blue sky its keen eyes caught sight of the group struggling on the cliff like ants with loads on their backs. All of a sudden, the group, in its struggle, shook with a spasm, and then, a desperate pause, a cry of panic.

'The cart's slipping! The brake! The brake!'

Instinctively the brakeman sprang up with clenched teeth, jumped to the side of the cart, and dragged the brake rope desperately towards his chest. Immediately, the brake lever bit fiercely into the axle. The axle grease caught fire and there was a deafening, thunderous noise. But the hillock of lime piled up by the greedy driver was too heavy, and the slope too steep. The four mules and the four humans were dragged on, sliding towards the edge of the precipice.

In despair, the driver shouted out,

'Brake-stone! Find a brake-stone! Quick!'

In a flash, without thinking, the brakeman tied the rope to an iron hook, dashed to the roadside and lifted up a big piece of stone the size of a pillow. At this very moment he saw the driver pulled down, his clothes caught on the handle of the brake lever; his body was dangling in mid air, struggling in vain, sliding rapidly forward and bumping from side to side. It seemed he was just about to be caught up under the iron hooves, then buried at the bottom of the precipice together with his cartload of lime. A cruel sneer appeared on the face of the brakeman.

'You and your ten thousand ancestors! This is Heaven's retribution!
Slide down, down! I don't care if I go down with you! It wouldn't
bother me!'

'Papa, find a brake-stone!'

The woman screamed for help, not realising that she should jump
off the cart.

'Screw your mother, you useless bastard!'

The brake lever and the axle were grinding, the whole cart was
groaning as if in bone-cracking and muscle-tearing agony. Suddenly
from the top of the cart came the high-pitched cry of the child. The
brakeman dashed to the rubber wheels, electrified. A crash. From the
edge of the precipice a cloud of white cloud of dust rose up mist. Then
everything came to a halt. After a while a man, covered in dust and
with blood dripping from his forehead struggled out from the middle
of the white cloud. The dust-covered man dashed to the head of the
shafts, and dragged his enemy out from under them, and shouting:

'You and your ten thousand ancestors! I should have let you fall to
the bottom of the precipice! I should have chucked you down myself.'

A rock loosened by the wheel started to roll slowly, slowly towards
the cliff edge, swaying from side to side as if unable to let itself go.
Then it plummeted down. In that instant, there was blue flash from
the very bottom of the precipice.

That evening, in front of the stable, after they had unhitched the
draught animals from the cart, the floral scarf whispered in the man's
ear, 'Late tonight, come to my home. I'll leave the door unbolted.'

The brakeman stared at him, uncomprehending.

The floral scarf laughed, 'Don't you still want to get your own back
on me? We've gone through a life and death experience together. No
reason that a woman should come between us. Tonight I am going to
let you get even.'

Now he understood. His heart beat violently.

In the deep quiet of the night, he went. Sure enough the door had
been left unbolted for him. Satisfied, he walked out of the room. The
floral scarf was squatting, his heels against the wall in exactly the same
manner as he himself had done the night before. He was momentarily
taken aback, then he smiled and tossed the words toward him, crisp
and loud, 'As for the money, I'll return it to you!'

He got home, his wife came to open the door with only a thin dress
over her shoulder. Desire welled up in him. Without explanation, he
pushed his woman towards the bed. The woman, tender and passive,
submitted to him silently. She could see clearly that the murderous

impulse was gone. The man had become once more the husband she knew.

In the dark, on the bed, two white shadows moved rhythmically together.

The moon had set. In the sky there were many stars.

# MISTAKES

## MA YUAN

### 1

THESE TWO KIDS, one had a mother and no father, and the other neither mother nor father. It wasn't that the father of the one with the mother had died, but that the mother didn't say who the father was — and the father himself didn't have the courage to own up. Thirty or so men were suspect, all except me. I knew I wasn't the father, so I can say as much. I'm bringing these old things into the open now simply to be able to write some kind of a story. The whole thing happened over ten years ago, in another world, so to speak. The two kids appeared on the same night.

I really can't stand using flashbacks. Why should I be obliged to start my story with 'at that time'? I don't know either the origins or the consequences of this affair; I don't even know if the two boys are still alive. If they are, they'll be old enough to cruise for girls and go disco dancing. About seventeen years of age, I figure.

That night something else happened. My army cap disappeared. Lost! Lost, so suddenly and in such a strange way.

You'll have to bear with me for a moment as I tell you about the place where we were living.

There were sixteen of us living in one huge room, with two of those large heated brick beds like you find in the countryside in the Northeast. The beds were facing each other, with a passage running between. There were eight people to a bed, divided up into different territories by a few meagre suitcases. Farty Zhao and I slept at the end farthest from the door. Our belongings lay side by side, with the cases on the outside. There was no electricity there, and if you wanted to do something in the evenings you had to fork out for candles. So someone just took his chance.

Thirteen lay down to sleep, so there were three to go. I was one, then there was Farty Zhao, and another called Doggy, who stopped at nothing with his light fingers and quick feet. He'd gone out. Farty Zhao and I were best mates, and every evening we'd have half an hour of wrestling before turning in. He'd had professional coaching and was

29

the number one champion for forty miles around. He'd been teaching me for a year. So you wouldn't imagine that anyone would dare to take my cap, and I left it on my case. We were just out in front of the building on a stretch of bare, chalky ground for an hour, and when we came back the cap had gone.

Just like that.

At the time army caps were all the rage. That was 1970 or maybe '69, I can't remember now. On the outskirts of Jinzhou, it cost you at least five *yuan* on the black market to buy an army cap, the equivalent in those days of five pounds of fresh, fat pork. The most important thing was that it was a symbol that a young lad could stand his ground in society. There was a craze at the time for nicking caps, and you were always hearing tales of someone killing for them. They weren't wild rumours either. That's how I lost my cap.

My priceless cap was simply lifted. What's more, those two kids were born that very evening. And with those two marvels to think about, everyone soon forgot about my little problem. The kid with the mother was Jiang Mei's. Jiang Mei and me and many others had all arrived on the same truck, and privately she was the woman I cared about most. I was probably the only one who really took it seriously when she was pregnant.

She was the first woman to have a baby on the youth farm. She didn't go to hospital. Afterwards, the question of who'd got her pregnant crossed my mind more than once, though naturally I'd no answer. She didn't even look at me; suddenly turned cold towards me. Being a woman, there's no way she wouldn't notice a man's attentions. And me such a tall strong man too, even if I was only nineteen at the time. We'd been in the same class from nursery right through to middle school. It was that strange night that Jiang Mei bore a son.

2

FARTY ZHAO SAID HE THOUGHT he'd seen Doggy come back to the building, but when we asked the thirteen who'd been in bed they all said they'd been asleep and didn't know anything about it. It's at times like these that no one'll volunteer to be a witness. Doggy swore he hadn't been back — though he wouldn't say where he'd been, or who could back him up. It was only later that I learnt why he wouldn't say. It would have cleared him from suspicion then and there if he had said. But if I were in his place I wouldn't have said anything either. No way. The problem was the cap.

I've a bit more to say about the cap. It'd been brand new the year before, and when I got it I vowed to wear it till the end of my days. I'd bitten my finger and signed my name in blood on the inside. For a whole year the cap had barely left my head, and everyone knew that cap was my life. I thought the whole farm knew that I'd tear anyone limb from limb to defend that cap. You can imagine how new it looked when I'd been wearing it for a year.

The whole problem was the signature in blood. But more of that later.

After our careful search had failed, Farty Zhao and I decided to wake up everyone in the dorm. I went up to each of the thirteen who were fast asleep and shook their heads.

'Hey, get up.'
'Hey, get up.'
'Hey, get up.'
'Hey, get up.'
'Hey, get up.'
'Hey, get up.'
'Hey, get up.'
'Hey, get up.'
'Hey, get up.'
'Hey, get up.'
'Hey, get up.'
'Hey, get up.'
'Hey, get up.'

It was about seven minutes before they were all up.

I was standing in the door frame, my body blocking the way out. Zhao's face had darkened and he was sitting on the edge of the bed nearest the door. I began to speak:

'Sorry about this, brothers, but my cap's gone. During the past hour, Farty and I were just outside for a short time, and we would've seen anyone who'd come into the building. I'd like to ask first off if anyone's taken it by mistake? A mistake's a mistake, and if there's been a mistake there's still time to hand it back. Has anyone taken it by mistake?'

I was prepared to give someone the benefit of the doubt at first, and had decided to wait for one minute. But Farty Zhao wasn't going to wait, 'Fuck this! If you've got it, get it out quick, or there'll be trouble.'

I waited for a minute then said, 'I'm sorry, but I'm going to have to ask you to open your cases ...'

31

Black Date cut me short. 'If you want to go through the cases, it's all right with me, but what if you don't find anything?'

'Whoever's got the cap in his case can answer for himself, and if it's not there, then I'll have to answer to whoever. You can do what you like, I don't care.'

Black Date said, 'As long as you keep your word. Got that everybody?'

Of course everyone had understood, but no one said anything. They weren't looking for trouble. All thirteen battered cases were open in a flash. They were all beat up, you couldn't hide anything in them if you wanted to. Naturally my army cap wasn't in any of them.

It was at this moment that I realised the wretchedness of our situation; none of us had a thing to call our own. I didn't see anything worth five *yuan*; no clothes or anything. It made me even more determined to get my cap back. Maybe I had a few worries about what Black Date might do, but I certainly wasn't afraid of him.

I knew he wasn't the sort to put up with things like this.

Something was going to happen, and I resolved to see it through to the end, even if I was wrong — I began to go through all their belongings. I was offending everyone. I knew even before I started looking that I wasn't going to find the cap, and I couldn't imagine how I was going to make up for it afterwards. But everything has to come to an end sometime, and I was waiting for the end.

Most of them kept quiet, and showed no sign of resentment or disgust. They didn't want to have anything to do with what was happening. Except for Black Date and Farty Zhao. Zhao was sitting there quietly waiting for the outcome, while Black Date had his hands hooked round the top of the door frame and was doing pull-ups. Black Date was a wiry man with guts and great strength, who rarely said anything much, but more than made up for it in other ways.

I felt my heart begin to pound.

I was hoping for a miracle, though I was the last person to believe in miracles. But I was still hoping. There was no miracle. I'd been through all the stuff. Except for Doggy's. He wasn't there.

Just when I was wondering whether or not to go through the Dog's things someone came running over from the girl's dorm saying that Jiang Mei was having her baby.

3

I DOUBT IF ANYONE FELT WORSE than I did about Jiang Mei having the baby. We'd all watched as her belly grew bigger day by day, yet I hadn't really prepared myself to face the consequences of her pregnancy. All I could think about was that she'd been screwed; someone had got her pregnant, and that it hadn't been me. That was all I could think about.

And now it was on its way. It was then that I had this funny feeling that something was missing, absolutely and completely missing. I forgot all about my own real loss, and can't remember how I was swept along with the crowd over to the girls' dorm. There were a hundred and twenty of us at that door, and there wasn't a sound to be heard.

The baby had been born, and someone in front of me said it was a boy. It meant that none of us men had anything to avoid any more. Jiang Mei lay wrapped up in her quilt on the warm bed, with a patterned hand towel round her head. The little bastard who'd arrived only minutes ago was wrapped in another towel, curled up close to her side. I couldn't help looking through the bedside window at the fire raging inside. I wondered who'd have been able to gather so much firewood in such a short time. Firewood was something that was most lacking in that place. You don't get much firewood on chalky land.

If I'm not mistaken, it was June.

From then on the little creature became a son to the whole farm. He was lovely, and I have to admit that I was fond of the little bastard. All the men would say, 'Come to Daddy'. And he would go to every one of them. All the men would say 'Call me Daddy', and he would make them all happy, by calling them Daddy, which was what they wanted to hear. But more of that later.

Jiang Mei died not long afterwards, or so I heard. When I'd gone back to Jinzhou, she stayed on at the farm, and I heard that she killed herself in the end. But more of that later.

That night she had so many presents. I think all one hundred and twenty people on the farm gave her something. Mostly tins and jars of food, and some new towels and scented soaps and so on from the girls. The average age of the Sent-down Youth on the farm was twenty at that time. It was increased slightly by the accountant Tian who was of Poor Peasant birth, and the storehouse keeper Li of Lower Middle Peasant background. They were in their fifties, and this raised the average by nearly a year. I didn't give anything because I hated that little bastard and I hated her as a result.

Another reason I didn't give anything was because on my lonely way back to our dorm, I was seized once more by grief over losing the army cap. And I knew there was something else coming. Soon, the others would all be back, with Black Date.

'If you want to go through the cases, it's all right with me, but what if you don't find anything?'

These words have been with me nearly twenty years. I'm not such a coward that I cower at a threat, and the words of this threat themselves seemly hardly threatening.

Black Date was scared of no one. And me? Me neither. Especially with Farty Zhao on my side. I didn't think Black Date had anyone on his side. The facts of the matter (as the facts emerged) proved me right.

Everyone made their way back; the last was Black Date. Farty Zhao didn't return. He never came back. I don't believe he died; he must have had something that he needed to do. Anyway he disappeared.

When Black Date did come in he was holding a long handled spade. He looked listless as he came in, as though there was nothing in particular on his mind. He didn't look up, didn't look at anyone, just squatted in front of the door patiently moving the nail that held the spade to the handle backwards and forwards. The others thought there was nothing more to come, began to put their things away and went back to bed. I was sitting in my place, watching Black Date from the corner of my eye.

He seemed to be quite calm, not at all hurried. He moved the nail to and fro slowly, until he could pull it out. Then pulling against the door step he tore off the head of the spade.

I knew the action was about to start. I can't remember the details as it was so long ago. I ended up getting my ankle smashed to pieces by the wooden handle, and was lame for life.

I remember telling Black Date word by word how I was going to rip his tendon from his leg. I remember Black Date smiling without a care in the world. He wasn't a deceitful enemy — he was a man. He'd kind of warned me before he made his move, and given the five feet of hard, wooden handle such a forceful swing. I'd tried to block it with my arm, but I didn't have time, and just as the handle was heading for my waist, his target suddenly shifted, and he hit me, smack, way down on the leg.

It was too far to go to hospital. They'd sent for a local witch doctor to look after my wounded leg. He used bone powder from black-boned-chickens in his medicine, or so they said. His recipes were secret. He was a hundred and seven when he died, they said. He was also the one who treated Black Date.

4

I'VE LEFT THE MOST WRETCHED part of the story to the last, my original thought was to whet the reader's appetite, and another reason is that I'm hesitant. I don't know if it's really appropriate to go on. It's even more wretched, as I've said. Yet I can't judge it from the point of view of original sin or morality, can I?

Shall I go on? If so, how?

These are all tricky questions that I'll deal with later. I believe that when it comes to the crunch problems just sort themselves out. For the time being I'm not going to worry myself more than I have to.

When I said I was going to rip open Black Date's legs, that was after the event, because at the time I was stretched out in front of the door, and the story of that night seemed to have come to an end.

The attentive reader will point out straight away that the story is not over yet, and that at the beginning I'd said there were two boys. True, it's not over. The second boy hasn't appeared yet. He will though, and soon.

But there was someone who appeared before him, who didn't appear earlier on in my story: Doggy.

Doggy crept in like a ghost, first moving around Black Date and then around me. I was in a terrible state, having just suffered under the stick, and I didn't look at him properly. He went over to his place and for about three minutes didn't make a sound. I was finished. No one gave a damn about me, they were all asleep (or pretending to be).

Three minutes later I was shocked (as, of course, was Black Date) by the first sound from that quarter. A baby crying! And from where Doggy was sitting!

My first thought was that he'd taken Jiang Mei's baby. The second was that it was his bastard. Without thinking, I said, 'Will he survive, if you take him away so soon?'

'Don't know. I'll give it a try.' Doggy hadn't looked up.

'And Jiang Mei let you?'

'Jiang Mei? What's it to do with her?'

'Well, that's odd. Nothing to do with her? And she let you take it?'

As I spoke, Black Date was already making his way over towards the baby, and was looking at it just like Doggy. Then Black Date suddenly spoke, and asked Doggy whose cap it was. Doggy muttered something, but didn't answer him. Black Date looked at me.

'Have a look and see if it's yours.' Then he looked back at Doggy. 'Put the baby on the quilt.' When he saw Doggy's face fall, he spoke even more viciously, 'Are you going to put it there or not?'

Doggy hesitated. 'The quilt's cold. Could you help me look for some firewood to warm the brick bed?'

Without saying anything, Black Date took the baby and put it on the quilt. It started wailing. Black Date threw the cap that Doggy had wrapped the baby in at my feet. 'See if it's yours.'

I said, 'From the way you were speaking, Doggy, this one isn't Jiang Mei's.'

Black Date said, 'Hey, see if it's yours.'

Doggy said, 'You mean Jiang Mei's had one as well?'

I said, 'Didn't you know, Jiang Mei had a baby boy tonight?'

Black Date said, 'If you're not fucking going to see if it's yours, then I don't give a shit any more.'

Doggy said, 'When?'

I said, 'Strange how the whole farm was all excited and you don't know about it. So whose is it?'

Doggy said, 'I'd just gone out ...'

I said, 'Whose? Whose is it?'

Doggy was quiet, then said firmly, 'I found it.'

'Found it? Where?'

Doggy wouldn't say any more. Then I realised where we were, and saw the blood soaked army cap Black Date had thrown at my feet.

My face must have gone white.

Doggy had only just noticed I'd been hurt, and walked over and quietly asked what had happened, at the same time squatting down and lifting up the bottom of my trousers. What he saw made him scream.

To see that awful blackened and swollen ankle already thicker than my calf would have made anyone cry out.

His shriek woke the others, and the twelve shot up from their sleep. Some jumped straight out of bed, complete with bare bottoms, and there was a crowd around me.

Even now I still don't know why I got angry, really angry, and yelled at everyone viciously, 'Just fuck off, all of you.' So they fucked off, as their friendly concern was obviously doing no one any good.

Only Doggy was still there at my feet. That was what I wanted.

5

THE ARMY CAP WAS NEITHER OLD nor new anymore. The stench of sticky blood went straight to my nose. The cap was completely drenched in blood, yet I could still tell it was mine. I had another close look at the inside, but my signature in blood had been soaked in so much new blood that there was no longer any trace of it.

I said nothing. I gripped him by the collar and kicked him right in the groin with my good leg. He fell straight over, rolling and howling on the ground like a lunatic.

The others jumped to their feet again. I remember people kept on coming until it seemed that the whole farm was gathered at our door. I don't remember much as I was soon delirious. I lost consciousness for a while, but I'm sure I wasn't in a coma.

Later I learned that the farm had ordered a cart and horse, and sent Doggy back home to Jinzhou that night. Lots of people accompanied him all the way there.

Doggy had to rest at home for three months, but he was, nonetheless, disabled. This wasn't my fault. He'd asked for it. He'd never be able to find a wife and give her children now, and it was retribution for all the stealing he had done.

If it hadn't been me, someone else would have done it. I'm sure of that. This reminds me of an old saying: There are three types of unfilial behaviour, and the worst is to have no descendants.

Later I went to see him, and neither of us mentioned that night. He didn't come back to the farm. He recovered his city residence and worked making wire netting at a small community factory.

Later on he got cancer, of the rectum. He had bad luck, and was twenty-three when he died. Over ten years have passed since then. In the short time before he died we became friends. But there was always some distance between us. We were not the sort of friends who share every secret. There was always a barrier. That year, the year when the incident happened, he was eighteen.

6

JUST NOW I FORGOT to mention a rather crucial detail, that before Doggy was lifted on to the cart, he yelled out to me, 'Farty Zhao told me to tell you he's gone, and he won't be coming back.'

I yelled back, 'Why? Did he say why?'

'No. He just told me to tell you. He also said to tell you to look after Jiang Mei and the baby.'

'Which one? Which baby?'

Then he was up on the cart. He didn't answer, perhaps because he didn't hear me. We didn't see each other for another six months.

## 7

SO THERE WERE TWO KIDS. Jiang Mei fed them both. It was good that they had so many fathers. When there are thirty daddies looking after two sons, it's not such a hard job.

I got things straight in my mind afterwards. Jiang Mei had had a baby; Farty Zhao had gone. He said I was to look after Jiang Mei and the baby. It was of course her baby, which meant that it was Zhao, who hardly ever said anything, especially to women, who got Jiang Mei pregnant. What's more, he knew I was in love with her, and yet he still had to come between us. What kind of man is that? A man like that shouldn't be given the customary equipment.

I wasn't going to clean up his shit for him. He'd have to do it himself, and him the wrestling champion too. From then on, I didn't look after Jiang Mei, though we stayed on at the farm, and seldom went back to Jinzhou. Then I was admitted to a technical college in Shenyang, and haven't been back since. I heard that Jiang Mei died, but nothing about the two boys.

Even now I still can't work out why Doggy waited to the very end to say those things. He could have said them earlier.

If he could've said something earlier then the story might have had an earlier ending. That wouldn't have been a bad thing.

Now when I try to remember exactly what happened that night, I know I'm not going to get anywhere, and I know there's something that blocks my memory. It's hard to say what, though.

One thing I remember quite clearly is that Doggy hadn't been there in our dorm, and when he did come back he stayed only for ten minutes, until he was carried out again. What I couldn't understand is how he'd seen Farty Zhao, why Zhao had left without saying anything; why he hadn't said anything himself, but had singled out Doggy to pass the message on.

I left the farm just over a year later. Everyone came out to see me off, out of the village and past the little wooden bridge that might've fallen in any time. I noticed Jiang Mei there in the crowd, but she didn't look at me, apparently her mind was elsewhere. I shook hands and said goodbye to lots of people, but not her. I couldn't think how she had the nerve to come and see me off. Who can understand how a woman's mind works?

And I remember that the two toddlers weren't there.

## 8

I NEVER KNEW DOGGY WAS SO POPULAR. All twelve from the dorm walked behind the cart to Jinzhou. It was about fifteen miles away, a good four or five hour walk.

There were just the two of us left in the sixteen man dorm, myself and Black Date. I couldn't stand up, let alone walk with the others. Black Date went out, then came back when the others had left.

He went back to his place and smoked hard, at least five pipefuls, I'd guess. So he was smoking non-stop for over an hour. It was nearly dawn.

I was still half sitting up on the ground, no one looking after me, and unable to look after myself. The pain was so bad I couldn't think of sleep. The tobacco smoke smelt good, my heart was calm like a pool of dead water.

In the distance a cock crowed. At the first sound Black Date leapt to the floor, and as he walked past me I sensed something in his steps. He took another two steps then stooped to pick up the spade. Before I realised what he might do he'd already taken the spade to himself, with what looked like real force and brutality — his left heel was sliced open, the blood pumping out. Then he keeled over, without losing consciousness, and smiled at me, a beaming, contented smile. 'We're quits now.'

## 9

I HAVE TO SAY THAT FOR A WHILE I really didn't understand. He'd just ripped out his own tendon and was curled up in a heap. Neither of us uttered a sound, and after that night neither of our left feet would walk properly again. I'd heard that once the tendon's gone you can't stand up any more, but hearsay's never too reliable. The witch doctor joined the severed parts of his tendon together again — a horrendous operation — with Black Date, who'd not made a sound since ripping his heel, screaming the whole way through. Afterwards the witch doctor said he was in good health, that he'd have no problems chasing women or working as a smithy, but having shortened the tendon he'd find himself walking unevenly. And he joked:

Swaying like a distant willow in the breeze,
Close up, like a fast horse resting its hoof;
Standing up, he strikes a pose to shoot his arrows,
Only lying down, one leg will be longer than the other.

Even Black Date smiled.

My operation was a lot simpler, and what I'm left with isn't too bad. I've got a slight limp, that's all. If you didn't know you wouldn't notice it. If I was really lucky I could still perhaps be an astronaut. I'm as strong as an ox.

Black Date is quite lame, and he swings heavily left and right as he walks. But, just like the witch doctor said, he soon found a woman in the village near the farm and had two children, both daughters. His life's happy enough, and he's a capable, well-off farmer. Later we used to enjoy seeing each other. To use his words, we were quits.

It was Black Date who told me the news of Jiang Mei's death, though as far as I was concerned she'd ceased to exist long ago.

'You know, you ... Why didn't you love her?' Black Date's tongue faltered. 'Just because she had Tian the Accountant's ... Tian the Accountant's child? Why should it bother you so much?'

I was stunned, 'What do you mean, it was Tian the Accountant's? It was Farty Zhao's.'

'The Farty's? Come on! The Farty wouldn't even look at Jiang Mei. He knew that Jiang Mei was fond of you. It was Tian the Accountant's, and no mistake.'

'How do you know?'

'Later Jiang Mei told me. She said she was sure you didn't love her any more. Later on she got pregnant again. That was also Tian the Accountant's. What could she do? So she died.'

I was speechless. It was a huge blow.

10

AT THAT MOMENT the circumstances of Doggy's death began to slither back into my mind like a snake.

Only then did I realise it had all been a mistake.

Doggy was conscious even on the morning before he died, and when I got there he said he should have died a day or two earlier, but he couldn't. He wouldn't close his eyes before I came.

I grumbled about his not telling me sooner, and he smiled bitterly saying there hadn't been time, he'd known from the moment he'd walked in that there was no time, and as that was the way it was, there

40

was no point in saying anything. 'I was already done for, so what difference would it have made?'

'You wouldn't be like this if you had said.'

'You thought Jiang Mei's baby was Zhao's, but you were wrong.
The other one, the one I brought back, was his. His and the young
widow from the village, Zhang Lan's. No one knew about it — I only
got to know that night. I'd gone to the village to pinch — I can't remember what now, and heard these strange sounds coming from
Zhang Lan's room. I didn't realise till I went in that she was having a
baby. You know she lived on her own, quite a way from the village.
No one else knew she was having a baby. I asked if I could do anything, and she told me through her tears to go and get Farty Zhao. I'd
just gone out of the door when she burst out screaming. I rushed back
inside but she was in such mad pain that she rolled off the bed on to
the floor. I didn't know what to do, I didn't dare take off her pants,
I'd never touched a woman.

'Then she went quiet. I was standing there like an idiot watching
her die. I was so scared I didn't think of the child until she'd breathed
her last breath. Then I didn't care about taking off her pants, once she
was dead. You could see the baby's bottom squeezing out, but its head
and its body were inside the woman. I know now that it was a breech
birth.

'I pulled that baby out, and cut the cord with a knife, gave the baby
a quick wash in the dirty water in the basin and brought it back with
me.

'I met Farty Zhao on the way, and wanted to give him the baby but
he wouldn't take it, said he had to go and see the last of Zhang Lan,
said he wouldn't be back, and said to tell you to give the baby to Jiang
Mei to look after. I didn't even know then that Jiang Mei had had a
baby as well.'

'Yet at the time you said he'd told me to look after Jiang Mei and
the baby. At least I thought that's what you said.'

'I was shit scared. I stumbled back like a drunken idiot. Then the
Fart called after me and thrust the army cap at me saying I should give
it to you, and tell you that you'd left it outside on the ground while
you were wrestling. I forgot to tell you when I came in. I slipped the
baby into the cap, and it was still covered in blood. I couldn't tell you
this before, but now that I'm dying …

'I didn't think you'd be able to take it, not that I haven't suffered
myself from keeping it all inside. Perhaps I shouldn't be telling you at
all?'

'Doggy, you should have told me earlier. A long time ago.'

'Don't cry. It's awful seeing a grown man cry. Please don't cry. Please …'

I was at his side when he died. Cancer's horrendous. He was small to start with, and now he was no more than a bundle of bones. After the cremation, his mother kept the ashes.

## 11

I THINK WHEN FARTY ZHAO heard that night that Jiang Mei was having a baby, it must have reminded him of his young widow. But where could he go once she had died?

# THE MAD CITY

## WEN YUHONG

A DOG WAS HANGING upside down in a tree, a great gash torn in its belly. Two young men were in the process of tearing out the hot, seething innards — one grasping a dagger dripping with blood, the other's hands caked in blood. They were working with intense concentration. The spectacle was so horrible that passers-by could not bear to watch.

These last few years they must have slaughtered some four hundred dogs. Their techniques became more and more sophisticated. Every time they butchered a dog their spirits were soothed and they felt a special kind of pleasure. Whenever they saw a living dog leaping about or jumping up and down, they stared as if they couldn't believe their eyes. How could any dog be as happy as that, how dare it have the nerve to shake its head and wag its tail like that — right under their very noses. Their fingers would start to twitch as if they could already see the animal dismembered and subjugated, struggling powerlessly — its fresh blood dripping down. It was as if they could already see the steaming, palpitating organs and intestines — as well plate upon plate of over-stewed, dog-meat chop suey.

They were blood brothers, totally inseparable and united by a bond of total dedication to one another. I don't know when, but there certainly must have been a time when they started this business of slaughtering dogs. They would hunt through the lanes and alleys of the town, and at each Korean noodle-house they'd be asked to go off and butcher a couple of dogs. The expenses they received were meagre, just a dish of casseroled dog-meat and something to drink. Drinking was something the brothers really did well; they could put away oceans of booze. They didn't eat much, but could easily get through several pints. They would drink till their faces were flushed, their heads swollen, and their foreheads covered in beads of sweat which dripped down onto the dining table.

Their lips were a dark purple, the corners of their mouths were fat, and they each had a mouthful of great, healthy, yellow teeth. It didn't matter if the beef stew wasn't tender, their sharp teeth would twist and grind away at it, gnashing backwards and forwards this way and that, and in no time they'd manage to gulp it down. When they were on

43

the booze they could drink half the night away, and there wasn't a single Korean noodle-house that dared to kick them out. There was nobody who had seen the brothers drunk. They didn't talk to other people but once in a while would yell at the landlord to get them some food — 'Hey landlord, more food!' — in their rude voices, snapping their thick, yellow fingers. Afterwards they would talk to each other, saying things nobody understood and laughing uproariously in their vulgar way.

When dogs saw the brothers coming it was as if they could smell the stench of butchery coming out of them. They would tear off, as fast and as far as possible, leaving not a trace of their existence behind. In the evenings, if the brothers went past houses where dogs were raised, the dogs inside would let out the most frantic howls — as if they never expected to live to see another day.

The brothers would invariably look at one another and burst out laughing, proud of their reputations.

They always kept gleaming daggers tucked into their belts, so the police didn't dare to meddle with them. The brothers both had official licences for this profession of specialist dog-butchers.

They rode huge motorbikes, wearing helmets and dressed from top to toe in leather. They would zip past your head tossing out great peals of laughter.

AS soon as the tradesmen saw the brothers coming into the market they would start to get agitated. They would rush forward to welcome them and exchange a few words of greeting, then give them a few samples of their goods.

When their hearts were set on the prospect of blood the brothers could not sleep. Their minds were focused on one thing and one thing only — butchery and more butchery. If there were no more dogs, they would make do with cats or even hunt rats. These creatures they would pin out on wooden planks, cruelly ripping open their bellies, and with their bare hands pull out the moist, slimy, sticky and still pulsing insides. At such moments they felt profoundly satisfied and to-tally forgetful of worldly things. They would hold the innards in their hands for a long time, gently squeezing them and delicately savouring the feel of the slippery organs, and only when they were cold, their vi-tality quite sapped, would they throw them away and rip out some more. Their greedy mouths would split wide-open, erupting with great belly-laughs. That was what they were like — a pair of hands still dripping blood onto the ground, and nearby, little corpses, still stretched out on the board, bellies completely voided. Hearts, livers,

intestines were scattered any-old-where, on walls, floors, ceilings —
here a string of intestines, there a large pool of bile — and a rising
stench of rottenness which filled the whole room. Then they would sit
down at the table, staring at their hands and watching intensely as little by little the blood there darkened and hardened, while the corpses
slowly stiffened on the boards.

Then they were dead tired, their strength as exhausted as if they had
fought some heroic battle or subjugated some band of marauding in-
vaders. After a while, when their fatigue had abated and they were fed
up with admiring their spoil, they would gather up all the bodies and
innards, scrape the blood and bile off the walls, and toss the whole lot
into a large cauldron of boiling water, sprinkle it with a pinch of salt
and pour black soy sauce over the top.

THIS was the strangest city I had ever seen in the entire course of my
life. I've been to all sorts of places, and passed the time of day with every kind of character — I've been genuinely shocked, frightened and
disgusted by abnormal psychology, paranoia and barbaric cannibalism.
But I have never before seen such a place, one with such a multitudinous population, yet all enveloped in such a suffocatingly negative
pall.

A winding river coiled around the outside of the town, always
threatening to flood. Inside, there was only a shallow, all but dry
stream. I went to look at it, and even in summer, on days of torrential
rain, it barely came up to a person's waist and was only something like
a metre deep. The brackish water glinted in the sunshine. Wide banks
of anaemic yellow sand were piled up along the shores on both sides. A
reinforced steel bridge rose out of the sand. It was suspended high
above the water, extending end to end fully a thousand metres. In
summer the local kids played naked in the water. On both sides, the
steep banks were overgrown with tall artemesia.

Other parts of the town had no stream at all. Of course the public
park had a lake where rubbish floated — scraps of bread, ice-lolly pa-
pers, clumps of grass and other things people chuck away. The lake
was the size of a mere pond but was crammed with innumerable pleasure boats, all bashing into each other, crashing and banging, sometimes producing a peculiar shrieking sound. A moat was in the process
of being constructed around the outside of the city. I wondered if it
was fated to become like the lake — filthy, stinking water and annoying scraps of waste paper.

You can imagine how dry the town was, mad winds and dust making everyone irritable. Huge numbers of chimneys gushed thick smoke

out over the town, and the stench of sulphuric acid from the chemical factories spread everywhere. The city was so big, with such an enormous population and such strange varieties of madness. Truly I've never seen anything like it.

THE day came when the brothers' behaviour suddenly became the established norm in the city. Every young person copied them, studying their good example. Dog-slaughtering hadn't existed as a mania till then, but in the twinkling of an eye it permeated every corner of the city. Every day the door of the Trade and Industry offices were crowded with people trying to wangle licences to set themselves up as professional dog-butchers. They queued up in long lines, all packed together. And hosts of young people streamed out of factories, institutions and schools, rejecting their previous work or study, and swaggering onto the streets to join the flood of frenzied dog-butchers. Each of them rode a great motorbike and zipped past your head. They had daggers tucked into their belts and they crowded into bars to drink themselves silly. They muttered streams of weird nonsense and let off peals of obscene laughter. And they began to hunt rats and cats, tossing intestines and internal organs about all over the place, afterwards throwing them into great pots of boiling water, stewing them till all the goodness was boiled out of them, and then gulping down the soup.

What the brothers did one day became all the rage in the city the next.

ONE day at a street market in the western part of the city, a young man arrived who wasn't acquainted with the place. He was a beef trader, tall and strong, clever and capable. When the two brothers entered the market at noon, the other tradesmen dropped their businesses and rushed forward to greet them. One after another they let the brothers pick out whatever goods they fancied. The young beef-trader, however, just stood in front of his carving board, wondering what all the fuss was about. Why on earth should anyone want to lick the boots of rat- or cat-catchers. He and the two brothers stared at each other. The brothers' huge, gamblers' mouths and flat butchers' cheeks made the young man shudder.

That afternoon a mad wind started up, lifting the sand and even turning stones. Bits of cabbage, shreds of paper, rotting vegetable leaves, everything was whirled up suddenly into the sky. In front of the crowd, the two brothers tied the young butcher up, stuffed his mouth with pig offal, and hung him upside down from the branch of a tree in

46

the market — in the same way they had done with the dogs. At that time of year the tree was almost bare. At the base of its trunk there was a huge, pitch-black hole full of creepy-crawlies. The brothers stripped the young man naked, tossing his clothes into the hole, then with a single slash of their knife, slit him from stomach to gizzard. His pale green intestines burst, slip-slopping, out. The mass of people crowded together in the market watched with the greatest relish. A gang of young men who were the brothers' particular fans didn't miss the least nuance of expression or movement of hand, keeping tabs on even the least discernible details. Some of them even acted out the scene at the same time.

That evening the exciting news of the brothers' deeds reverberated round the town. The business was discussed with glee in every household.

Like the eyes of wild animals glaring out from the jungle, lights blazed from every building, every house, penetrating the murky haze of the dimly-lit streets. Out of every window poured great gusts of laughter, as well as sounds of cursing. This went on till well past midnight when the lights were finally extinguished. On the streets outside it was pitch dark and a cold wind was blowing. Laughter just like the brothers' laughter, continued to spew out from the lips of the sleepers, bursting out of windows, ricocheting around and echoing wildly. Sleep-walkers rose from their beds, grabbed their food-choppers and began to whet them against the sides of big pickled-cabbage pots.

All night long the dreamers' ravings kept pouring into the dark sky above the town. They mumbled unspeakable horrors. There was the ceaseless rasping sound of sharpening knifes. And on top of it all there was a continuous cackling of blood-curdling laughter.

THE following day in different markets across the city, sixteen real attacks on customers actually happened, one after another — all of them just like the brothers'. Customers were seized, strung upside down from the branch of a tree — and butchered.

Within the next few weeks the whole town was infected with this madness. Not only young people but even those of more advanced years were butchering right, left and centre. All night long terrifying sounds poured out from the city. The dreamers' sleep-talk became more and more horrifying, making your flesh creep. All night long, the awful sounds of knife-sharpening became more and more oppressive and nerve racking. It was as if the whole town had been filled with a crazy singing and dancing — the slashing of hundreds of icy, gleaming knives.

THE municipal government sent in the local police to capture the brothers. But some people noticed that even in the ranks of the police there were many who had been responsible for butchering their 'clients'. The police stormed the brothers' residence, kicking in the front door, assault weapons at the ready. But the place was empty — just a cauldron of rat meat and innards stewed to a pulp. The police put down their weapons and shouted to the inn-keeper next door to bring them a pot of something alcoholic, then wrenching off rat thighs and scooping up portions of their innards, they sat down to feast, gorging themselves with great mouthfuls.

WITHIN a few days the brothers had reappeared in the city. They were still just the same, daggers tucked into their belts, riding great motorbikes, and rampaging about with a murderous look in their eye.

THE city was constantly enveloped in dense yellow smog. In the doorways of every shop there were fortune-tellers and palmists, young and old, men and women. Each of them clutched a great wad of gaudy cards and was dressed in a black padded coat covered with grease, stains and dust. They yelled loudly, bustling about this way and that through the crowd. The rain dripped slowly down from a grey sky, and yellow leaves covered the city, flying about or sticking soggily all over the black tarmac on the roads. The roads were pot-holed and loose stones rolled about on them. Every day the people flowed back and forth to work in great winding serpents; gathering, then disappearing into fathomless nooks and crannies.

In front of the cinema and the theatre, people were bored stupid. Particularly since the theatre's doors had remained tightly closed for years. At the cinema they showed the same film, day in day out, three hundred and sixty days a year. The soundtrack coughed and spluttered out of a broken-toothed old projector. The ushers, both young and old, who were supposed to look after things, just fumbled about in the dark playing poker.

There were two occasions every year when there would be a remarkable hubbub on the playing field. This was when there was a national or international football match. Several hundred spectators would be crushed to death or trampled flat as they tried to catch a glimpse of the exciting battle. The young men who came out onto the field over successive months were like wild, unbridled horses. They would dash about hither and thither, bumping and bashing, twisting and turning, frothing at the mouth, hair all dishevelled.

THE first time I came to this town it happened to be right in the middle of the season of mad winds, during the time of year they called 'the fall that just *kills* you'. Gust upon gust of buffeting wind had demolished all the houses. Even hotels and large buildings which had been built to withstand earthquakes — all had collapsed. Spirals of dust swirled around on the road lifting a frenzy of waste paper, rotting wood and bits of old roof-tile. Enormous trees had come crashing down and lay silently on the sides of all the roads. Slender willow twigs flew up and danced proud in the angry wind. And on top of everything there was the black smoke rising silently from the rubble, the mad wind fanning it out everywhere.

I saw crowds of people, huddled group after huddled group of them, all sitting in the broken shells of the razed buildings. They threw poker cards down on the table with exaggerated force. On the corner of the tables a dark, carelessly-stacked pile of bank-notes was already heaped up. These people were dressed in long woollen coats and sucked hard at their cigarettes. Their brows were lowered and their foreheads furrowed as they clutched their cards in a death-like grip. The dark smoke painted their faces black and yellow, and the northeast wind, hooting and whistling from the rafters, came in bursts of hot waves. I saw small children huddled at random amongst the crowds. They too were smoking like old troopers, their penetrating, childish screams grating on the ears. All around were pieces of rotting wood, crumbling bricks — and right under their very noses, a tide of cockroaches and other insects scuttling back and forth in unbroken currents.

ON an empty part of the square, the two brothers had set up a boxing ring. Anyone who came to see the fight had to pay ten dollars. A great beast of a dog was brought out into the ring. Wearing only the scantiest of trunks and grasping their daggers, the two men did battle with the dog. The brothers had specially trained these dogs, and every day fed them wildcat, hare or rat — alive. This had turned the dogs into savage beasts. When they were hungry their eyes blazed, they bared their fangs and their ears pricked up. Their cavernous red mouths hung wide open, long tongues lolling out, and they let out blood-curdling howls. They would leap at the brothers immediately, their sharp claws stripping bloody scales from the brothers' bodies and reducing their skimpy trunks to tatters. The men too became like wild animals, mouths hanging open and revealing their strong yellow teeth. Ducking and diving this way and that way, they would await the moment to seize their chance — to plunge a dagger down into the dog's throat. With the dog's claws still deeply embedded in their skin, there would be a little glugging noise, and gradually the dog's grip would relaxed. It would stretch out and its body stiffened.

The audience watched goggle-eyed. Holding their breath, bodies utterly still, they would stare unblinking as the dogs leapt at the brothers.

Whatever the weather, whether it was blowing a gale or pouring cats and dogs, every day at mid-day the brothers would bring a dog into the ring for a performance. In order to experience the exquisite spectacle of this fierce battle, people would come from all over — some even by train from several hundred miles away. It didn't matter whether gales had destroyed their homes, or if they were soaked to the skin, their whole attention would be riveted, just waiting for the destruction of the howling dog.

EVERY day a battalion of girls trailed after the brothers. Their lips were painted bright red, their faces plastered white as paper, and dressed in the most fashionable clothes. Facing the crowd, they and the brothers would egg each other on with the most vulgar obscenities — and raising a storm of laughter from the audience.

There was one girl who had been with the brothers for a long time. Whatever the time of the year, she always wore the same black dress. She was one of the town's best-educated girls. People said her parents had agreed to her marrying a young man who had money as well as education. The townsfolk were green with envy.

But in this town, things are always twisted. The young man had graduated from university not long before. People used to say — look at him, he'll go far. He began to frequent bars and dance-halls, cleaning up with his talk and his dancing. People still said that he was intelligent and capable, and sooner or later he'd be a high-ranking official. But the next morning he was discovered having committed suicide on his bed.

On the evening of her wedding the girl came running out. The following day, wearing a black dress, she appeared on the square with the brothers.

Like the brothers, she chain-smoked, which turned her nails yellow and made a green light shine in her eyes. She drank one glass after another too. She drank until steam came out of her mouth and she couldn't think any more.

But she remained both lovely and exquisitely elegant. Her eyes became darker and colder, like the light in the winter sky. People often discussed her, and said that these eyes were strange. Her gaze seemed out of focus as if she wasn't looking at anything, and yet at the same time as if she could see everyone. Even when she looked at the brothers she appeared at a loss, as if looking at them without seeing them. She didn't laugh or cry, and didn't get angry; her voice and expression revealed nothing about her, but made it seem as if she was endlessly dredging the bottom of the ocean for a lost needle.

She got on extremely well with the brothers, thinking up ideas for them, as well as giving them her body. On New Year's Eve she got them to buy five hundred dollars' worth of fireworks, and then in the evening let them off in one fell swoop. The sky was lit-up for all of three hours. She got the brothers to wrap up a dog's heart — bloody, dripping and still warm from the little bit of life left in it — and send it off to an old boyfriend. When he received it the young man nearly died of fright, and screaming for an ambulance, was rushed away to hospital. And she got the brothers to put on masks and rob a bank. Then, taking the bills they had snatched out onto the square, she threw them up in the air, watching with immense gratification as people leapt as high as twin-storied houses, a forest of arms reaching up to grab the beautiful notes. She and the brothers all wore daggers, and whenever they saw a parked car, they slashed deep holes in its tyres, then faded away into the night.

She also got on very well with the gang of girls who trailed after the brothers. She never interfered with them, just stood quietly to one side, watching as they and the brothers teased and flirted with one another. She never wore make-up and seldom dressed up, but was, nonetheless, wonderfully turned-out, with her glossy hair swept back off her face naturally.

She liked to drink till she was tipsy, and would run out completely naked and roll in the snow. She liked to go out in summer storms, without any protection — the rain-drops all whipped up in the streets by the wind — running through the heaviest rain and get soaked through.

The other females in the gang were jealous of her status with the brothers, and practically the whole town detested her, but each time they thought of murdering her, she was saved by the brothers, who discovered the plot in the nick of time and put a stop to it.

THE police started a hunt for the brothers and for her. They put an end to the fighting in the square, which set everyone complaining. The brothers' dog-butchering licence was revoked. And at every Korean noodle-house a platoon of policemen was stationed to keep watch over the landlords so that they wouldn't hire the brothers to go dog-butchering.

IT seemed to be the most peaceful day of my stay in the city. Every street, large or small, was flooded with yellow uniformed policemen. They grasped electric batons, had rifles slung from their belts, and their shouts thundered out everywhere. The landlords were forever putting glasses of beer into their hands. 'My dear officer. Sir, please do have one on me. Have one on me.'

It appeared that the young people with daggers slung at their waists were no longer to be seen. Nothing was to be heard except the policemen's motorbikes hooting eerily. At the doorway of the cinema, people were still bored stupid. The theatre was closed fast.

NOW it is winter, and the murky yellow waste gases are still spreading out over the city. The choking smell of sulphuric acid, of dust and of coal smoke is denser than ever, permeating every corner of this place. The trees on either side of the main roads have become pitch-black, and heaped up by the side of the road, even the spoilt snow is pitch-coloured, ulcerated with a thousand holes. The biting north wind blows right through people. And at night-time the city is still filled with stories of horrors recalled by the dreamers, and the sound of sharpening knifes.

I thought the city really would quieten down for good. On the day I left, I asked a policeman standing beside me — the same kind of young man as the brothers — 'Have you really killed them as people say?' He gave me a sly look and told me in a low voice that the brothers had secretly joined the police long ago. Seeing my surprise, he went on with even greater pride. 'The brothers are going to start up again in the spring — this is just a period of rest and consolidation. The cat is hibernating now. It's like this every year.' He spoke without the least trace of caution. 'And the girl?' I asked. 'What about her?' 'What girl?' His brow furrowed with distaste. 'They killed her ages ago.' 'Killed her? — the brothers?' 'Ah, no — it was the gang. When the brothers were off their guard, they took their chance and killed her.' He put his hands round his own throat to show me. 'She was a real pain in the arse you know,' he added.

# THE DRY RAVINE

## YANG ZHENGGUANG

NO ONE EVER COMES to this dry ravine. It's not far from the village but no one ever comes here. The ravine is overgrown with scrub — trees that never grow into usable timber — no one knows their names. They grow leafless on the slopes of the gully at this time of the year, bare twigs entwining and entangling one another. The full length of the ravine can only be seen from the top of the hill. Once inside it, you feel something ominous — that you might never get out, that you might dry up there yourself.

That was what he thought the moment he entered the dry gully. He had just plucked a few hairs from his nose and felt a sort of emptiness inside. He pinched his nose and looked into the gully. There wasn't a sound. Every now and then a wolf howled. Only occasional howls, very far off. But he couldn't make out the direction they came from.

Day was about to break.

He felt a little cold. He knew day would soon break. At dawn it was chilly. The moon was like a ghost dangling from a gallows over the hill top. He could see it. He felt the branches whip his face, like a stone being scratched, without any feeling. He tried to push them away with his hands. He thought he would trip on the twigs, fall over and never be able to get up again.

They wouldn't arrive so soon, he thought. He could have a short sleep before they came. He pushed aside the undergrowth to make space and lay down on the slope. He put his hands behind his head and looked at the moon for a while. The moon seemed brighter. He fell asleep, gazing at it.

'LET'S GO,' he said. He looked at the back of La'neng's head. La'neng was his sister. He saw her turn her head and look up at him. They had come to see the film. He saw La'neng sitting on the mud path, in the arms of a geological explorer. There were many men like him amongst the prospectors who enjoyed caressing the village women. Their own women were back in town, so they embraced the women hereabouts and gave them money and nylon stockings. They were looking for minerals in the mountains. They said that once they'd found these minerals, the people here would all be rich. They were shameless, shameless in their hunt for stones!

He saw the prospector running his hand along La'neng's body. La'neng's eyes were fixed on the screen. She let him grope her without flinching. Later, she too felt for him with her hands. La'neng wasn't watching the film any more.

He didn't look at the screen at all because he was thinking of that guy, Luo Shanzi. That morning Luo had come to their house. La'neng was cooking. He saw La'neng give the man a smile.

He didn't want to eat. He went out, feeling as if he had swallowed a fly whole. He went to Pockmarked Gui's cave-house to see about their frozen beancurd wager. Gui had told him that he wouldn't have to pay if he could eat it all. He saw the confident expression on Pockmarked Gui's face and felt like gnawing a chunk out of the wretched thing. Without a word, he kept on eating in big mouthfuls. The ice made a grinding sound between his teeth. He felt as if there were insects inside his mouth, and that his tongue was being peeled. He thought he was eating the beancurd together with slivers of his tongue. To begin with Pockmarked Gui was smiling at him, but he soon stopped. Gui's face looked as frozen as the beancurd. He finished it, all three pounds of it. He knew that he mustn't wipe his mouth. His lips would rub away too if he did. He left Pockmarked Gui's cave and ran back and forth along the valley several times. Then he went up the hill and rolled down. He kept rolling until it was nearly dark. He saw a few people going up towards the prospectors' camp to see a film. La'neng wanted to go. He thought that he wanted to go too.

'Let's go,' he told La'neng.

La'neng rose from the ground, brushing the dust from her bottom. He saw the explorer roll his eyes and stare at him. He heard the guy swear, 'Fuck your mother backwards.'

These people cursed like that, 'Fuck your mother backwards.'

They set off for home. They heard people moving in dark corners, snogging. People hereabouts go in for casual affairs. Women even go with strangers. One tug on a girl's pigtail is all it takes. Manners here are simple. And women don't have to worry about thugs. There aren't any thugs.

'That Luo Shanzi came this morning,' he said.

'Mm,' was La'neng's reply.

'I saw him.'

'Mm?'

'That guy is really disgusting.'

'Mm?'

'Mm! Mm!' he said.

'Will you marry him?' he said.

'Mm.'

'I knew you'd marry him.'

His began to breathe heavily. His nostrils were itching. Some of the hairs in his nose were too long. He thought he should pull them out.

They walked home. The film wasn't yet over. He didn't realise then that anything was going to happen.

DAD WAS ASLEEP. He could tell from the sound of his breathing. He was blind. When Mum died he had become blind. Dad slept on the wall-bound side of the brick bed. They slept on the other side. There was only one room in their cave-house.

'Don't marry that Luo,' he said.

'Don't,' he said.

La'neng didn't answer. They heard the paper in the windows flapping. There was no wind, but it kept on flapping.

'I won't let you,' he said.

'I will,' La'neng said.

'He's disgusting,' he said.

'He says he's got wheat flour in his place.'

'If you marry him, you won't be able go out with that prospector any more.'

'I didn't go out with him.'

'He was feeling you up.'

'Brother dear,' La'neng protested. He heard her exclamation. Every time she raised her voice at him, he felt a little better.

'And you were touching him,' he said.

'Brother dear!'

'I saw it,' he said. He heard La'neng pulling up the quilt. La'neng was trying to hide her head under it.

'When he started feeling me it made me want to touch him too,' said La'neng.

'I don't mind you touching him,' he said. 'But don't go and marry that guy, Luo. I don't want you to marry him.'

'I will marry him. I have made up my mind. I've told him so. I've made up my mind.'

'You'll be finished if you do,' he said.

'I don't think so.'

'I knew you wouldn't agree.'

'I don't.'

'I tell you, you'll be finished.'

'And I don't think I will.'

He heard La'neng fall asleep. Dad was tossing about on his side of the bed. Dad snored. Dad ground his teeth in his sleep like a cow chewing the cud. Sometimes he gritted his teeth as if in hatred.

HE AWOKE to people talking. They were talking somewhere above him. He could tell from their voices that they were from his village.

'They didn't cover her. They didn't cover her at all even when they brought her out,' someone said.

'I'd never seen a woman's body before. Honestly, I'd never seen one,' the other said.

'Everyone was looking at it. Fucking hell, everyone was looking at it.'

'Not much blood. Bloody strange. She was stark naked.'

'Her face was ugly. The faces of the dead are always ugly.'

'So you did see it?'

'No. Why should I have seen it?'

'Then how do you know?'

'I didn't see. You're putting words in my mouth!'

LA'NENG FLUNG AN ARM OVER onto his stomach. There was a smell to her arm. He knew it well. Every time he smelled it, it made him hot and bothered. His throat felt unbearably dry. He considered putting La'neng's arm back under the quilt. That would make it easier to bear. But he didn't. Instead he pulled La'neng's arm around his own neck. La'neng woke up. La'neng called out.

'Brother dear.'

He listened to her cry. He didn't answer. He held her arm. He knelt in front of her. He felt an urge to do something.

'Brother dear, you're an animal.'

He was kneeling there, looking at La'neng. He felt something crawling out of his eyes.

He didn't want to use the cleaver, but there wasn't anything better, so he picked it up. It was the cleaver La'neng used to prepare the meals. But La'neng would never know. The cleaver was cold. The paper on the windows rattled again and again. There was no wind, but it would not stop rattling.

'I don't want to,' he said to La'neng. 'I really don't want to. I have no choice. Don't blame me, La'neng. Otherwise I really would be an animal.'

He pulled the quilt up for her. It was worn and ragged. There was a pungent smell of sweat. He pulled the quilt up to her neck, and stroked her neck with his hand.

She flinched and shuddered at the coldness of the cleaver. That was something he hadn't expected. Suddenly she opened her arms and pulled him down against her. He felt a force surging up inside him and into his hands. He pressed down, and she embraced him. He felt her close embrace. He heard her utter a groan.

'La'neng, you mustn't blame me.'

He pulled up the worn quilt. After a time he heard a sound beneath it. He realised that it was the stuff flowing out of her neck and seeping into the quilt.

La'neng had groaned once. He remembered she had groaned once.

'Dad. Dad.'

He stood where the brick bed met the wall and looked at his Dad. He felt an itching inside his nostrils, and gas in his stomach. He got hold of a long hair and pulled it out. There was a little twanging noise.

He heard the hair come out of his flesh. It was still dark and dead quiet. So he could hear the sound of the hair being plucked.

'Don't you try to find me,' he said to his Dad.

'How could I, a blind man.' His Dad turned over. He didn't stop grinding his teeth.

'HE MUST HAVE RUN AWAY. What would be the point of hiding here?'

The two men were sitting there, without moving. They were sitting somewhere above him, talking.

'I don't believe it,' the other said.

'I must have a piss. Wherever I go, I have to have a piss. But when I saw La'neng's body, I forgot.'

'Get on with it then.'

He heard the sound of pissing above him. He had a lump in his throat.

'This ravine is frightening,' said the guy who was pissing. 'I really think it's scary.'

'How can a ravine be frightening?'

'Aren't you scared? Just think it over.'

'I don't think he'd hide here.'

'Who knows?'

'I don't want get killed. Just think. If he jumps out at us, he'll try to kill us.'

'Listen!'

'A hare. It must be a hare.'

He heard them push aside the branches. After a while he couldn't hear anything. He wanted to call out to them, to call them back. They were from his own village, those two. They'd be back, he thought. They could be back anytime.

But he was wrong. Later he realised that he was wrong. It was days afterwards when he crawled up to the place where the two had been talking. There was a huge rock. He realised they had been talking on the rock.

He propped himself up against this rock. He didn't have the strength to crawl any further. He opened his eyes. He wanted to find the place where the man had pissed. He couldn't find it. He was slumped against the rock, not moving an inch. After a while he heard two crows alight in front of his head. Their wings brushed his face. He felt them pecking at his eyes, pecking deeply. Then they flew away. Somehow he knew that they were proud of themselves. He felt something oozing from out of his eye-sockets. The sun was a deep red. It was winter, but the sun was a deep red. Before long his eye-sockets would dry out and turn into two round holes.

# IN A LITTLE CORNER OF THE WORLD

LI HANGYU

IN THE EARLY SUMMER OF 1934 excessive rains in the Gechuan River basin had caused a disaster. At daybreak on the last day of May, the thirty thousand inhabitants of the town of Common Prosperity, who had been besieged by flood waters for seven days and seven nights, all heard, at almost the same time, a curious and inexplicable kind of 'shooshing' noise.

The noise seemed to originate outside the town. It seemed both faint and far away, yet also strangely close at hand. It alarmed the town's many householders. Some thought it sounded like the gentle and refined murmuring of spring silkworms as they ceaselessly spun their silk; but others compared it to a couple of shards of broken porcelain being rubbed together — an irritating and oppressive rasping.

An expanse of pitch-blackness extended beyond the houses. The people were lying out in quilts which were so damp that they were growing mildew. They shivered with fear, but tried to look on the bright side.

Was the flood retreating?

Perhaps the wind was getting up. If there was a typhoon the dampness they had suffered for months non-stop might be driven to the north.

The blind soothsayer, who'd returned earlier, had pronounced that, according to his interpretation of the almanac, this was going to be a year of decay. However, because at the beginning of the year the Xuantong Emperor had been elevated to the throne for a second time,* there would, after all, be a degree of benevolence about. Things were unlikely to be excessively bad. The common people would not be desiccated, like the grasses, to within an inch of their lives.

THE BEGINNING OF SPRING had not been very propitious. First there was the large group of ragged and lousy men and women from

---

* In 1934 the Japanese set up Puyi, the former Xuantong Emperor of the Qing dynasty, as 'Emperor' of the Manchurian puppet state they controlled at this time.

north of the Yangtze who had tramped in, fleeing famine. The streets were filled with their cries for food, and Common Prosperity, which had been a refined and pleasant town from ancient times, was turned into something as disorderly and odorous as a fish market. Its bad luck was entirely due to this 'northern riff-raff'. Before the plum blossom season it had begun to rain non-stop, and, in the event, this continued for more than two months. Not only had the River Gechuan discharged its flood water all over the place, but the rain water had even made the nearby uplands to the north and west of the town so soggy you could squeeze half a bowl of water from every handful of earth. Now the city was cut off. Hearing all around them the strange rustling which began that evening, no wonder the panicky and distressed citizens couldn't prevent themselves becoming even more distraught and confused.

At the foot of the North Gate was the Camel Bridge, and under the hump of the arch was a flickering shadow in a coolie hat, a straw cape and grass shoes. A night-watchman strolled slowly along the embankment casually banging a bamboo tube and shouting every few steps in a voice that sounded hoarse with cold, 'All safe and sound ... sleep safe, sleep sound ...'

The watchman, who was hard of hearing, ignored the 'shooshing' sounds around him. From the North Gate he swayed along step by step to the South Gate, dallied for a moment under the Young Scholar's Bridge, then turned back on the same road, doing all sorts of ill-mannered things as he went. At the tightly locked wooden door of Lucky Zhu's he spat out a glob of phlegm. Then he smeared some snot with his fingers onto the gilt-etched sign board of the rice merchant, Prosperous Chen. He swayed along under Phoenix Bridge in the centre of the market where, deciding to relieve himself, he simply spread his legs and aimed a stream of hot piss straight into the 'Chastity Gate' erected in honour of the grandmother of the madame of 'The House of Pleasures'. What the hell, there was only him going back and forth along the street at this time anyway. Wagging his head he idly hummed a Shaoxing Drum Opera — but the cold made him shiver. Suddenly his toe was stopped by something dead in its tracks.

'Aiya, Mama. Help, hey, I've been bitten by a ghost. Help ...'

His terrified, shrill cry was like a bolt out of the blue, it spread through the empty lanes and dispersed into the roads beyond, awakening the dazed citizens and setting their hair standing on end. Womenfolk begged their men-folk not to go out, grown-ups told their children not to utter a sound ...

60

Now, old folk with good memories say that night seemed exceptionally long.

Not until dawn did people realise exactly what had happened during the night. Rising early, they went out, and found the whole town crawling with crabs.

Crabs beyond number roamed the streets and alleyways at will. Along the rows of stonework, crabs clambered up and down the bridge-arches. From gaps between paving slabs, along ditches and dikes, crabs poured out.

To the east, Common Prosperity faced the Gechuan River estuary. To the west, it abutted the vast expanse of the rich, hundred-mile long Water-chestnut Lake. To the north, the large and small Mei and Xi Rivers flowed from the Heavenly Buddhist Mountain, travelling side by side, twin streams threading through the town and out of the North Gate to join up with the Beijing-Hangzhou Grand Canal in the west. The countryside was chequered with lakes and ponds, crisscrossed with creeks and canals. In a good year, the paddy became a sheet of yellow, the mulberry-trees so many dots of green, the grain crops were abundant, and fish and shellfish flourished It was usually at the Dragon Boat Festival in May that the 'Wheat Yellow' crabs were at their most marketable. This was when the mother crabs produced their roe. In a normal year at festival time there would be a bustling crab market under the Sky High Bridge at the West Gate with crab stalls lining roads and alleyways, even coiling round the better half of the central part of the town. You could drop in for a meal anywhere, and everyone had the chance to appreciate the seasonable crab roe's fresh flavour — even more delicious than fresh wine. There was not a home where they didn't indulge in this seasonal treat and, following the custom of the place, there wasn't anyone who refused the pleasures of alcohol.

But now the entire place was a crab market. The stalls this time were altogether excessive. Armies of crabs were everywhere, clogging up the streets without leaving people a single place to set a foot down. Even without all the tongues set wagging with alarm, this spectacle by itself was enough to make people believe that calamity was about to descend upon their heads. And in fact because of the great flood surrounding the city, their thoughts were already constrained by fear, their minds stuffed full of every kind of bad omen and evil notion. This left little room for thoughts of fresh crab and gluttony. It was like being suddenly faced with a world blanketed in gold coins where even

the out and out money-grubbers shrunk back in fear, unable to work
out how to gather them.

In every directions growing numbers of crabs were clambering over
the city walls, entering into the very heart of the market place and
converging on Blue Hill and Rice Market Port where the terrain was a
little bit higher. It was as if there was a crab king commanding all
crabs under Heaven. Of course they were really only doing what
comes naturally to a crab. They liked to climb embankments and they
dread deep water or turbulence. Now that the world had become a
boundless ocean, there was only Common Prosperity which still
counted as a piece of solid land. So there they came to rest.
'Shooshing' their frothy spittle, string after string of foamy bubbles
were caught by the wind, blown up from the ground to waft over the
city. Everywhere there were hairy crab legs; everywhere the gleam of
dark, shiny pincers. When they encountered a pedestrian obstruction,
the crowd of crabs would raise pair after pair of neat, swishing pincers,
fan out, display their strength in numbers, commandeer the street and
move on — the front advancing while the rearguard took their places.

Crabs crawled into houses and rooms, into the corners of walls,
onto stoves, inside children's cradles, some did a turn around a room
and then crawled away, but others set their sights on getting their
share of people's homes and took lodgings in their rooms, even
climbing onto beds and into cupboards …

At Flourishing Ye's chicken-hatchery on Magistrate's Street about
five or six hundred male crabs burst into the shop. In the ensuing
hoohah feathers flew and eggs were broken. Clucking noisily, mother
hens pecked father crabs to death one after another, while many of the
newly hatched chicks, sheltering under their mothers' wings, were
pinched to death by the crabs. Hearing the commotion, Proprietor Ye
came rushing noisily downstairs from his bedroom, hauling on his
trouser belt, thumping his chest, stamping his feet in desperation, and
bellowing to his two wives to quickly go and bar the door and not to
let a single extra crab inside. Looking at the floor all covered in
twitching chicks, he cursed them with a sob in his voice, 'Damn that
mob of crazy crabs.'

The crazy crabs even stormed the Local Party Headquarters. At the
Town Hall the old doorman knelt reverently at the bottom of the
steps in front of the committee rooms, banging his head on the
ground, kowtowing non-stop to the crowd of crabs which were crawling around everywhere, while intoning over and over again, 'Amitâbha
Buddha, I'm a wicked sinner', as if he were in front of the Great

Temple of Buddha. As the sutras reveal, amongst the endless forest of Buddhas there was certain to be at least one enlightened and incarnate crab.

If the crabs were going mad, the people were becoming completely crazy.

The vast majority of the citizenry followed Proprietor Ye's methods, each standing guard in their own doorway and trying to prevent the mad crabs from invading their homes. They waved carrying poles, fire tongs or pokers, and beat to death any crab that tried to cross their threshold. One battle over, they would await the next round.

Although the mass of frenzied crabs risked life and death with absolute abandon, because they crawled too slowly, there were periods of calm when the front was annihilated but before those behind had had time to replace them. One bout over and nothing to do, many of our manly heroes guarding their doorways were forced to sit and rest. But idleness made them jittery, and finally it dawned on the brighter ones amongst them that, quite apart from defensive tactics, they could take the initiative and attack. So seizing their weapons, they charged out of their doorways and started killing crabs all over the street, one stick one crab. Soon there was crab roe spattered about on all sides ...

Eventually, others of even more astonishing astuteness simply put on hard-soled shoes and trampled the crabs as they went along the street. This saved considerable trouble, and was also much more fun.

Despite everything, by mid-day the townsfolk had still had not exterminated all the crabs. The road surfaces were covered in a sticky crust of festering crab meat pulp and smashed crab shell, but even so, everywhere from between cracks in the uneven stones of the Mei and the Xi embankments, countless numbers of live crabs were just waiting to climb out. A few crippled crustaceans managed to escape from the sticks and cudgels, or from beneath the hard shoes. Others, minus a large pincer or a pair of hairy legs, escaped over walls and up onto roofs, squealing as they climbed along the rows of tiles, and sometimes boring down between the cracks in the tiles to make their way along rafters and uprights, invading people's homes at will. They were simply impossible!

Because of this, decent and devout men and women like the town-hall porter were once again in the ascendancy. A few old women who believed in ghosts and spirits went around everywhere advising people to paste up more talismans of exorcism in front of and at the back of their houses. They even succeeded in persuading the townsfolk to carry the Boddhisatva Guanyin out of the Iron Buddha Temple.

Tramping down roads covered in dead crabs they brought the iron Guanyin out to stand guard at the Camel Bridge by the Mei river. There, crowded together along the two embankments, the townsfolk kneeled and kowtowed, praying, in a continuous, muttered incantation, to the crowd of squirming crabs, while smoke billowed up from the innumerable incense candles which had been lit along the banks of the river. A day later this had become the most enjoyable topic of conversation amongst the citizens of Common Prosperity, just as Port Arthur folk relish stories about the Russo-Japanese war, or people from Western Hunan lap up stories about robbers and bandits. And even though it is now years and years ago, whenever young people today hear old folk talking about this ancient affair, they still cluck with amazement even though they harbour deep resentment. Amazement that there should have been enough crabs all those years ago to allow such a situation to arise, and resentment because the older generation finally, stupidly, exterminated the crabs — just as the 'Four Harmfuls', flies, mosquitoes, lice and mice, were exterminated — leaving children, grand-children and great-grand-children who saw the price of Common Prosperity's crabs reach three *yuan* a pound before their very eyes, and they could no longer afford to buy them.

Throughout the last fifty years of Common Prosperity's history and even now, that day when so many extraordinary and interesting things happened has been used by successive generations of the town's men of letters as material for their 'Words from the History of Prosperity', 'Folk Anecdotes' and 'Choice Specimens of Country Lore', and so, of course, for the enlightenment of future generations.

It was on this very day that a certain Mr Zhong from north of the Yangtze, driven by the wind and rain, sailed across the canal and arrived in Common Prosperity. He had his wife and son on board, but his boat's name was blotted out.

He was about thirty or so, tall with broad shoulders, and thin as a rake. He had a pair of serious, indifferent eyes and a face like hardened steel. Bare-chested, he stood beside the mast at the prow of his boat. He was so tired his arms hung down lifelessly, both shoulders covered in symmetrical, bloody scars, like the epaulettes of an army officer. They were the result of rope burns as he hauled the boat along from the canal-side. His boat threaded its way along the many bends and curves of the winding stream through the outskirts of the city and sailed gently in through the North Gate, finally coming to rest on the river beyond the Camel Bridge in the moorings crammed with every kind of wooden craft and now turned into temporary homes.

This shanty-town was made up chiefly of people who had fled the famine in the north. Some were skilled boatmen, like him, who had sailed there, but many more were peasants who had trudged in on foot. There was no place for them to settle on land, so the only thing they could do, copying the example of the boatmen, was to steal a bit of timber here or a bit of straw there and cobble together some kind of a shelter for themselves on the river. Boat to boat, shack to shack, a continuous line stretched almost all the way from the North Gate to the Camel Bridge. Children skipped along gang-planks, threading their way through their dwellings as if they were on dry land. The outsider's fear of a strange country made these disaster victims stick together. Those who had arrived in Common Prosperity earlier had been settled there nearly half a year, but had still never ventured north to take a turn round the area where the rich merchants were concentrated. They clung to each other, establishing themselves in this town's most filthy and dilapidated north-west corner, which they now looked upon as their homeland.

'Hey mister, what is it like further to the south?' the newcomer, Zhong, addressed an older Huai'an compatriot on the boat alongside his.

'No kind of place at all. In the south it's all mountains — huge mountains ... what's the matter? Don't you like this Common Prosperity?'

The man laughed, 'What's there to like?'

'The whole place is well-off. They really live off the fat of the land.'

Zhong leaned back against the mast and looked into the distance at the crowd of people dimly looming out of the pall of black smoke by the Camel Bridge, and asked lazily, 'What the hell's going on over there?'

'They're crab-worshipping I guess.'

'Crab-worshipping?'

'Yes. Just get a load of that.' The old man pointed to the rough stones on the side of the embankment where the crabs were thickly crowded and milling about. 'You see? Today the crabs have staged a rebellion against Prosperity.'

Zhong stood gazing stupefied. For ages he couldn't utter a word. The wet crab shells were spread out, gleaming darkly. The noise of their frothy spittle seemed long ago to have merged with the native noises of the town's general hubbub. It was only then that Zhong remarked that the people around him on the water were all eating crabs, and, moreover, that some of the children had already given themselves tummy ache and were squatting with their little bottoms stuck out over the water.

'It's fine with a bit of ginger. Ginger helps warm the stomach and stops indigestion.'

'My God! Why the hell are there so many crabs?'

The old man answered as if he had considered his reply, 'They're refugees, the same as us.'

His old lady was just putting a pot of crabs to boil on the little wood stove she'd fixed up behind the cabin awning. He banged the lid of the pot to get Zhong's attention, 'Hey little brother, why not go and get a few to boil up yourself? They're free. Only a donkey refuses to eat when he gets the chance. You may say they don't satisfy, but still, one way or another, it fills up the emptiness. Though according to my taste, the crabs here aren't a patch on ours back home in Huai'an.'

Zhong turned and was just about to climb the bank to get some crabs when suddenly his seven-year old son burst out of the cabin, all of a fluster, saying, 'Mum's about to have the baby, she wants you to come down quick.'

He raced down after his son into the cabin. His wife was rolling about all over the place clutching her huge stomach, her waxen face distorted with pain. Beside her on the plank bed, her little three-year old son was stunned into complete silence by her groans of agony.

'Is it going to be born now? It's not time yet.'

'Quick dad, go and get a midwife. Quick, quick ...'

'Where the hell am I going to find a midwife!' He was really in a fix. He'd just arrived in this place for the first time and didn't have a clue.

'Please, I'm begging you, go quick!'

'I mean, can't you just hang on another day or two?'

He'd no sooner spoken than he realised how absurd it was. He dashed out of the cabin and, standing on tip-toe, peered out at the nearby embankment, as if by straining his eyes he could pick out some old lady passing by who might bear some resemblance to a midwife.

'Is your woman about to give birth?'

'Hmm!' He didn't feel like passing the time of day with the old man just now, and eyes fixed, he went on scanning the alleys by the embankment.

'What are you looking for, little brother?'

'You don't know where I could find a midwife do you?'

'A midwife? Well my old woman's a midwife.'

The old lady, hearing someone calling her, limped across, and with a severe expression scolded Mr Zhong, 'What's up with you then? It's not the first time your woman's had a baby, hey!'

Then she rounded on her husband and started abusing him, 'What do you think you are doing craning your neck like that? Want to see a woman give birth? You shameless creature. Go and put a pan of water on the boil, quick.'

The old man smiled, abashed, and ran to the back of their shelter. 'The crabs aren't ready yet.'

'Throw them away and put on a fresh pot of water,' the old woman commanded while crossing over onto Mr Zhong's boat.

'Isn't it a pity to just throw them away?'

'The crabs are free. There's plenty more.'

'But ...'

'Hurry up you old devil, the baby's about to be born,' she growled as she hobbled deftly down into the cabin, and had another go at Mr Zhong. 'You "heroes" are all useless, good for nothing. Go outside and wait there.'

The cabin door slammed shut.

The small boat rocked gently on the water, its oar-sockets making characteristic squeaking noises. The river water was murky and choppy, so high it flowed almost level with the embankment. Squeezed together on either side of the bank, row upon row of arched eaves and tiled roofs extended outwards, narrowing the waterways between them into dark troughs. Sometimes the embankment followed the left bank, sometimes it twisted over a little bridge and followed the right bank. When the embankment crossed to the other bank, that side's bank became the one with the riverside houses, back doors opening directly onto the water. Women sifted rice, washed vegetables or scrubbed out night-soil pots, while gossiping with neighbours about the weather, the price of rice, this neighbour's marriage or that neighbour's funeral.

The old man boiling water was grumbling furiously, 'I'm really an unlucky old bastard, my old woman's as mean as the devil. But going back to what I was saying before — a good-for-nothing gets his just deserts. Little brother, don't worry about her limp, she really knows her stuff, in fact I've got a cushy life.'

Zhong hadn't said a word. His face was creased with worry. Looking at this spectacle, the old man ventured, 'Just look at the water everywhere. This year's harvest is going to be a disaster.'

'Huh?'

'I mean, this child is being born at the wrong time.'

Zhong was thinking the same thing. And he was worrying about something else too — his original idea had been to go further south to a little town called White Sands in the upper reaches of the Gechuan River where a clan relative had opened a boat business, and where he might find a secure job. But he had only got part-way, and now his wife was having her baby early. He was afraid that her frailty after childbirth would mean she couldn't cope with lack of food while they were travelling, and so they would have to kick their heels here, where they had no family or friends.

'Is there much of a livelihood hereabouts for a boatman, mister?' he asked.

'It's not bad. The first couple of days after the flood surrounded the town, I brought out a boat-load of jewellery and valuables for Mr Chen, the boss of the Chamber of Commerce. Dear me, it was enough to make your eyes light up.'

'Don't people here try to rip off strangers like us?'

'Well, if you take the name of this place at its face value, you wouldn't expect them to be hard on outsiders.'

'What do you mean?'

'Think about it. Common Prosperity gives the idea that the whole world's a single family, everyone enjoying good fortune together, sharing the common bounty.'

Zhong smiled. He was utterly exhausted and couldn't help flopping down to stretch out on the deck. His mind started to drift and he was soon heedless of the old man's tittle-tattle. Having brought the water to the boil, the old man stepped across with the pot in his hands and passed it to his old woman who had been demanding it impatiently. Zhong just went on lying there, unmoving, and little by little fell asleep, as if all the fuss had nothing to do with him.

He was unaware of how long he'd been asleep. Suddenly, there was a baby's cry from inside the cabin. He jumped up violently, setting the boat rocking.

He wanted to do something.

But no sooner had he had this idea, than he changed his mind and lay down again.

The lame old woman emerged from the cabin, covered in sweat.

Impatiently, the old man asked, 'What variety of goods is it then?'

'One with two more ounces of flesh — a boy.' Fed up, she waved him aside dismissively. 'Another woman is doomed to suffer.' She went to where the man was still lying down, and lifting her bad foot, gave him a kick. 'Hey you, get up, go and see your wife.'

He got up, making way for the old woman, but he really didn't want to see his wife just after she'd given birth. At such times she always had a filthy, disgusting, half-alive look. There was nothing pleasant about it. Every year she had a child, and out of five, three had died. Hadn't he seen her comic face before, clucking happily like a mother hen just after she's laid an egg? Not a pretty sight. He thought, it's better to climb onto the bank, gather up a few crabs and start to get her back to health.

The baby's birth was timely. The crabs would help provide him with milk.

From that afternoon, the general hatred of the crabs amongst the citizenry of Common Prosperity began to be redirected towards the 'northern riff-raff'. This was because this gang of beggars and outsiders was taking advantage of others' calamities, and feasting on crabs.

Common Prosperity folk were spoilt by their habitual good life in this land of milk and honey. Their nerves were rather fragile and they couldn't cope with the torment of a day like this. They went completely insane.

Rampaging around and flourishing the weapons they'd been using to kill crabs, they took to the streets. They didn't ask what kind of person it was, if it was 'northern riff-raff', then they bashed it in. They even snatched up dead crabs from all over the streets, throwing them into the strangers' faces and spitting through clenched teeth, 'Eat, you northern pigs, stuff yourselves to your hearts' content!'

Rich merchants like Proprietor Ye did everything they could to encourage this bigotry. The prosperous citizens, fearing that the crab catastrophe would reverse their luck and bring bankruptcy, found their nerves in an even more unstable state than usual. They got together to sign a petition demanding that the police order the expulsion of the refugees, and drive away, once and for all, the 'northern riff-raff' who'd brought bad luck to Common Prosperity. In this way the town might rediscover its former, elegant and flourishing self, restore the old worldly charm of 'the town with the little bridges and flowing water', safeguard the tranquillity of its many homes and preserve the prosperity of its multitudinous businesses.

For one reason or another the authorities were not able to meet the demands of industrial and commercial circles, but, by giving tacit consent, they assisted the gradual escalation of the atrocities.

On the second day the townspeople again stormed the two em-bankments near the North Gate, showering a hail of paving stones, roof tiles and rubbish down on top of the water folk's house-boats. Even more serious, one hooligan who liked a bit of horseplay, set light to a roll of cotton yarn soaked in kerosene, tossed it through the roof of a thatched awning which had been rigged up on the water, and set off a raging fire which enveloped one whole stretch of the river in a thick, rolling pall of darkness. Propelled by the wind, the great blaze spread quickly to the other boat-shacks. In the midst of the explosion of crackling noises, grass roofs caved in and ash-filled smoke surged up. Through this thick smog the light of the fire glimmered, now faint, now bright. Refugees ran hither and thither, crying out in every direction, their shouts adding to the chaos. Some people fled onto the embankments, others dived into the water …

The great fire raged for one whole day, until all the shelters and shacks had been reduced to ash, and every single one of the boats on that stretch of the river had vanished from the town.

To the west of the town a gang of valiant northern boatmen who had been attacked earlier, rose to defend themselves. They took up their boat poles and charged up the bank. Both sides went at it ham-mer and tongs. Long poles and short staves were flailed about in the mêlée, leaving almost a hundred casualties. The local people who were of a naturally feeble disposition felt sick when they saw a drop of blood, so each of the 'northern riff-raff' was worth ten of them. Becoming braver and braver the more they fought, the northerners pressed the townsfolk right back into the inner district around Phoenix Bridge. The police came out to intervene, opened fire and wounded the boatmen's leader. They arrested any northern boatmen who dared to retaliate.

For two whole days there were continual small-scale conflicts all over the city. And naturally, in the end, those who suffered the most were the outsiders.

After the third day, the flood which had surrounded the city began to subside. The crisis passed. Common Prosperity began to return to normal. Wasting no time, the peasants from round about seized the opportunity to pick up their carrying poles and speed their vegetables and pork into town to get the best prices and so make up for the losses they had suffered during the flood. Hard on the heels of the producers, the stall holders hurriedly set out their wares, and the principal streets started to bustle again. Everything flourished just as before. Even the gentle breeze sprang up again, which wafted through the trembling willows hanging down into the water by the little bridges over the winding waterways. But the townsfolk had to face a new and different spectacle. The orphans and beggars on their streets were more numerous than ever. The streets were so full of desolate cries that it sounded as if every house in the town was in mourning. The northern refugees who had their shacks burnt down and had no home to return to, were huddled everywhere — in street corners, under eves — their bedding spread out, sleeping rough. Emaciated and ragged boat-women sat outside the police station all day long, sobbing, crying and pleading for the release of their men-folk. Around them their silent children crouched, huddled by the base of the wall beside the road, so starved already they no longer had strength to cry. Pair upon pair of eyes fixed on the passers-by like little lambs in shock, full of bewilderment and fear …

Usually the citizens of Common Prosperity were neither totally heartless nor evil. Faced with the importunate pleas as well as the pathetic, wordless looks, they started to revise their thinking. Many people began to regret the atrocities. They avoided the glances of the orphans and widows who filled the streets with their countless pairs of eyes all swollen with tears, and, their hearts filled with shame, they hastened home. Good-natured citizens would take advantage of darkness to sneak out and bring a few titbits of food to the starving kids — cake-dumplings, palm-wrapped sticky-rice *zongzi*, that sort of thing. There were even those who went so far as to bring some roofless 'northern riff-raff' back to their homes for the night. They did their best to succour them in the darkness to make up for the suffering they caused them in the daytime.

But it was now too late The seeds of hatred had already been sown.

Night brought a breath of hot damp wind which made the reeds rustle on the lake surface, and at the mouth of the tributary outside the suburbs, the fleet of sailing boats which had gathered there swept gently past. Up above there wasn't the glimmer of a single star. It looked as if it would rain again tomorrow. This time of year with storms, cold, dark and muddy roads, the prospect was even more depressing for those who had to take to the road and travel afar.

The outsiders who had been beaten up had almost all decided to leave this place. Some of them were going south to seek a living; other honest folk, filled with despondency after trying to earn a living in a strange place, were turning back towards their old homes in the north.

'A golden nest or a silver nest, Nothing beat your own straw nest!' After supper the old fellow from Huai'an took his leave of Zhong. His

71

old woman was tidying their boat and getting the dry food ready. 'Little brother, is there any message you'd like me to take back home for you?'

'There's no one left there now. Anyone with any breath left in them came away too.'

They sat for a long time, staring silently, woodenly, each of them thinking his own thoughts. Going south had its particular hazards, while returning had its own problems.

'Anyway, since nowhere leads anywhere ... its my opinion, better to go home.'

Mr Zhong shook his head.

'Once we get through this bout of spring famine, perhaps things will start to get better gradually.' The old man gave a glance towards the city gate. 'As things are at present, it really won't be much fun here.'

Zhong nodded his head again. In fact he hadn't had any intention of staying in Common Prosperity.

'Little brother, don't you think it'd be better to go home? We can give each other a helping hand on the way.'

'I can't go back now.'

'*Can't* go back?' The old man was thoughtful. He appeared to have worked something out. 'You must be in some kind of trouble with the law. Are the authorities on your tail?'

'Nothing of the sort.'

'Don't worry, I'm not a grass.'

'Stop talking rubbish.'

'What sort of trouble is it?'

Zhong didn't want to go into it. He realised the old man was on to him and changed the subject, asking, 'Who are the big wheels in the underworld around here?'

'It used to be the "grain protection mob". I heard their chief was from Fujian, a fourth level gangster from the Yellow Section. They had eight thousand members and links with the Nine Songjiang Halls as well. They were really something. Later on during the Taiping rebellion, their boss was rubbed out. After that the 'Xin' lot got on top and the old gang were done away with.'

'And the Red Section?'

'There's no leader, not even any small fry.'

'What about a local?'

'The people around here all live in cloud cuckoo land, they're good at playing drag acts in the opera, and that's about it.' The old man saw

Zhong smile knowingly, so he probed further, 'What Order do you belong to brother?'

'The Fourth Order — the women's,' said Zhong, laughing.

The old man nodded, and ceased his questioning, while the younger man quizzed him carefully — probing gingerly one minute, pretending indifference the next — and generally beating around the bush. But not another drop of information could be squeezed out of the old man. Some people were really difficult to deal with. Those days it was hard for folk to get on with one another. Even idiots had turned into smart-alecks. Hearing the cry of the baby coming from inside the boat, the old man got up to say goodbye.

'Wait a bit,' Zhong said holding him back. He made a deep bow and respectfully requested, 'I would have great faith in your blessing, honoured sir. Would you be so good as to name our child?'

'What ... what ...'

'We trust in the good fortune your years have bestowed on you.'

The old man tried hard to wriggle out of it, but in the end, with evident pleasure, he gave in and consented. 'What's the child's place in the family?'

'The youngest son of three.'

'A third son ... ah! And he was born during the great flood as well. Let him be called Sanmiao.'

'Which characters are they?'

'"San" meaning "three"; and "miao" using the three dots of the water radical.'

'Sanmiao?'

'Three times three equals nine. "Great water" will play an important role in this child's fate.'

'Great water ...'

'In the life of a boatman, great water is good for navigating.'

'That's so.'

For the first time Zhong laughed heartily.

'I wish you smooth sailing honoured sir.'

'Many thanks, and smooth sailing to you too!' The old man remembered that he'd planned to follow the Gechuan River upstream. 'I hope everything will be fine in the south and that you will make your fortune ... Little brother, if things really are good down there, just send me word, and I'll set out again to see the world.'

'Of course, of course ...'

Zhong agreed readily, and took his leave of the old man.

Actually he didn't even know the old man's name, or even what county or village he came from.

But that was hardly important, and anyway he'd decided not to go to White Sands now. Instead he'd decided to settle and strike root here in Common Prosperity, to set up his home and bring up his family on this patch of ground where he had experienced all the humiliation of being an outsider, a place which was still filled with hostility towards him. The more other people drove him out, the more firmly he resolved to stay. 'That's the kind of animal I am.' He smiled grimly in the darkness.

Behind him the boat door creaked open and, stretching her head out, his wife asked, 'Aren't we leaving, father?'

'Yes, let's be off,' he agreed and went to the helm to pull up the anchor, then taking a punt in his hand he slowly pushed the boat away from the bank.

Gently he brought the boat's head round into the bend of the river.

'Where are we going, father?'

'Into town.'

His boat was laden with his woman and his kids, and those crabs which had crawled secretly on board. In the clear night air he headed for the dark shadow of the city wall, punting forward, hand over hand.

The
*LOST*
*BOAT*

o

LONGER
SHORT
STORIES

# THE LOST BOAT

## GE FEI

*ON 21ST MARCH 1928, an advance task force from the Northern Expeditionary Army suddenly appeared on the banks of the River Lian. Sun Chuanfang's forces, who were defending the area, surrendered without a fight, and the NEA swiftly took control of the strategic town of Yuguan, where the River Lian and the River Lan meet. Sun Chuanfang, while concentrating large numbers of troops at Linkou, also moved some of his crack divisions to defend a strategic pass in the mountains of Qishan, on the lower reaches of the River Lian. Late one night, Xiao, the commander of the 32nd Brigade, which was part of this defence force, slipped into the village of Little River, on the bank opposite the Qishan mountains, and seven days later suddenly vanished. His disappearance cast a mysterious shadow over the rainy season campaign which began a few days later.*

## PROLOGUE

XIAO RECEIVED SECRET INSTRUCTIONS from Divisional HQ on the morning of 7th April, telling him to take the 32nd Brigade and garrison the village of Little River, on the opposite side of the river from Qishan. This village, which consisted of only a few dozen peasant households, stuck out like a horn at a bend in the River Lian, and was an ideal spot for defence. According to his orders from HQ, he was to slip into the village in the small hours of the 9th and find out as quickly as possible all that he could about the situation there. HQ reminded him, 'Since we have spotted this strange area of open land, it is unlikely the NEA will miss it.' On the day before he was to set off there, by boat, something unexpected happened.

On 8th April, the oppressive afternoon sun made everyone lethargic and drowsy. Xiao was riding alone in the willow woods on the bank of the River Lian. As he passed a dazzling array of military tents in a valley on the northern slope of the mountains, a chestnut horse caught up with him.

His bodyguard reined in his horse at an angle to him on the left. The sun was shining full in Xiao's face and he could not open his eyes very wide. The bodyguard sat up straight on his still restive chestnut horse and smartly raised his right hand to brush the peak of his cap.

'There's an old lady waiting to see you at Brigade HQ.'

Xiao let his horse continue smoothly, steadily forwards for a few paces before turning its head around. The weather was extremely muggy. A cool breeze came over the ridge and passed over his head, but the air in the valley was thick and heavy. The bodyguard, still at the same spot, did not put up a hand to brush away the drops of sweat which kept rolling down his face — he just stared at Xiao nervously, waiting for his reply.

'Find a way to get rid of her —' Xiao waved his hand impatiently. The bodyguard urged his horse forward a few steps, lowered his voice and said rather timidly, 'She says she comes from Little River.'

Xiao gave him a brief glance and said nothing in reply. He whipped his horse to a gallop in the direction of Brigade HQ, his bodyguard trailing him some thirty yards behind in a cloud of dust. The war had made him weary of these minor nuisances. He knew that it was quite common for the relatives of soldiers killed in action to turn up unexpectedly at HQ, and that these strangers clutching notes with the names of their sons or husbands written on them would make ridiculous demands — asking for the belongings of the dead men, or trying to find out all sorts of details about the soldiers' last hours. Because this undesignated unit had never kept a list of the names of any of its officers or men killed in action, these poor folk often went away angry, sworn at by the junior officers and intimidated by their rifle butts. Even though Xiao's unit were crack troops under central command, they frequently had to fight at the front line when the supply situation was particularly bad. Sometimes all his men had to be replaced, as night replaces day, and a crowd of peasants who had hitherto only shot at birds was called up temporarily to carry out extremely tough sniping missions. On this afternoon, though it was almost as quiet as usual, he was deeply troubled by an ominous presentiment about the great battle which lay ahead.

When he walked into the provisional Brigade HQ, whip in hand, he immediately recognised the old lady from his home village. She was Mrs Ma, the village match-maker. In the few short years that he had been away from home in the army, this woman who had been so attractive and so full of life had suddenly grown old. The passion and generosity she displayed towards the men in the village had provoked endless disputes among the women. During intervals in the fighting, she had often been the focus of his recollections of the past in his old village. She had come to bring him the news of his father's death.

His father had been lighting the stove at dusk one day, when the choking smoke coming back into the room reminded him that they had not swept the chimney for a long time. The old man of seventy-eight had climbed, very shakily, onto the roof, carrying a bamboo pole with a bundle of rice-straw tied to it. He broke three tiles and two rotten beams before falling to his death in the water-tank by the kitchen. When the match-maker, in her shrill voice, had given her almost comical account of his father's death, Xiao appeared exceptionally calm. He felt no sudden pangs of grief or fear. He cast his mind back briefly over his father's life, and asked his bodyguard for a cigarette. The fingers with which he struck the match trembled a little, but he knew it was from lack of sleep, not from grief.

Oblivious to the people round him, he walked out of the command-post and over to the old poplar tree where he had tethered his horse. As he untied the reins he heard behind him the sound of footsteps on the thick, uneven grass. It was his bodyguard who, feeling uneasy, had followed him out. Xiao turned to glare at him, which made him stop in his tracks.

It was already dusk as Xiao rode alone from the northern slope up onto one of the lower peaks of Qishan. It had been drizzling for the last few days but now it was sunny. The dimly visible village on the far bank of the River Lian was dyed orange in the rich evening light. The long narrow path at the bottom of the valley was covered with wild flowers. All around, the countryside was open and peaceful. He thought of the past, of the ruins under artillery fire, and a strong desire to write poetry welled up in him. His father had been one of the lucky few survivors of the Small Sword Society, and one of the handful of leaders who knew how to handle a gun. His experience of warfare, and his large collection of books on military strategies meant that Xiao had been exposed to the atmosphere of war from an early age. The neighing of horses and the rumble of guns often featured in his dreams. Finally, he went up to his father one day and asked him why he had committed himself to an army which was defeated. His father flinched, but his reply was casual: there were no such things as defeated armies or victorious armies, there were only wolves and hunters. His mother was a born worrier. For her, the continuous fighting and the rapid maturing of her children were a constant anxiety. The day before his elder brother was to go off to the Whampoa Military Academy, she wept her heart out and cursed her husband vociferously for letting the boy have his own way and putting him on the road to death because of his own ridiculous expectations about the war. All of a sudden she became very high-handed and determined, and shut his skinny brother up with a couple of goats for three days. On the third day, at the dead of night, Xiao stole the key to the gate in the solid wooden fence. His brother walked away in the moonlight with hardly a word to him. Their parents were fast asleep at the time. After that, his mother was worried that Xiao might go the same way as his brother, so she sent him off on a small boat to the busy little town of Yuguan, to learn medicine from one of his uncles. It was a blazing hot summer. Xiao had gained a good deal of experience from all the trouble over his brother's departure. When he was about to start work as an orderly to one of Sun Chuanfang's officers he went back to the village wearing a very stiffly starched shirt. Because he said nothing when he left, his mother thought he was going on a visit to the next village, to size up a possible bride.

Dusk was all around him. The cool evening breeze brought with it a breath of dampness from the River Lian. His white horse was moving about restively on the hilltop, its hooves scuffing the earth. Far away, the village opposite was already submerged in darkness. As his horse went leaping down the hillside, he remembered the report he had heard a few days earlier, when he went to a meeting at HQ — the unit which had taken Yuguan on 21st March turned out to be his brother's.

## DAY ONE

XIAO AND HIS BODYGUARD crossed the river before dawn. As they reached the far bank they heard the first cock crowing in the village. Xiao rowed the little boat towards some leafy camellia bushes which hung down over the bank — it would be a good place to hide it. The water gurgling by rocked the boat gently, and a black waterbird suddenly emerged, flying low along the river bank and away. Xiao could feel a slight coolness among the dew-pearled creepers, and the heavy scent of the flowers and the smell of the water filled his heart with wonderful, peaceful fancies. He was quite unaware of the catastrophe which, before long, this beautiful village would bring him.

After climbing up the bank, he passed a grove of dense bamboo and went into the village which he knew so well. Behind the village, the crescent moon was sinking into the west, and in the east dawn was about to break over the river. The women drawing water at the well did not recognise him. Now and again old men, up early, walked past him coughing, and disappeared into the thin mist. The villagers had long since ceased to take an interest in strangers, and reserved any warm feelings that they had for the bellows of the tinker, the horse-headed combs of the men who came to tease the cotton, and the whistles of the traders who came for the malt sugar. Xiao passed through the long, narrow lanes and between the thatched huts, and nobody paid any attention to him, although he did provoke a long drawn-out bout of frenzied and rather spine-chilling barking from the dogs. A few ripples disturbed the tranquillity of his heart, but he was soon revelling once more in the clear scents of the peach blossom and the young wheat.

His family's house was on the western edge of the village. From far off the gate appeared to be closed, and it was only when he got closer that he realised that a length of black mourning cloth had been hung over the open gateway. When he lifted up the cloth and walked into the yard, his mother was there with a kerosene lamp in her hands, and it gave her quite a start when two black shadows suddenly picked up the curtain and burst in — although she still kept her grip on the lamp. But when she recognised her son, now wearing a trim little moustache, she threw the lamp into a drain about ten feet away from her. She looked at him for a long while, and found that he had changed completely. The expression in his eyes was exactly the same as the expression in her husband's eyes just before he died: they were deep-sunken eyes, without a glimmer of brightness. The feeling of foreboding which she had had when her husband had fallen off the roof into the water-tank welled up in her once more. When she took her son into the room where the body was lying, she burnt three more wads of funeral money, not out of grief for her husband's death, but to ward off calamity for her son. Xiao knelt heavily by his father's coffin. His tranquil mood was not disturbed by the solemn atmosphere of the room; as he saw it, his father had been dead ever since his unit had ceased to exist and he had shut himself away in this village north of the River Lian. The one thing he felt guilty about was the way he himself had deceived his mother and treated her so badly before he left home. Staring fixedly at her thin shoulders, he became conscious of all the changes that the war had brought about in him. He felt as if a very fine goose-feather were stirring up things from the past which were hidden deep in his heart, but the feeling passed almost at once. He stood up and took a deep breath. The air was full of the scent of burnt incense and paper money.

His mother noticed that his face looked old and pale, and his hair was untidy, so she got out a wooden comb and a pair of scissors and made him tidy up his moustache. He asked, puzzled, why the room where his father's body lay was so deserted, and his mother said that in the latter half of his life his father had hardly ever left the house, and did not like mixing with ordinary people. Because of the war, they had had no news for a long time from any relatives, near or far. She only ever went into the spare rooms and the back yard at the Double Ninth festival, to get rid of the rats. By now the damp ground there might already be covered with water-weeds and moss. Xiao remained unmoved by his mother's sobs as she spoke. He asked her some more questions about the funeral ceremony, but she seemed not to have heard, and for a long time did not reply. He took a deep breath and then fell silent.

This was the longest conversation he had had with his mother.

In the afternoon, Xiao and his bodyguard checked every corner of the village and found no one there who came from outside. He thought to himself how fortunate it was that the NEA had not yet noticed this remote village north of the River Lian. The village had been untroubled by the flames of war for at least a thousand years, and the villagers believed that this peace would continue far into the future, just as the river went on flowing past, day after day. They did not make the slightest connection between the two strangers who had made the dogs bark early in the morning, and the war. All they ever spoke of, among the sounds of the cattle being driven home by the herd boys in the twilight, or beside the well as the shadows under the eaves gradually lengthened, were the things which never changed over the years. Just as the sun was about to sink behind the hills and Xiao was getting ready to go out onto the river to make a survey of the terrain, the bodyguard reported to him that there was a Daoist priest of unknown origin on the fan-shaped piece of ground used for drying grain in the centre of the village, and his fortune-telling was so accurate that an increasingly large crowd was gathering there.

The crowd on the drying-ground, out of the respect due to strangers, made a small opening for Xiao and his bodyguard as they squeezed in among them. The Daoist was in the middle of predicting what the fortune of the village would be. He had lost nearly all his teeth, and spoke very indistinctly. A thick layer of grease had accumulated on his heavily-patched gown. In front of him, an old yellow flag was spread out. The divination characters on it were very blurred, because the writing had run. He was sitting cross-legged on the ground, with piles of tortoise-shells, snake-skins and medicinal plasters beside him. In addition to these, he also had two revolving discs and a bamboo scoop sprinkled with glutinous millet.

He pondered for a while, then murmured something which no one could possibly understand, and waved his hand in the direction of the pious village folk as they waited to find out what was in store for their village: the Heavenly Scorpion was travelling south, the Two Fishes were going north, Capricorn was settling in the west, and the Maid would marry in the east — the war was past.

A barely perceptible smile of disdain hovered on Xiao's cheeks. He felt that people always lived in a world of illusion. For him, the future was already quietly reaching into the present, and the war had begun. His pity for the villagers did not sweep away the shadow of his perplexity about himself — like them, he too lived in a sort of illusion. Before dawn today, when he had stepped into that little boat in the thin mist and looked at the soundly sleeping village far off on the opposite bank, an inexplicable excitement welled up in him. He did not know if his impatience to go home was because of his father's death or because he missed his mother, or perhaps it was a yearning to revisit the village which bore the record of his childhood. He felt as if some even greater, more significant force was urging him on.

One by one, the people on the drying-ground went away, and the sky slowly grew dark. Xiao felt that the Daoist was unlikely to be a spy for the NEA, and he tossed a copper coin down at the old man's feet as he was collecting up his bundles and the rest of his paraphernalia. The Daoist paid no attention to the coin as it rolled noiselessly along the ground, and did not pause in his tidying-up, but he raised his head and shot a glance at Xiao.

'Does that mean you would like me to tell your fortune, sir? Is it marriage or money?'

'Life and death,' said Xiao. He lit a cigarette. He was gazing beyond the low-growing thickets of mock indigo to the motionless mist which cloaked the far-off River Lian, and while the Daoist was working out his eight 'natal characters' on his fingers, it grew completely dark.

The Daoist mumbled a single sentence, 'Beware of your wine-cup.'

That evening, the bodyguard brought in two bottles of the local liquor and a packet of beef. As usual, he laid out a pair of bamboo chopsticks and a china wine-cup in front of Xiao, then sat beside him, his hands on the edge of the table. Xiao pushed the cup towards him and poured him some of the liquor, then lit himself a cigarette.

Just like a girl, the bodyguard fluttered his fine, long eyelashes, stole a glance at his commanding officer, and, with some hesitation, picked up the cup. Xiao saw once again, in his eyes, the cunning gleam which had been in the eyes of the Daoist.

He thought that the bodyguard must have detected his nervousness and, despite the fact that he was just an unsophisticated boy, Xiao still felt an anxiety and a melancholy he could not suppress.

As his mother pushed open the door and came in, Xiao saw behind her the graceful shadow of a woman slipping into the gloom of the mourning-room.

## DAY TWO

THE WOMAN WHO HAD VANISHED behind his mother the previous day sparked off endless thoughts and associations for him, and he breathed in as greedily as if he had smelt the fragrance of fruit on the hot summer wind. It was not until they met again at his father's funeral the next day that he recognised her.

That evening he went to sleep amid the clamour of wailing in the room where the corpse was laid. After midnight, the sound of a *huqin* tuning up woke him. No one in the village had died for a long time and the musicians who played at funerals had lost their previous rapport. This neglect of their skills meant that all they could produce were a few intermittent screeches. When Xiao sat up in bed, the discordant music made him sneeze several times in a row. By the light of the moon, pouring in through the rotting lattice, he discovered from the hands of his pocket-watch that it was nearly three o'clock. When his father's funeral ceremony formally began, he followed close behind the musicians, still not fully awake. The moonlight was obscured by scudding black clouds, and his steps faltered slightly. The smells of thorn-trees and grass on the night breeze were a heady mix, all round him. He gazed at the shadows of the hills looming in the distance and recalled the sweltering summer he had spent in his uncle's home.

Due to his brother's sudden enlistment in the army, and under duress from his mother, he had taken a passing boat to Yuguan, which stood at the junction of the Rivers Lian and Lan, and studied medicine with his uncle. His uncle was an honest, good-natured doctor of traditional Chinese medicine. Formerly, it had been his habit to earn his living by wandering from place to place and practising medicine, but his wife had died in childbirth and, because it was difficult having no one to look after his daughter, he had opened a herbal medicine shop in a street near the river in Yuguan. For the first few days after his arrival in Yuguan, Xiao felt extremely restless and impatient and the only things which vaguely interested him as he leafed through tome after yellowing tome on medicine in the bamboo hut by the river were the occasional illustrations of the human body. Under the rays of the blazing summer sun, he would look out of the window at the motionless reflections of the sails far away on the river. The sound of rapid, clattering horses' hooves was often in his ears. Time flowed quietly by, as the shadow on the sun-dial grew longer and shorter, and his uncle, detecting that he had little interest in pharmacology or in books, let him study acupuncture and moxibustion instead. One day, at midday, the sky suddenly filled with dark clouds, and the rumbling of thunder made him restless inside the bamboo hut. His uncle had not yet come back from seeing patients, and Xiao was practising sticking needles into a winter-melon when his uncle's daughter came up into the study. She was looking for a red oil-paper umbrella. When she had found it and was about to go downstairs she saw Xiao stabbing needle after needle into the winter-melon and producing puddles of clear juice. She went over to him and showed him the right way to do it. She had come with his uncle to meet him when he stepped off the ferry onto the quay in Yuguan that day, and he had missed a marvellous opportunity of getting to know her. Because of the resentment that he was feeling towards his mother, and the scorching heat, he had not spared her a single glance. And now, this girl called Xing was turning the fine silver needle with her index-finger, thumb and middle finger, and he suddenly felt a slightly bitter, salty taste rising up in his throat. He could not take his eyes off her pale, slender hand. It was as if the needle had entered one of his veins, and he could smell a fresh fruit fragrance in the room, getting stronger and stronger. She left the room, having spoken no more than a few sentences to him. When she had gone, the odour she left behind seemed to solidify inside the room. In the whole endless, solitary summer which Xiao spent there, this scent never disappeared.

Xiao's uncle went to a lot of trouble to arrange a series of practice sessions for him, based on his own experience of medicine. After two weeks of sticking needles into winter-melons, his uncle let him practise on a rabbit, and his mood rapidly became even worse than it had been before. This animal leaping about in his hands was harder to handle than the winter-melons. When his uncle was there, he could manage, very cautiously, to insert the needle into its neck or its stomach, but once his uncle had gone, he would immediately stop concentrating and stick the needle in quite carelessly, killing off a rabbit nearly every day. His uncle shook his head and sighed over him more and more often, and in the end abandoned the idea of making him learn acupuncture and started him on learning how to make a diagnosis from a patient's pulse. Much to his uncle's surprise, Xiao mastered this in two hours.

One day in late summer, he went into the yard below the house at noon, while his uncle was having a siesta in the study. Xing was asleep on a deck-chair beneath the gingko tree. She was holding a book of legends about annual festivals — it lay open on her chest, rising and falling as she breathed. Xiao sat, mesmerised, on a bamboo stool very close to her. Its creaking brought him out in a cold, nervous sweat. Her other hand was hanging limply over the back of the chair. Xiao could hear his own heavy breathing, and the sound of the oars coming up from boats being rowed on the river. A drowsy white butterfly flew in front of him, as he lightly touched her soft fingertips, then put his hand on her pulse. He could feel the blood coursing swiftly beneath her milk-white skin. He was sure that she would not wake up.

And, indeed, she didn't.

When, during his later, rather turbulent, military career, he lay in some quiet hollow in the hills, looking at the starry sky and swallowing the bitter juices of grass-roots and leaves, he would sometimes remember how time had drifted by on that stifling afternoon, and recall how his finger-tips had lightly stroked her smooth arm, and the intoxicating feeling he had when he undid the top button at her neck, suddenly sensing that she might perhaps be awake. That realisation had never left him since.

Now he had smelt that fruit fragrance again.

When the coffin had been put down safely in the graveyard, the ranks of mourners slowly surrounded the gentle slope covered with pear blossom. Xiao sensed that Xing was somewhere among the scattered groups of people, and it seemed as if an ice-cold water-snake was climbing up his spine. After the funeral ceremony, he heard from his mother that Xing had married into the village a month previously. Her husband, San Shun, was an expert on treating sick animals. This young man, who had the strength to floor an ox, was crazy about veterinary medicine. He had read the *Medical Dictionary* and the *Compendium of Materia Medica* from cover to cover, and had also made a special study of the *Classic of the Yellow Emperor*, a book which very few people understood. When he ran into Xiao's uncle in the street in Yuguan, the old man was drawn to him at once because of his erudition. When the old doctor of traditional medicine found out that San Shun had successfully transferred to animals the methods used for curing people, he could only deeply regret the fact that they had never met before. They talked deep into the night in a corner tea-house, and this chance meeting had helped to bring about a very satisfactory marriage for the young man.

Xiao's father's coffin was placed gently in the grave, where a lot of copper coins and funeral money had been scattered. An elderly undertaker, leaning on a stick, handed Xiao an iron shovel. He shovelled up a lump of earth and sprinkled it over the lid of the coffin. Suddenly, he sensed that there were eyes burning into him from behind. He very slightly altered his angle of vision, turned round and saw Xing, dressed in mourning, standing beside his mother. Behind her were the deserted fields and, perched on a solitary silk tree, a magpie and a green-headed flycatcher.

One by one, the mourners in the grave-yard dispersed. Xing and his mother planted a few speckled bamboo and a snow pine in front of the grave. Xiao stood next to a field of brilliant yellow rape, and the wordless affection between Xing and his mother gave him a flicker of consolation. He fished a box of matches out of his pocket and walked over to the grave, where he set fire to the remaining yellow, dew-sodden funeral money. He poked with a stick at the bits of paper which lay curled in the ashes, and the April breeze lifted them up. Some little balls of pale grey ash rolled as far as the newly planted snow pine, and Xing's feet. She was just bending down and stamping the earth level over the roots of the tree, treading the ashes of the paper which had blown over into the soil, when she raised her head in the direction of the wind and glanced at him, very quickly. He squatted down not far away from her, and his eyes saw nothing apart from the silhouette of her graceful body.

When they went back to the village, his mother and Xing walked ahead of him. The bodyguard must still have been fast asleep, for Xiao could not hear the familiar sound of footsteps behind him, which seemed rather strange. But the sky ahead suddenly became broad and spacious, and he felt that now he could see everything.

None of them spoke. Behind them, the sun had just risen.

## DAY THREE

WITH THE FUNERAL OVER, the village regained its former peace and quiet. The fresh sunlight gradually increased its heat as noon approached. It was now the slack season, when the wheat was not yet in ear, and the tender young willow leaves had not yet completely unfurled. The farmers, who found it hard to cope with all their leisure-time, were unhurriedly pruning their peach trees and mulberries. In the afternoon, the village was even quieter than at night. Xing went to the grove of tea-bushes behind the village, to pick some of the green tea which was now in season, and when her slender figure had become a motionless black dot beside the distant, sparkling irrigation ditch, someone else also crossed the wooden bridge behind the village, and headed for the tea-bushes by the same route that she had taken.

This was a very long day, but it seemed to pass quickly. As usual, Xiao had risen early. When Mrs Ma came into the yard, he was squatting by the drain and brushing his teeth with salt. The bodyguard was still sound asleep. Because he had had too much to drink the night before last, he had not been woken by the blaring sounds of the horns and the noise of the crowd in the funeral procession. Now that the war had suddenly begun to develop so rapidly, every man in the army was feeling more worn out than ever before. Xiao was usually extremely strict with his subordinates, but he did have a deeply hidden softer side to his character. In the past he had been furious with this ignorant youth for being so slow on the uptake, but now, as the war took away the familiar faces round him, one by one, his faithful bodyguard had become his sole companion in the holocaust. He found that as he became gradually more tolerant of the boy's stupidity, his relationship with this uncommunicative subordinate of his had grown closer every day. Mrs Ma had come to borrow a fine sieve. She said that the rapeseed they had kept from last year was full of weevils, and she was going to sieve it before taking it to the oil-mill. She did not leave immediately she got the sieve, because there was something that she wanted to say to Xiao. But just then his mother came back from weeding in the fields, the scarf on her head covered with wet petals. Mrs Ma hastily began a conversation with her, which ranged from the rose of Sharon blooming in the yard to the rise and fall of the River Lian. While she was talking to his mother, she kept glancing at Xiao. The former matchmaker may have lost her earlier good looks, but her surreptitious glances still reminded Xiao of what she had been like in her youth. In the autumn of the year in which she had married into Little River from a distant mountain village, her husband had suddenly gone off on a passing boat, and had never been heard from again. Village gossip had it that he had fallen for a skivvy who washed dishes on board the boat, and that was why he had left. But people who knew told her that her man could not stand their unending and increasing poverty and had gone off to join the army. This conjecture was proved correct three years later, when his body was brought home by some strangers. While the village women comforted the meek young woman with their tears, the village men comforted her in a different way. And so, before long, the village women fell out with her. But even though she had made enemies of almost all the women in the village, the young widow had a relationship of mutual respect with Xiao's mother. Xiao remembered how his mother often used to take him to her solitary little hut by the river. At that time, he was unable to understand many of the things that women talked about. Very late one night, his mother, puffing away at a cigarette, and Mrs Ma had sat opposite each other, and they had both cried. They told each other in low voices of some things long past, but for most of the time they did not speak: each of them mulling over her own worries, sunk into lengthy reminiscence. They were accompanied by the chirping of the insects at the foot of the wall. Xiao was bored by the silence of these women in their shared intimacy, and he fell asleep with his head in his mother's lap. The sound of the night-watchman's gong woke them when it was nearly light. Xiao distinctly remembered the sight of Mrs Ma's soft breasts, wrapped in her blue blouse, hanging over the table as she bent forward to blow out the guttering oil-lamp, and the early dawn light seeping little by little into the room.

Mrs Ma brushed the petals off his mother's scarf, and she went into the inner room. Mrs Ma led Xiao outside. They stood by an apricot tree in full bloom at the corner of the wall, and after glancing all around, Mrs Ma lowered her voice and said,

'San Shun has gone fishing a long way upriver. He won't be back for two days.'

When she had said this she went off, carrying the bamboo sieve. Xiao felt deeply embarrassed. He had felt the same sort of embarrassment when his mother had scrubbed him down in the bath-tub just when he was becoming dimly aware of what happened between men and women. Women always thought complex things were so simple, and imagined simple things to be terribly complex. He stood for a long time by the corner of the wall, wishing that he had found out more about Xing from the match-maker, but her figure was already receding from view. Angrily, he went back into the house. He sat in the yard next to two pots of ornamental bamboo and watched the clouds moving slowly across the sky. He felt tremendously agitated, and not at all sure what he ought to do. This mood stayed with him until he caught sight of Xing, carrying a bamboo basket and walking towards the back of the village from the willow copse by the river.

Behind the village of Little River was a broad expanse of open plain. The far edge of the plain was hidden by the dark line of a windbreak forest. Xing's tea-bushes were on a mound a long way from the village, and to the east of this mound was a very deep ravine. The water at the bottom of the ravine was full of green plants. Xiao saw Xing's distant figure disappear among the tea-bushes. All around was open and still. The tips of the grass and the leaves of the young wheat drooped slightly in the midday sun, and a hunter, out after pheasants with his light brown dog, walked lazily along by the winding river. Xiao saw him stop beside an old man who was collecting cow-dung, apparently to ask for a light. The light brown dog raised a front paw and licked the old man's trouser-leg. The men chatted for a while, then each went his own way. A barely perceptible breeze brought with it the rich scent of tea.

Xiao sank once again into the confusion which Mrs Ma's unexpected morning visit had created. He felt that her words had uncovered a mystery long hidden in his heart, but that it now seemed to have changed into another, even deeper kind of mystery. He had no idea how Mrs Ma had turned up out of the blue at the little-known HQ in Qishan, or how on earth she had divined what was going through his head. Had Xing ever been to that isolated thatched hut by the River Lian? The scene from his summer in Yuguan was puzzling him again, deep down in his mind.

The tawny mound resembled a bare island emerging from the middle of clear water. As Xiao approached it, Xing was not aware of him. A swift which flew up and skimmed the water in the bottom of the ravine alerted her to his presence.

Very gently he pulled her down.

He could smell the scent of the earth coming from the shady spaces between the rows of dark green tea-bushes. His agitation suddenly vanished. He lay on the sun-baked, weary earth and heard its strong voice, throbbing gently from near and far. There was a breath of warm wind, and he silently recalled an old folk-rhyme. This feeling of tranquillity did not last long — soon he was once more dissolved in a sense of boundless loneliness. Xing was sobbing in his arms. He felt as if her weeping, and her arms clasped tightly round him, were sucking all the marrow out of his bones, and his whole body was icy cold. Her eyes were closed tight, as if she was fast asleep. The closer he held her, the further away from him she seemed to be. He felt himself sinking into a vast quagmire, his struggles serving only to exhaust his vitality. Then his whole body was bathed in warmth, as the sense of separation to which a man is born spread swiftly through him as he lay in the young woman's embrace. He experienced a tension and then an exhaustion that he had never felt before.

A water-buffalo's horn appeared at a bend in the ravine, followed by another. A herd-boy was sitting on the buffalo's back, driving the gadflies away with his bare feet.

The young ox-herd did not notice them.

## DAY FOUR

XIAO MADE HIS WAY to Xing's red house as if he were walking in his sleep.

San Shun was not yet back. At dusk, a strong wind began to blow on the River Lian.

## DAY FIVE

THE RAIN CAME in the middle of the night. In his dreams, Xiao heard the thunder which presaged the spring floods on the river. When he woke, the cocks were crowing everywhere. The big buds on the thorn trees, gorged with rain, had fallen all over the sandy ground, now scoured clean by the downpour. A combination of the enticing scent of the flowers, and the sun, blazing after the rain, made him very keen to go fishing. He rummaged around and brought out his father's long disused fishing rod from under the bed. It was made of Hebei bamboo which had gone mouldy, and the iron ferrules were covered with damp, brown rust. He got some chicken feathers from the yard and trimmed them into floats. While he was sorting out the line, the bodyguard collected a small jar full of worms, for bait, from under the trees near the house. Soon they were on the river-bank.

Little River village was on the lower reaches of the River Lian. At the bend in the river before it joined the River Lan, the flow of water was quite turbulent. The leaves and willow-catkins which had been peacefully floating along the surface were suddenly swept into eddies when they passed over the masses of uneven boulders which lined the river-bed. When the women washing clothes on the stone jetty in the river saw him casting his line at a spot on the opposite bank where the current was very swift, they could not help laughing. They said,

'He's only been away from home a few years, but he's forgotten all about fishing! In water like that, he'll only catch weeds.'

He did not hear the women's comments, but he did hear the advice his hitherto taciturn bodyguard gave him, 'The water here is very fast.

It might be better to go downstream a bit and find somewhere where the water is calmer.'

'But you can catch arrow-fish and shuttle-fish where there is a strong current,' said Xiao.

The bodyguard did not utter a sound after that. Xiao lit a cigarette. He knew that fishing in this kind of water demanded great patience. He remembered that his father had often fished that stretch of water when he was alive, from sunrise to sunset, and come home empty-handed almost every time. He sat in the deep shade cast by the hazel trees, gazing at the columns of geese flying past from the village, and the motionless clouds. Gradually, his gaze shifted to a right-angled red wall to the west of the village. It was Xing's house. Xiao knew that only by sitting in this place could he look over the red wall and get a clear view of everything in the yard.

The sun was already high in the sky. The spacious yard was silent and still. The door to the central room was shut, and there were a few hens pecking for food below the porch. Last night, when he left her yard, Xing had leant against the door, just staring at him. The south wind brushed over the water and made a rustling sound in the groves of bamboo. Up amongst the cold, distant stars, there was a hazy moon with a halo round it. The buttons of her blouse were undone, and her hair was loose over her shoulders. Xiao looked at her long and hard, and the chilly spring night made him shiver repeatedly. As she shut the black-painted gate she said that if San Shun did not come back that night she would hang a basket on the clothes-line in the yard next day.

The spring sun shone warm on the water. Xiao gazed uneasily at the rain-scoured courtyard. He did not see a basket hung on the clothes-line in the yard, but he did suddenly make out Mrs Ma, signalling to him from the clump of willows in the village on the other side of the river.

'The bait you got are too small,' Xiao said to the bodyguard. 'And they're dark. The fish move fast in the water here, and it's hard for them to see dark-coloured worms. Come on, let's go back.'

Puzzled, the bodyguard glanced at him. He was bored just sitting there, and the windless weather made him sleepy. He helped Xiao to bring in the line, bewildered by his brigade commander's changeable moods, as if he had no clue as to what Xiao was thinking. He had, apparently, been unaware of all the things that had happened to Xiao in the few short days since they had come to Little River.

He's just a child, thought Xiao calmly, as they walked back.

Mrs Ma was bubbling away at her water-pipe. She dragged him to a deserted spot and for a long time said nothing. He noticed that her eyes were frightened and kept avoiding his, and her dainty little feet were trembling slightly. The match-maker lowered her husky voice and, looking very upset, told him that his affair with Xing had been discovered and that all the neighbours had been alarmed by her screams and sobs the previous night.

San Shun had come back very late, not long after Xiao had left. The overdue spring rains were beginning to fall intermittently. The clever young animal specialist had scented something unusual in the atmosphere almost as soon as he stepped through the gate. Neither the strong smell of fish which he gave off, nor his weariness after several days of fishing prevented him from putting two and two together. He set his heavy nets down on the chicken coop in the yard, ignoring the bowl of hot water Xing brought to wash his feet in. Her halting walk, and the flush which was still on her cheeks, aroused his suspicions. He took her indoors and let down the blinds. Xing's legs were trembling slightly, but she patted his rough, stubbly cheeks affectionately and said she would go into the kitchen and get him something to eat. As she made to leave the bedroom, San Shun caught hold of her. He gave her a gentle push and she fell back a few paces onto the edge of the bed. He deftly removed her clothes and shoes, picked her up and threw her onto the bed, letting down the bed-curtains as he did so, and blowing out the lamp on the table. In the darkness, Xing heard him take off his leather belt, but the sound did not excite her as it had before — instead, it warned her of imminent catastrophe, and in spite of herself she started to cry. As soon as San Shun's clammy body touched her skin, her own went rigid, as if electrified.

Xiao fished out all the coins he had in his pocket and put them into Mrs Ma's hand, not to reward the old lady for all her to-ings and fro-ings during the past few days, but to try and calm her down while she was speaking. But she was unable to hold on to them — her fingers were twitching like small animals, and two of the coins fell to the ground between them.

San Shun strung Xing up from the roof-beam with a thick rope, and after he had broken six willow-branches on her, she told him Xiao's name. By then it was midnight, and the neighbours were woken by her screams and cries. They flooded into the red-walled courtyard. The door to the inner room was bolted, but through the cracks in it they could see Xing's naked body hanging there, and they began trying to smash the door down. It was made of new gingko wood, and they flattened the two great circular iron handles and broke a hole in the door. They were going to reach through this opening to draw back the bolt, but suddenly they stopped short. All those who were looking in through the cracks and the hole in the door held their breath. Behind them the others had no idea of what was going on inside the room: San Shun had heated a small pig-gelding knife in the flame of the oil-lamp and swiftly gouged out part of Xing's lower belly. He did it with a practised ease, as if he were scooping the flesh out of a papaya. Xing no longer had the strength to cry out. Her body jerked violently several times and then she lost consciousness.

Mrs Ma's water-pipe had emptied long ago. She seemed to be stunned by her own story, as if she would never get over the awful act committed by this hitherto good-natured and unassertive young man. At dawn that day, some kind women had taken the still unconscious Xing back to her family's home in Yuguan, by boat. The villagers saw nothing strange in the affair — unfaithful wives were quite often sent back home mutilated like this. But there were some other things which Mrs Ma did not tell Xiao. The most important of these was that San Shun had told everyone that he was going to kill Xiao, and he was now missing from the village.

## DAY SIX

EVEN THOUGH XIAO KNEW that San Shun had disappeared from the village, he went to Xing's house on the afternoon of the fifth day and walked around inside its red walls, his pistol in his hand. The yard was empty and spacious, as it had been before. Just as he was about to leave the red house with its strange fruit fragrance, he noticed a figure dart past in the bamboo grove. He unconsciously gripped his pistol more tightly. There were six bullets in it. He had grown extremely irritable and wished he could find someone to shoot them at. The dense foliage of the bamboo grove gave what seemed like a shudder, and out walked his bodyguard. Xiao let out a long sigh of relief.

After they got back home, the bodyguard very cautiously reminded him that perhaps they ought to return to Qishan, because the big battle was about to begin. Xiao angrily pounded the table with his pistol butt, and his mother, alarmed by the noises coming from the room, pushed open the door and came in. She already knew about everything that had happened, and was looking for an opportunity to have a talk with her son. She was very scared when she saw Xiao glaring at the bodyguard, and she went over to the table, grabbed the gun and slammed it into the nearest drawer.

Xiao stood up and walked out without a word. Very gingerly, his mother followed him. She felt it was imperative to talk to him, because she was convinced that if San Shun had threatened to kill him, he was sure to succeed. She knew very well how unpredictable his family was. San Shun's father had also been a meek and law-abiding fisherman, but because of some minor quarrel he had once caused a brawl involving thirty or forty people. Xiao was unaware that she was following him. He went into his father's study and closed the door.

No one had been into this dark, dusty room since his father's funeral. He lit the oil-lamp on the table and raised the wick, which was covered with grime. He sat at his father's desk, gazing at his father's portrait on the wall. A black frame had been pasted round the edge of the portrait. It had been carefully cut out of a square of gauze, and he could almost see his mother, painstakingly sewing it in the lamplight. The people in their village did not know that the art of photography had been invented a long time ago, and so his family had asked a doctor who sold medicinal plasters to paint his father's portrait. The itinerant artist had not made his father's eyes quite deep enough, and his jacket looked very ill-fitting, but, although the portrait was so unlike its subject, Xiao could tell that the painter had expended a good deal of ingenuity on his father's expression — that calm, profound expression in his eyes was one he had known well. The day before he left home, his father had been lying on a cane chair in the yard, reading a book of poems copied by a reciter of ancient verse called Mei. He used to pick up this book nearly every day in the latter half of his life. Xiao knew that when his brother went to the Whampoa Military Academy he had gone with their father's tacit consent, and he had hoped very much that his father would be able to discern his own intention of joining the army in the same way, and give him some guidance. He hung around for a long time that day, but his father had not paid him any attention. Through the gate he could see the river, dazzling in the sunshine, and the small boats beached on the ochre sand along its edge. One of the fellows who was going with him to enlist was waving to him. By then, it was twilight. He had never been sure whether, when he was appointed orderly to one of Sun Chuanfang's officers, his father had silently approved or not. Later, in all the frequent fighting, he wondered more and more if he had not unwittingly gone against his father's wishes.

His father's reddish-brown chair had been worn a light brown. You could still see your reflection in the tall, shiny bookcase made of carved redwood. He casually picked up from the desk some writing which his father had been doing just before he died, and looked it over. It had been underneath an ink slab with the words 'River Lian Coarse Ink' incised on it. As he flicked through the bamboo-paper book which his father had used for copying out Han and Wei dynasty stone-rubbings, he suddenly noticed that there was a copy in it of a letter from his father to his brother. Because his father's brush had not taken up much ink, the writing looked exceedingly bold and sparse. Xiao found his own name in the last few lines of the letter.

His father had written, 'I no longer dare to hope that I will see him again. His unit will soon be wiped out. I am not as anxious now as I was before, but I do worry about hearing the news of his death.'

Xiao felt as if someone had stuck a needle into his spine. Even though his father had not really meant to imply that he blamed him, he still felt ashamed. He sat blankly at his father's desk. The afternoon slipped away like so much sand. His innate pride and stubbornness forced him to calm himself, and for the first time he seemed to wake up from the nightmare of the last few days in Little River. He had had no hopes or expectations of any sort before, but now an intense desire for victory made him eager to hurry back and rejoin his unit at once. He remembered seeing all those reports from the front line not long ago, which said that Sun Chuanfang's troops were on the verge of total collapse under the onslaught of the NEA. The surrender, without a fight, of the 72nd and 31st Divisions had cast an indelible shadow over the men, whose morale was already low. Xiao was assailed by an ominous presentiment, but it soon vanished, and his headstrong and totally impractical nature meant that he put all his hopes into the campaign which was just about to begin. He believed that since there was no other way out for him, he should take the risk. He could not tell whether this absurd desire had grown out of the resentment that he felt towards his father, and a wish to mock him, or if it was an appeal to his father's soul in heaven to forgive him for making the wrong choice. He made up his mind to hurry back to Qishan at once.

Just as he was getting up to leave his father's study, a faint thought slipped through the recesses of his mind and made him change his plans once more.

He thought of Xing.

Her gentle, perplexed gaze came before his eyes. A cool fruit fragrance seemed to waft by him. He remembered the baking hot summer he had spent in Yuguan, and the dispensary built of bamboo near the water. He thought of all the occasions when images of her had flashed in front of him in the swirling flames of battle, and of the catastrophe which he had brought to her during his few days in Little River. A profound sense of original sin was dimly developing in his heart.

At dusk, he told his mother that he was going to Yuguan that night. She was not surprised, for she knew that ever since he had gone there to study medicine he had secretly lost his heart to her uncle's daughter. She sat at the table and said nothing, looking at him dully and trembling a little. The bodyguard was dead drunk, but did seem to be vaguely aware that Xiao was going to Yuguan and struggled to stretch out his legs. He made an attempt to get up, but no sooner had he raised his head slightly than he slumped back onto the bed, and fell into a deep sleep.

Yuguan was seven miles from Little River by river, and it was possible to get there and back in one night. When Xiao walked out of the gate, it was already nearly dark.

He walked past the deserted, fan-shaped drying-ground in the middle of the village and saw the scattered lights at the river's edge as the lamps of the fishing-boats were lit. He took a deep breath and quickened his pace. The sound of wooden pestles hulling rice in stone mortars came to his ears in the gathering dusk.

He reached the bank of the River Lian and was on the point of going into the dew sprinkled camellia bushes to untie his boat, when all of a sudden there seemed to be several dozen black shadows dodging about swiftly behind him. He turned his head and saw San Shun and several men he did not recognise all closing in on him clutching butcher's knives.

The black shadows slowly moved a few steps forward, nine-inch knives dancing in their hands. Xiao had by now retreated to the edge of the river. He could hear the water clearly as it murmured peacefully by. He patted the empty holster at his waist, in vain. Because he had been in such a rush when he came out, he had forgotten to bring his pistol. At that moment, it was shut up with its six bullets in a drawer in his bedroom table. San Shun had not moved over to him — he was leaning against a thorn-tree, chewing on a leaf and calmly watching his henchmen surrounding Xiao, ready to stab him to death. All at once, he spat out the chewed shreds of leaf and walked rapidly over to Xiao, as if he had suddenly had a thought.

'What about your bodyguard?'

The black shadows round him also seemed to become suddenly alert. They left him and went into the bushes, searching carefully all around. They were convinced that the bodyguard must be close by. San Shun raised Xiao's chin with the point of his knife.

'Where is your bodyguard?'

'He's drunk,' Xiao said, very calmly. San Shun snorted softly and said no more. In a while, the men who had been into the bushes darted out again, one after the other, covered with dew and cobwebs. The moon appeared from behind the clouds and now each side could see the other clearly. San Shun realised that his men had found nothing.

He looked at Xiao very suspiciously, because he could not understand why he would be returning to his unit without his bodyguard. He peered closely at Xiao's face, and a barely perceptible expression appeared suddenly at the corners of his mouth.

'You're off to see that whore in Yuguan, aren't you?'

Xiao did not reply. He was calmly watching everything that was happening, realising that the sombre, terrifying future had already stolen up on him.

Silence enveloped them once more. After a long time, Xiao heard a faint, drawn-out sigh. San Shun threw his butcher's knife into the river, turned on his heel and left. Before he went into the bushes, he looked back, and gestured to his minions to let Xiao go.

It may have been that he was affected by Xiao's blind love for a mutilated woman, or perhaps it was just an inexplicable change of mood deep down inside him — but San Shun abandoned the idea of killing him.

While these thoughts were passing, rather hazily, through Xiao's mind, the men melted away into the night.

## DAY SEVEN (THE END)

IT WAS VERY EARLY THE NEXT DAY when Xiao came back to Little River from Yuguan. The horizon was suffused with pale, purplish-red light as he moored the boat among the camellia bushes, in the same place as before. The contours of the village were hidden by a hazy mist, and water-buffaloes were snorting among the willows on the bank. It was a pleasantly cool day of the kind typical of the rainy season. As he made his way softly through the lanes, the sound of his footsteps reverberated in the deep, narrow alley-ways, but the dogs curled up beside the bamboo fences of the village did not bark — they obviously looked on him now as someone familiar. Inevitably, he recalled the almost exactly identical early morning of the first day be came to the village. Having escaped death so narrowly on the riverbank last night, he felt very good in the warm dawn breeze.

When he reached the gate of their house, his mother was already up and sweeping the yard. They greeted each other, and he went straight into the inner room.

When he stepped through the door, his bodyguard was sitting at the table, waiting for him. He was just exclaiming that this was the first time the young fellow had been able to drag himself out of bed so early, when the bodyguard quickly pulled open the drawer, grabbed the pistol and aimed it at him.

At first, Xiao thought he was just fooling around, but he soon realised the seriousness of the situation from the slight sneer on the boy's lips. Then he heard him make the longest speech this usually inarticulate lad had ever made.

'Ever since the 31st Division abandoned the town and surrendered, I have been obeying orders and keeping a watch on you. It is your brother's unit which has taken Yuguan, and if anyone supplies him with intelligence the whole plan for the defence of the Lian valley will be ruined. The day before we left Qishan to come here, I received a secret order from the divisional commander: if you went to Yuguan, I was to shoot you.'

Xiao could almost smell the gunpowder and sulphur already. He tried to force himself to be calm, but because he was so exhausted after several consecutive nights of rushing about, and so tense in the face of this sudden threat of death, his legs began to shake violently and uncontrollably. All his nerves felt taut, and there seemed to be a ball of cotton-wool stuffed into his throat. Everything he wanted to say was stifled in the depths of his consciousness. This must have seemed an admission of treachery. Finally, his voice faltering, he managed a single sentence:

'You could take me back under arrest and let them interrogate me at Divisional HQ.'

The bodyguard gave a crafty smile.

'Executing a brigade commander in the camp would be bad for morale. Besides, the big push is about to begin — there's no time left.'

Before he had finished what he was saying, Xiao very deftly kicked the table over and, with a sideways bound, was out of the room. As he dashed into the yard, his mother was just shutting the gate so that she could catch a chicken. Like a weary wolf, he fled to the gate, but it was already too late to unbolt it. He turned round, helplessly.

The bodyguard walked up to him, holding the gun.

It had got light very quickly. The dim red glow of dawn had disappeared, and a fine rain was drifting in the air. As Xiao stood facing the unfathomably deep muzzle of the gun, all sorts of scenes from his past flashed in front of his eyes, like so many petals scattered on the river, moving past and then vanishing. Once again he was lost in a trance of helplessness, sunk in the terror of dying so unexpectedly. He recalled the Daoist's ambiguous advice — only now, it was not a cup of fine wine that was forcing him through the gates of Hell, but the black muzzle of a gun. He felt a vague sense of regret. He saw his mother, watching him in alarm from beside the chicken coop nearby. She had caught her chicken. He looked at her slight figure — she had feathers and dirt all over her creased trousers from trying to catch the chicken — and a strong desire to hug her welled up in him. In the split second when he heard the shots ring out, he felt something wet and sticky running down his stomach and thighs.

The bodyguard, standing only three paces away from him, very deliberately fired all six bullets.

# FABRICATION

## MA YUAN

*DEITIES TEND TO BE BLINDLY SELF-CONFIDENT. This is how they acquire their overweening sense of mastery. Each thinks he or she is unique, but in fact they are remarkably similar, as the various genesis myths demonstrate. The gods' method is fundamentally one and the same — repeated fabrication.* — Apocryphal Buddhist Sutra

1

I AM THE PERSON KNOWN AS MA YUAN, a Han Chinese. I am a writer.

I like to write in a style which is free, unconventional, astounding — like the proverbial 'heavenly horse roaming the clouds'. My stories are always more or less sensational. I tell these stories in Chinese. Reputedly, the characters of Chinese constitute the writing system which is the most difficult to reconcile with language itself. I take some satisfaction in being able to write in Chinese characters. None of the great figures of world literature were able to do this. I am the exception.

The implication seems to be that I would like to call myself a great writer, perhaps even to claim that I am the only good writer who writes in Chinese characters. This sounds like excessive self-confidence. Arrogance? Who knows!

Anyone as self-confident as I should be able to demonstrate their confidence by relying entirely on their own writing. I shouldn't have to force you readers to go through to my list of publications if I have real confidence in myself.

Now I am going to tell you what I've written. I don't believe you've read any of it (or very little). Don't feel unhappy or ashamed on my behalf. I want you to know that I feel complete equanimity on this score.

Some say I went to Tibet for the sake of my writing. This is not the place to discuss the truth or falsity of such an assertion. That I *have* been to Tibet is a fact. And it's also a fact is that I have written tens of millions of words about Tibet, all in the language of the Han people, in other words, Chinese. It is true that I was in Tibet for a long time, without learning a single word of their language. What I have been talking about is the people there, the environment, and stories that might be in that setting. A careful reader will notice that I have used the word 'might'. I think such readers might not notice that I did not use the word 'occur' Where others use 'take place', 'occur', I use the verb 'be'.

This is not a language course, so let's drop the subject.

Once I wrote about a female deity, the Goddess of the Lhasa River. I didn't mention the painstaking effort it cost me to choose the gender of the deity. I wrote about men and women, but I deliberately avoided writing about the things man and woman do when they are alone together. I wrote about brown eagles, bald eagles, kites; I wrote about bears, wolves, leopards and other ferocious animals like them. I wrote about small animals, scorpions (the vicious), lambs (the meek), foxes and marmots (neither vicious nor meek).

Of course I also wrote about the life and death of my fellow human beings, about the way they live and the way they die. Naturally, the writing was fabricated in a way I thought proper. Perhaps this is a way of proving myself to be out of the ordinary. Who knows?

In fact, there isn't an essential difference between me and other writers. Like them I must observe life, and then create fabrications based on the things I've observed. To write like a 'heavenly horse roaming the clouds' one has to have a horse and some clouds.

Take, for example, the story I am fabricating right now. I stayed in Maqu village for seven days, risking my life. This Maqu village is a designated disease zone, a leper colony. Mine is a story about lepers.

What I simply wish to do is borrow this leper-filled village as the backdrop to my story, and weave a sensational story from the observations I made during those seven days. I dare say that writers who are unable to find knock-out subject matter would be envious of my good luck. Are there any envious writers among the readers of this story? If you are one, please write to me. My name is Ma Yuan. It's my real name. I have used pen names before, but not in this story.

Of course, there are others who would rather give up their writing career than run certain risks. They are quite right not to take such risks. So the envy is unnecessary.

To be honest, I am now living in the Peaceful Repose Convalescent Home. 'Peaceful Repose' is a public designation. People in the know can tell you that the place is a lunatic asylum. I am staying here in order to write. Around me there are old people. This is a ward for geriatric patients. The room is spick and span, twenty metres square with six beds in it.

At first I was completely steeped in romantic ideas, trusting in the unusual powers of my imagination, and firmly convinced that I was capable of creating a truly immortal piece of work, one which would last forever.

I am not the sort of person who, like Hemingway, is content with 'Isn't it nice just to imagine?' Whatever I imagine, I do. That's why I did it. That Hemingway was an American.

I cannot boast that I was the only man fit for such adventures. The first person I met when I entered the village of Maqu was another such person, and he told me that he had not been the first.

2

'TELL ME HOW OLD I LOOK. Give me your immediate impression based on a first glance. Don't go easy on me. Don't say anything just to make me feel better, please don't.

'There are mirrors, water pools. I can see myself every day of the year. But I don't know if I really do look decrepit. I can't imagine how other people look at my age. Be honest with me. You won't offend me, you know. I withdrew from your world long ago. Your world belongs to you.

'Thirty years have passed. Maybe forty. I have no way of counting. Time cannot be measured. Yesterday was like today, tomorrow will be like today. One fails to remember mornings and evenings that have been repeated so many times. Mountains turned green and then yellow. I just can't remember.

'I'm a deaf-mute. Anyway, the people here treat me as a mute. I have not uttered a single word since I came here. I was afraid that I might have forgotten the Chinese language. Now that I'm talking to you, I realise that I must have retained it. Some skills, once learned, are never forgotten. Swimming is like that. I learned to swim at the age of seven, which seems to be over a hundred years ago. I am not a hundred percent Han Chinese. My father was an Indian merchant.

'I began by not speaking and now nobody wants to speak to me. Forget it. What does it matter what they call you I've lived all these years without a name. Nobody calls me by my name. Nobody knows my name. They take me for a deaf-mute.

'You really do have good judgement. No one here could tell that I'd been to school. My father was rich. It was me who didn't want to carry on with my education.

'Do you want something to eat? You've got something with you? That couldn't be better. It's years since I've tasted biscuits. Delicious. Let's go back now or we'll miss lunch. All right then, let's walk on a little towards the ravine.

'I haven't been thinking about such things. They don't seem to concern me much. Maybe they've never concerned me. Whether it's something to do with me or any one else, what does it matter?

'I know for sure that you'd never believe that I have a gun, a Mauser which takes twenty bullets. You'll see it soon enough. Seven bullets left. After this long I wonder whether it will still fire. Not a speck of rust on it. I keep it where the rain can't get at it. Nobody knows where it's hidden. Nobody bothers to climb up the mountain. If I go up the mountain, they think I'm a fool. Let's start climbing here.

'From the very first day I arrived, I started climbing the mountain. I blazed this trail. No one ever bothers to come here. If you're tired, we can rest a little. It's still quite a distance. I tried to get as far up as possible. I couldn't stop worrying about the pistol. Are you ready to go now? We'll take another rest if you feel tired again.'


3

WE CHATTED WHILE CLIMBING. He looked really decrepit, but was more sure-footed than I was. I hadn't been expecting miracles, but I wasn't averse to the idea. Walking and resting, we finally got to the place he wanted to show me. He asked me to wait.

All of a sudden, he was miraculously transformed and a fully armed highwayman appeared in front of me, swift in movement and ferocious in expression. His voice and appearance told me the pistol was no toy. He aimed it at me and I remembered the seven cartridges. My legs started to tremble.

'Take out all the food from your sack! Be quick!' he said, 'Didn't you hear me?'

I was thunderstruck. My head was unable to function and my eyes were glued to the dark hole of the muzzle. It was much bigger than I had imagined, like a cave. I could just walk into it. I reached into my sack, and threw the first tin out onto the ground; then the other two tins, a packet of chocolate and some hardtack.

I was on the point of taking out my camera when he burst out laughing, 'This was my livelihood for many years. After such a long time I just wanted to see how someone would react. Just like it used to be. Nothing has changed. Ha! Ha! Nothing.'

He was laughing. I couldn't. The dark cave in front of my eyes made me forget what laughter was. What he said made no sense to me.

My brain refused to function.

Slowly the muzzle moved away from my eyes towards the ground. My consciousness stirred like a snake in springtime. I began to sense the lingering implications of his words; to recall the part of the day that had just passed.

No. My brain was still half awake. I couldn't make out the meaning of his subsequent gestures.

Once again he took the gun in his hand, holding the handle in his left hand and unlocking the safety catch with his right. He lifted his left arm skyward. What was he up to?

I stared at his left index finger on the trigger, watched as he squeezed and the gun went off.

The air shook violently. Echoes resounded from mountains far and near. I felt as if the whole world was looking at us. Maqu village looked tiny at the foot of the mountain — so tiny that it appeared unreal, like a model in a sand box. No villagers were in sight, but somehow I could feel all their eyes on our backs.

'What a pity. Only six left. Not bad really, after several decades.'

I understood these words at once and knew that the nightmare was over. At the time I didn't realise the role this incident would play in my story.

Before I knew it, he'd disappeared among the mountain rocks. When he reappeared, the pistol was gone. He seemed to have forgotten all about me. Scampering, light-footed down the mountain he passed straight by me. You could see him, leaping between rocks, disappearing behind them from time to time. He seemed to have grown smaller.

I bent down to pick up my tins. By the time I stood up again he had disappeared completely. It occurred to me that I should look for the gun.

I had a premonition and I wanted to make a trial of it. My premonitions were never wrong — I would never find the pistol. It may never have existed or perhaps existed only in my imagination.

Not until I was walking downhill did I remember the problem of leprosy. Was he a leper? He'd lived in this leper colony for decades. I wondered why I'd met him of all people; why I didn't enter the village first.

## 4

I WASN'T SURE whether I'd be able to obtain a medical permit or not, so I'd slipped into this forbidden area on the quiet. I had heard beforehand that there were two doctors in charge of Maqu village. They were two young Tibetans. One was a woman. The man was said to be very handsome.

The leper colony had no wall or fence of any kind. No patient could be prevented from leaving, and no outsider hindered from entering. I took advantage of this fact.

A highway ran the length of the river bank, although there were no other human dwelling places to be found for over a hundred miles. That was why the two stone buildings seemed unusually desolate. The one on the west was for the highway maintenance team, the other was the Maqu hospice. As for the village itself, that was still miles away, in the distance, at the foot of the mountain, separated from the highway by a vast expanse of boulders. Looking northward from the highway, the small village could be seen clearly at a glance, lying there in the far distance. There was nothing to block the line of sight. A little tract, zigzagging like a tapeworm, connected Maqu with the outside world.

I hitched a ride in a truck. So as not to alarm the two doctors, I entered the village on foot after the truck set me down. I was sure the doctors could never have dreamt I was there.

I'd kitted myself out with a sleeping bag and some food and aimed to solve the problem of longer-term food and lodging myself. I wasn't clear about how long I would stay, but, at any rate, I wasn't going to leave the same day.

The mountains to the north of the village were very high, with many gullies which became flood-control channels as they reached the foot of the mountains. These channels divided the expanse of boulder-strewn plateau into a criss-cross of rectangles.

I began to look for a place to sleep, somewhere close to the village, but out of the way of the inhabitants. After some searching, I finally discovered a deep, narrow ravine. I buried my rucksack and most of the food supply at a place where the ravine turned a corner. Then I went into the village with just the knapsack and my camera.

The afternoon sun was hot enough to leave you parched. The village was unusually quiet. There were no domestic animals. Only a few dogs could be seen sleeping in the shade.

All the houses were made of stone, in the characteristic Tibetan style, with low, flat roofs. The layout was no different from any other village, but the mud tracts were too narrow for horse-carts. I wandered about at my leisure. There was no one in any of the courtyards. I walked into every corner of that village without seeing a single soul. I reminded myself not to run the risk of actually entering any of the courtyards or buildings unless I had to.

What fascinated me was that none of the dogs barked at me. Not even the dogs were interested in me. I sank into a kind of deep melancholy.

If I hadn't known better, I could have mistaken this place for a ghost town. But it wasn't. At least one hundred and twenty souls were living here. I'd learnt beforehand that these people didn't have to farm or keep animals. Food and daily necessities were supplied free by the State.

I saw my first sign of human life in a two-storey building. By this time I'd discovered the 'back' of the village where the only two-storey building was situated. The stairs leading upward were on the north side of the building. It was the piercing cry of a child which came to my ear. Without hesitation, I climbed the staircase and pushed open the door. I never expected to see women in there.

Three women were leaning drowsily against the wall next to one another. I was so embarrassed, I'm even blushing now as I write. I can only tell you that none of the women were wearing anything below the waist. All they had on were thread-bare Chinese-style cotton blouses. Their breasts were exposed. One of them was suckling. Clearly, her child was the source of crying.

I knew immediately I had blundered into the wrong place. But the women didn't seem to have noticed me. Only the eyes of the little boy turned towards me. The women were enjoying the warmth and comfort of the sunshine with their eyes closed. Like any sensitive young man, I took particular note of the way they deliberately sat with legs apart, as though sunning that particular place. Obviously I couldn't stay there staring at them, but neither did I run away like I'd seen a ghost.

Strictly speaking, this building shouldn't be called a two-storey building. It was just a compound with two small rooms built on top of the roofs of two of the lower living spaces. This inhabited room was on the roof of the lower room to the east. On the roof of the north room there was a stone wall about five feet high around a communal living space for the female inmates. On both the east and west sides of the compound some brushwood for the fire was stored. There didn't seem to be any male residents.

I stood at the door, neither coming nor going. I hadn't noticed the faces of the women. First impressions told me that the woman with the child was still fairly young. I felt I couldn't just walk in, I was about to turn away. Just then I heard a voice.

'I can speak Chinese.'

I turned around and found myself looking into the face of the woman with the child. She was the one who spoke.

I answered, 'I speak Chinese too.'

For all I knew, I was trembling. The face of that woman made my blood go cold and sent shivers down my spine. Her nose had withered with corruption, the rest of her face was scarred as though it had been burnt. The skin was unnaturally shiny and taunt.

Her expression was strange. The pupils of her eyes were askew and she seemed to be both looking at me and not looking at me. She said, 'You are from Lhasa. People from Lhasa speak Chinese.'

'Have you been to Lhasa?' I asked.

She said, 'Lhasa is a big place ...'

'Yes, it is a big place. Where are you from?'

She said, 'I've been to Changdu. I was told that Lhasa is bigger than Changdu, so I figure Lhasa must be very big.'

'How come you speak Chinese?'

'People where I come from all speak Chinese.'

'Where are your men-folk?'

'Which man do you mean?' she answered, 'They live in their own place. This place is for women ... and children.'

'How long have you been here?'

'Mountains have turned green and then turned green again,' patting the boy on the head. 'He was born here. Please, come in.'

'Do the doctors come to the village everyday?' I asked.

'I've been told they've been replaced, but I haven't seen the new ones yet.'

Unconsciously, without knowing what I meant, I stammered, 'Uh-huh ... I see ...' I didn't know what else to say and turned to go. Once outside I remembered that I should have asked if there was any-one else in the village who could speak Chinese. I turned to go back up the stone stairway when I noticed that all four of them were watching me from the door frame.

5

SHE WAS THE ONLY PERSON in the village who spoke Chinese

I had no other choice. I asked her to tell them to put on their clothes. I could see that none of them was old, but the other two were thin and weak. All three of them looked very much alike.

She had a little more life in her than the other two and was much less emaciated. I followed her to another room. This room was entirely hers, for her and her son. After some hesitation, I sat down on a wooden chair.

She said, 'The short one's retarded. The tall one has a bad back. Neither of them can have children.'

The child was only a toddler, but his eyes had a sort of fearful maturity. He looked at me out of the corner of those eyes and walked towards the door. The sun shone on his naked body, making it appear almost transparent.

'He understands things,' she said. 'When people visit me, he goes out.'

To our way of thinking, these words seem to be hinting at something. But I have to say that this is our mistake. She wasn't the kind of woman we're used to. That was the conclusion I came to after spending a few days with her.

I told her I was going to stay in the village for a while.

She said, 'No outsiders come to stay in the village. They come with the doctors, look around and then leave together with the doctors. There is no place for outsiders to stay.'

I told her firmly that I would be staying in the village for some days. Then I added, 'I can't speak Tibetan. I can only speak Chinese.'

'Then just speak Chinese.'

While she was talking, my attention was drawn unconsciously to the two holes which would have been nostrils if she had still had a nose. When I spoke I did so without thinking. I even forgot to be disgusted. I just felt that the two small nostrils on her face were very funny, funny to the point of being absurd.

'I came to this place on my own account,' I said. 'Will people here be unhappy that I've come?'

She said,' They won't even notice you. They aren't bothered about other people's business. The grain supply and film projecting teams are

LOST BOAT

the only things they notice. They don't pay any attention to anyone else.' After a while she added, 'You should go into the village. All out-siders go around the village. They all have doctors accompanying them. You're on your own, no one came with you.'

'I came by myself,' I said. 'I don't want any doctors with me.'

She said, 'I'll go with you to the village. You can ask me.'

'Ask you what?'

'You can ask whatever you want to,' she answered. 'I know more than those doctors.' She often stopped half way through what she was saying. It took me some time to get used to her way of speaking. 'I live in the village.'

Before we set off, I remembered something.

'Hold the child,' I said. 'I'll take a picture of you.'

'I don't take pictures. I don't understand what you mean.'

I took a photo album from my knapsack and showed her a colour photo of me.

She said immediately, 'It is you.'

I explained that I could preserve her image on that stuff like that. She shook her head.

She said, 'I understand. I won't "take pictures". I am not sure about this picture taking.'

Her words were contradictory, but I sort of guessed her meaning. What she wanted to say was that she knew photographs existed, but she didn't understand how people could be moved onto the paper. She didn't want anyone to take her picture. I remembered reading in a book that people who had not been exposed to modern civilisation thought photography was soul-snatching; that their soul would be cap-tured in the little box of the camera. I'd like this detail to appear in my next masterpiece. It seemed that she must have seen photos or videos of some kind.

She didn't want to be photographed. I had to leave it at that.

Later, I repeated the same error of presumption. I forgot that people here had seen movies. Photography was by no means beyond their un-derstanding. When she said she wasn't sure about photography, she had her own reasons. But more of that later.

6

IN THE CENTRE OF THE VILLAGE towards the south was empty space. Two simple basketball boards stood at either end of it. At twilight, people started to gather around the playground, which was probably the only public place in the village.

I stood with her a little to one side. She looked relaxed and easy, holding the toddler by his hand. I hadn't brought out the camera.

Just as she had said, none of the villagers paid any attention to the additional stranger.

Most of them seemed apathetic, incurious, without desire. I decided that the tight skin was not as horrible as it had seemed at first. The golden rays of the setting sun shone on these faces and lent them the colours of some bizarre fantasy. Gradually my tension eased.

Leprosy made them look alike. The same collapsed noses, the same shiny skin, even the extra wide distance between the eyes was the same. I noticed in particular how many of them looked at things askance.

'All of them seem to walk very slowly,' I remarked.

She said, 'They have no need to walk fast.'

'Does anyone here play basketball?'

She turned her head and looked, as if wondering why on earth I had asked such a question. I didn't understand. But it wasn't long before I did.

A young man bounced a ball out from the house to the south. Some other men responded immediately to what he was doing. They whistled and shouted, full of vigour.

I noticed that some of the men who joined in the game were no longer young. They all separated into two equal groups. No referee. The match was a complete mess, like a game of American football.

'All the men here come to play basketball in the evening,' she explained.

'Oh.'

'Go and play. Men should play basketball.'

I understood what she was getting, but I couldn't just go along with it, unthinkingly. I was a good basketball player, but I had no intention of showing off in front of her.

The game drew a lot of people. I followed the crowd to the basketball court. She stood in the inner circle carrying the child. I stood by her side.

Among the players was a little guy who was particularly agile. He was about forty, and was the only player who knew how to dribble and shoot properly. He scored several times on his own, each time winning cheers from the noisy crowd.

He lobbed in one more basket. Just as the crowd began to cheering, she nudged me with her shoulder, then patted the boy.

'This is his son.'

Not even a complete idiot would have missed the pride in her voice. 'Sometimes he comes over to sleep with me,' she added.

She didn't lower her voice in the slightest, even though there were many people standing near by. It obviously didn't bother her, but I blushed.

What happened next caught me unawares. The ball rolled towards me as if drawn there by some unknown force. One flick of the foot, and it was in my hands.

I immediately regretted my rashness, but I hadn't had time to think clearly. Standing on the side of the court, at least ten steps from the basket, I concentrated hard, lowered my elbows and shot.

As you may have guessed, with Heaven's assistance, the ball soared straight into the basket without touching the rim. What a pity there was no net to show off my triumph better.

It was thus that I finally caught the attention of the Maqu villagers, who started to cheer for me. I was now the centre of attention, under everyone's eye. I deeply regretted the unnecessary exposure.

At the same time I noticed the unfriendly stares of two men. One was the short basketball player. The other was a man of advanced years. He was tall and badly hunch-backed. The absence of a beard on his shrivelled face, made him look like last year's walnut. He was the only one amongst the villagers who did not share a dull expression. He was dark-skinned, so it was hard to detect the usual signs of leprosy on his face.

7

QUIETLY I SQUEEZED MY WAY out of the crowd.

What happened then almost made me forget where I was. I never thought that I could be so much at home amongst lepers. Now I felt myself being watched.

One's sixth sense can often be surprisingly acute. I recognised him at once. Seeing I had turned my back, he looked away. At the time I didn't know I would be climbing up the mountain with him the following morning.

I waited for him to turn back again, and he didn't let me down. He gave me the swift glance that you might expect from a much younger

112

man. Then he walked into the crowd without looking back. The sun was already on the ridge of the mountain. It would soon be dark.

As I was just about to say goodbye, she walked towards me, still carrying the child. Her steps made a heavy tapping sound on the ground. As she came closer, she put the child down.

She said, 'The mute always stares at strangers. Don't be afraid of him.'

'Which one is the mute?'

'The old hunch-back. He's very quiet.'

'Is he on his own here? I mean, does he have any relative here?'

'He is the oldest in the village,' she answered. 'He lives in the small house towards the western end of the village. He never has anything to do with other people. Everyday he climbs up the mountain to the north.'

'At what time?'

'Each morning at the time of eating *tsampa*.'*

'I'll come again tomorrow,' I said.

'It will be cold outside tonight. It's going to rain.'

I couldn't figure out why she had said that. I hadn't told her where I was going to spend the night. I didn't understand what she was driving at. What was more, you could even see a few stars twinkling in the deep, clear blue of the sky above.

I said, 'I'll say goodbye now.'

'It is going to rain,' she insisted, 'it will be cold outside.'

Cold outside? I was secretly laughing at her. She was still talking about the cold and the rain, while I was gazing at the stars with open eyes as I lay in my sleeping bag. The ravine wasn't so bad. It was sheltered from the wind and very quiet. I didn't notice when I fell asleep.

Still, I made up my mind before falling asleep to get up early and wait for the old mute who climbed the mountain every day.

I dreamed of Lhasa. I dreamed about my friends in Lhasa and the female pilgrims of Kanba. The cold wind drove me from my dream. So did the rain.

I struggled out of the sleeping bag in a fluster. The sky was black as a kettle, without a crack of light. Gusts of cold wind were driving heavy drops of rain. I was shivering with cold, and had to gather up my sleeping bag and provisions. The ground was too damp. I had to walk back and forth along the ravine to try and keep myself warm. I

---

* Pinyin 'zanba', a staple food in Tibet made from a type of roasted barley ground into flour.

was worried that rain might soak through to my food supplies. I had no where to go, although Maqu was not far away.

I was lucky that the wind soon blew away the rain clouds. The sky cleared again. I felt the ground with my hand. The rain had hardly penetrated the surface. But the temperature had dropped more than ten degrees.

I spread out my sleeping bag again and lay down. I didn't sleep much the rest of the night.

I was frozen to death and began to feel feverish.

8

I GOT UP AS SOON AS THE SKY began to lighten. I almost forgot to wait at the back of the village for the old mute. It was so cold that early in the morning. Perhaps I should have gone back into the village and let her know.

Once again I buried my rucksack. I didn't go to see her first.

When I came back from the mountains at noon, I could see her house a long way off. The building in which the women lived was situated just at the mouth of the ravine. I was surprised to find myself so anxious, and quickened my pace.

What an extraordinary night and morning I had experienced since yesterday! Just to be able to return to her room would be a miracle in itself.

The sun shone joyfully overhead. Her small door and the stone staircase were cast in shadow. What a cool, delightful shade it was!

As I drew near, I recognised her sitting on the threshold. She was sitting motionless, her silhouette like a paper-cut. I was about to enter the shadow of the house, when she stood up, walked inside and closed the door behind her. I stood at a loss in front of the stone steps.

I was hungry, and didn't want to wander around the village on an empty stomach. So I sat down on the steps and took out some cake and chewed it slowly. I was considering what to do next as I ate. If she refused to see me, I would be on my own. I had already raised one corner of the veil, I was sure I would eventually see behind it. But I was aware of the difficulties awaiting me, now that the only two Chinese speakers refused me help. How could I succeed without knowing their language?

I didn't have an answer. I was seized by a violent fit of coughing, perhaps because I had been sitting on the cold stone steps. The incessant coughing left me breathless. After a second violent seizure, my lungs felt hot, swollen. I was falling ill.

Then I heard the door behind me open. I stood up without turning round. I heard her footsteps walking down the stone steps.

One, two, three, four, five, six, seven, eight, nine, ten, eleven. she was now behind me, but I would not turn around. I was behaving like a child, like a child who refused to be the first to speak.

Another fit of coughing seized me. No matter how hard I tried I couldn't control it. I coughed until I was red in the face and my skull was ready to split. At this very moment, she spoke.

She said, 'Come upstairs.'

At first I refused, but I soon overcame this mean-spirited stubbornness. She was not my kind. She was not even from a world that was familiar to me. What right had I — Why should I?

I walked meekly in front of her, counting the steps mechanically — eleven steps. She followed me into the room.

The scene was exactly as it had been yesterday except that she was not in her place. Her place had been at the far end where her son was now. The other two were half asleep, still baring the lower half of their bodies to the sun. She indicated that I should go on in.

In the front of the room there was a lighted iron stove. On it a blackened teapot was boiling, giving out a delicious smell. I swallowed involuntarily.

I entered the next room and sat down on the mattress. And then what did I see? I couldn't believe my eyes — my rucksack! I put out my hand to touch it. No mistake. The soft sleeping bag was inside with the tins and the hardtack. I put the rucksack behind my back and used it to get comfortable.

She didn't speak, and I didn't open my mouth. She poured me a cup of tea and walked out of the room. Through the window frame I could see that she had returned to her place. She opened her dress to give the boy her breast. What made her different from the other two was that she wore a pair of trousers.

The tea was too hot. I waited for it to cool. But before the tea was cool enough to drink I fell fast asleep. I spent the rest of the day in a deep, dreamless sleep. Somehow I knew I was still coughing in my sleep. I could feel my throat burning. I was dying of thirst. But I could not open my eyes.

The first thing I did when I woke up was look for water. I grabbed the teacup off the table I finished it in one gulp. What delicious milky tea! Then I saw that it was growing dark. There was nobody in the room, and nobody outside it either. I recalled yesterday evening. They must've gone to the basketball ground. My head was aching terribly as if it had been hit by something hard. I had to lean back on my rucksack again.

Even then I didn't realised what a terrible thing I had done. I had drunk a full cup of tea from a leper's mug. I couldn't get back to sleep. I felt dazed, like a wounded bird, which could neither fly properly nor settle on the ground.

I started coughing again. My throat felt as though it was being torn apart. Maqu became something in the past, as if it existed a long, long time ago. I could not recall what the woman looked like. But I was expecting her, expecting her to return to my side. I dimly remember that I spread out the sleeping bag on the floor, and insisted that I sleep in it. But somehow the little boy ended up in the sleeping bag. I dimly remember her putting some white pills into my mouth, which, it seemed, she had got from a doctor. I dimly remember hearing her say the woman doctor had come to see me. It was the first time that I had lost all sense of time. My time-sensory nerve must have been misconnected. The entire night I was running a high fever. It was not until day-break that I fell into a heavy slumber. She said later that I had been raving the whole night. She said she hadn't slept herself. It was thus that I became her patient.

9

FOR TWO DAYS I DIDN'T GO OUT. She wouldn't allow me to and I was too weak anyway.

I was allowed to go as far as her door. I sat on the old wooden chair feeling bored and looked out onto the roof balcony. Watching the two neighbours from dawn till dusk, I discovered something interesting.

During the day she often went out, sometimes with the child, sometimes leaving the child behind. When he was left at home the boy rarely sunbathed with the two women. He would sit very still on the mattress watching me. I watched him. I felt that he was studying me. It is not very pleasant to be studied by a one year old.

He had very deep set eyes, and three wrinkles on his forehead. I enjoying gazing at him and having him stare back. It was reasonable entertainment, provided you did not always think of yourself as being under scrutiny. I determined that whoever blinked first would lose each match, and that ninety-nine matches would decide the winner.

Anyway I had plenty of time. But to my shame I lost confidence after nine matches. I only won once and that was after the toddler had beaten me six times running. In other words, he blinked once while I had blinked six times. The odds were stacked against me. I had no stomach for the competition.

My eyes were dry and sore. I shouldn't have started with this kind of game in the first place. The only good thing about it was that it made me forget that I was being scrutinised by the little imp. It was so unsettling.

I thought of something new. Because I was so bored, my ideas were often boring. I took him on my lap (he was surprisingly light) and made him look me in the face. I put my left index finger between my eyes and crossed my eyes by looking at the tip of my nose. This was my *pièce de résistance*, I knew I looked very funny. Sure enough, he was started to laugh. It was the first time he had laughed since I'd met him many days before.

When he was laughing he didn't look so precocious or so serious. I decided to teach him my trick. He was a genius. I only had to point my finger between his eyes and those lovely pupils of his would cross at once. I can't tell you how beautiful he looked.

I burst out laughing and he laughed with me, without stopping.

It was some time before I discovered that something had gone wrong. Long after I'd taken my finger away, his pupils had still not returned to their original positions. I ordered him to stop, I shouted at him, but all in vain. I took his head in my hands and shook him hard, but to no avail. I got really worried. Then I remembered a story about an old scholar who passed the official exam and went mad with joy. He sobered up only after his father-in-law slapped him in the face. Without considering the consequences, I slapped the boy. He burst into a loud wail, and roused the two placid women who looked in our direction. When I saw that he was bleeding I felt very uncomfortable. Anyhow, this clip round the ears brought an end to the boring story of the crossed eyes.

Didn't some philosopher once say 'Nothing is worse than boredom'? Two days of imprisonment had left me bored. What about these people who had been shut away all their lives? The word boredom is hardly strong enough. Take those two women, my 'neighbours' of the past few days. They really were her neighbours, in name and in truth. I was just a stranger, her temporary lodger.

I observed the two women for a long time. They didn't talk to each other. The short one was retarded, saliva constantly dribbled from her

117

mouth. In the morning she got up first. She went in and out of their room several times and out of the house once. She wore trousers in the mornings and when the sun come out she helped the tall one, who wore the same type of trousers to get up and out. Then she helped her to sit up against the wall. Once they got settled, they'd sit apart with little or no communication. By the time the short one looked up to see the time of the day, she'd be very dozy. I also noticed that they always sat in the same places.

After sitting like that for about two hours, they'd start fidgeting. The tall one would twist her neck while the short one put a hand inside her clothes to give herself a scratch. After shifting her position slightly, the tall one would take out a little metal box from somewhere inside her dress. With great care she would twist of the lid and gently pour out a little powder onto the thumbnail of her left hand. Then she sniffed it up into her nostrils. She did this with great effort, then tilted her head backwards with an odd expression on her face, and after some time, sneezed with full force and complete satisfaction. The short woman observed this whole procedure, envy all over her retarded-looking face.

I wondered whether this was what people know as 'snuff'. I could see it was a great pleasure for them. The tall one soon began to repeat her preparations, but this time for her roommate. As I watched her raise her thumbnail toward the nostrils of the short one, my eyes became moist with tears. The short one had deposited snot all over her finger, but the tall one didn't seem to notice. She was as attentive as if she was enjoying the snuff herself. She watched the short one sneezing with even greater attentiveness.

It was a great pity that this scene ended here. In days to come, I did not have the good fortune to witness it again. They resumed their normal positions, and sat there motionless.

Towards noon it became hot. Again it was the short one who began by taking off her trousers, and then baring her breast to the caresses of the sunshine. The tall one took off her clothes later. She was thinner than the short one. The skin on both of them had seen so much sun that it showed no texture. I could not make out why they were so infatuated with the sun.

Lunch was fetched in an enamel mug by the short one, a mugful of *tsampa* flour. She went and got a further mugful of water and then returned to her place. Without a word, each of them kneaded the flour and water into balls of dough, then put them one by one into their mouths. They chewed methodically for some time. Finally they craned their necks to ease the food down.

I could see they both had good appetites.

After lunch they would fall asleep in any old position. They slept so soundly that I doubted even a thunderclap would wake them. They didn't wake up for at least three hours. Then, after stretching their legs they would sit on until sunset.

Neither of them went to watch the basketball. Supporting one another, they'd usually go outside once to relieve themselves before coming back to their room and shutting themselves in until the next morning. They probably took their other meals in their own room. I noticed that the water they used was fetched by my 'landlady' in a small bucket. They did not boil water for tea.

Sometimes the little boy would go out by himself to the two women. Whichever one was closer to the boy would hold his hand. I noticed that they didn't take the child into their arms, but they did seem to be very fond of him. They were happy to give him some of their time. If he needed any help, they wouldn't say no.

At first I didn't notice that the ground floor was also inhabited, and by more than just a couple of people. They seldom spoke, and moved about very quietly. The first thing I heard was the clicking of a door and then learned that there was another world. I saw five old women. Each of them went about separately, going in and out without a sound, like extras in a dumb show, or ghosts in a haunted house. It was clear that they had no family. They lived together but they didn't communicate. I even began to think that their souls must be lonely, if they had souls. Their hair was turning grey.

She said that altogether there were six people downstairs. 'But one is completely paralysed.'

'Can they speak?'

'All of them can speak. They seldom do. There is nothing to talk about.'

'And how about the two upstairs? They don't talk either.'

'The short one wants to speak but she can't. The tall one can talk but she won't.'

'Are they all Tibetans?'

'Some are Han, Some are Muslims, some are Lobas.'

'I thought you said that nobody here speaks Chinese?'

'The Han Chinese who were born and brought up here speak Tibetan. Nobody speaks Chinese.'

'What do the old people go out for? All of them go out.'

'I go out too. We go to turn the prayer-wheels. There are two divine trees in the village. We go to the divine trees and turn the prayer-wheels.'

'Are you a Buddhist?'

I regretted the question as soon as I had asked it. I realised at once that I had made a mistake. The two trees were very tall, I had seen them in the distance.

'I have to do something. I can't be just like them,' she gestured towards the room next door, 'nothing but sun-bathing.'

Something tugged at my heartstrings.

## 1 0

'NOWADAYS PEOPLE IN THE VILLAGE say that the old mute has gone mad. He doesn't normally go out except for mountain-climbing. But these days he doesn't climb any more. Early each morning he wanders around the village, which he never did before. He keeps on and on walking. Everybody thinks he's crazy.'

'Why does he walk about in the village?'

'Nobody knows. He walks from morning till night, but he doesn't climb mountains any more.'

'Nobody knows why he climbed the mountain?'

'No. Nobody knows why he climbed the mountain. Nobody knows why some people go in for turning prayer-wheels and some go in for sun-bathing.'

I may be overly egocentric, but I'd say he was looking for me. I was the only person who had learned something of his secret and that made him anxious. Perhaps he wanted do something to make up for having shot his mouth off. I remembered that morning two days earlier and the 'mountain cave' one could almost walk into … I felt my skin coming over in goose flesh and my skull itching as if I had been needled.

'I said I'd been to school and know quite a few Chinese characters.'

'What did you say?' My head was spinning and I didn't understand the significance of her words.

'You're tired. You haven't recovered. Just lie down for a while. I'm going out.'

'Did you say you that you've been to school, and know quite a few characters?'

'You lie down and rest for a while. You still need to take a nap during the day.'

She helped me to settle down and then went out.

I did not want to go to sleep. Why had she suggested it? She was frank with me. She was never evasive. I noticed long ago that her speech was simple but unique. She asked no questions. If I were to transcribe what she said there would be no question marks. I am a writer of fiction. I pay special attention to the way people talk. I *know* that her way of talking was extremely uncommon. Her way of thinking differed from that of the vast majority. We make great leaps in our reasoning but there are always question marks. Thought without question marks is a marvel. To her, whatever was, was pre-existent, plain beyond question. Just now she said she had been to school.

Headache.

I'd been shut up in the room for too long. I wanted to walk around a bit. I figured that she must have gone out already. I didn't want to bump into her at the door or in the village. There was still some time before twilight, hardly anyone was about in the village. She didn't say anything, but I guessed that she must have gone to turn the prayer-wheels. She said the small guy who played basketball hadn't visited her since my arrival. Judging by way she said it, he was her man. Mightn't she go to him if he didn't come to her? Perhaps I was imagining things. I'd like to tell you that as I searched for the answer to this question, I did so without the slightest hint of jealousy, but I think I'd be protesting too much if I did. Anyway, I decided to go and look for her.

My arrival and presence must have been tiresome. Having me to stay in her place must have kept her from her normal life. Should I have thought of living somewhere else? These past two days I had been sleeping on the mattress, the boy in my sleeping bag. She seemed not to have slept at all. When I lay down, she was stroking the child to try and get it to sleep. By the time I woke up, she was already busy with something or other inside or outside the room. I was exhausted these days and always slept through till dawn. If the sky had fallen one night, I would have died in my sleep.

Someone was following me, not far away.

I didn't turn my head. I knew who it was. I slowed my pace, waited for him to get nearer. But he didn't. He'd probably slowed down as well. I didn't understand what was happening, so I decide to go on the offensive, make a surprise attack.

I gave myself a verbal command. I forced myself to turn sharply around like a well-trained soldier. We found ourselves facing one another. I went towards him taking large strides, sure he'd take fright

121

and back off, unprepared for my strategy. I was soon before him, standing face to face.

'For two days you haven't climbed the mountain,' I said.

To my surprise he ignored what I said and walked right past me. I was stunned. After some time I remembered that he was a 'deaf-mute'. He had played this role for several decades, and couldn't easily drop the pretence. I was being too hasty. Although there was no one in sight, we couldn't be sure that nobody would overhear us. I decided to walk past him a couple of times, and then waylay him. We both walked several times around the village.

After a while he stopped walking. He returned to his dwelling place.

I didn't like to follow him. I was sure that I *would* go to his place at least once. But we'll speak of that later.

Twilight had fallen again. I turned back. Then I remembered my unresolved question: should I move out of her place? This wasn't a matter for me alone.

I decided to let her decide.

I hadn't at all expected to meet the small guy who played basketball when I got up the stairs. He was playing with his son. He looked up and smiled. I found that I liked him.

I went into the room. Wrong again. She wasn't there. So she hadn't gone out to look for him. I sat on the mattress watching a picture of happiness and innocence through the window frame.

The father made all kinds of faces and the kid laughed. The father lifted the child up from behind to his height and the boy twisted his head round and tried to see his father's face. It was obviously one of their regular games. They played a kind of hide and seek in this way. The father tried to hide his face by keeping it glued to the boy's rear end.

Suddenly there was a dramatic change. The father gave up the game and put the boy down on the ground. I cannot forget the laughter frozen on the little child's face. The father became jumpy and inattentive. She had returned.

I watched the development of this incident closely.

She didn't greet him, nor did he look at her. His eyes were fixed on his feet. She walked right past him, stooped to pick up the baby, then went into the inner room. He cast a hasty glance at the mother and child, and was outside the gate in a wink. What did it all mean?

At supper, I opened a can of pork. I watched mother and child gulp it down. I was delighted. 'Delicious,' she said, somewhat embarrassed.

11

I DIDN'T FEEL LIKE SLEEPING that night, perhaps because I was slowly getting better. I lay down and covered myself as usual with the only woollen blanket the women possessed. In order not to disturb her, I turned towards the wall, and lay there without moving.

The room was dingy, and it was hard to make out anything. From the sounds I heard I guess she must have lain down on the floor close by me. I kept myself from turning to see what she had covered herself with. The night was cold, I felt uneasy about it.

I lay motionless, my eyes wide open. Gradually I got used to the dark. I tried to kill time by counting. A hundred was one unit. I counted up to three thousand three hundred and thirty three, but I was still unable to sleep. After hearing her fall asleep I turned over quietly.

I didn't expect to see the pale moonlight shining into the room through the window. It must've been a crescent moon. In the moonlight I could see her wrapped in fur-lined Tibetan-style dress. She was facing the door, deeply asleep. Only the sound of her breathing could be heard. One of her legs stuck out from under the dress. It was plump and glistened slightly in the moonlight.

The temperature had dropped — my exposed face was the best of thermometers. The tip of my nose was icy cold, so I curled up under the woollen blanket. Then I noticed that, in her sleep, she drawn her bare leg back in a little. She must have been much colder than I was.

After all, wasn't I a man, wasn't I supposed to be tough? How could I let this happen? There was my down jacket. Whatever the temperature, I should've been able to get through the night without a blanket. I didn't have any excuses. I sat up abruptly, feeling for some shoes with my feet. Gently, I placed the blanket over her, taking special care to cover the leg outside the dress.

I sat back on the mattress again, my heart filled with indescribable warmth. I sat still, watching the small window full of moonlight. I didn't feel like going back to sleep, or even lying down. I closed my eyes.

I thought about how she had been sitting on the threshold waiting for me to come back, how my mind ran wild when she closed the door behind her. I felt as if I had known her all my life. Everything seemed so strange yet so familiar. I couldn't figure out how she managed to retrieve my rucksack, or make her prognostication on the rain. The thought of the rain made me shiver and I remembered the feeling of being covered by the thick blanket. Just then I felt as if the woollen blanket, smelling a little of mutton, was covering me again. I didn't open my eyes for fear of losing this sensation.

The down jacket over my knees fell to the floor. I had no desire to pick it up. I knew instinctively that the shoulder touching mine was naked. We sat together under the blanket, not knowing what to say to each other.

I was the man, so it was up to me. I put my hand on her thigh, she put her palm on my hand. Our hands were pressed together. No words were necessary. She was completely naked. Why were we just sitting there? One woollen blanket would be enough covering for us both. The Maqu nights were warm and tender.

I shall never forget her passion in love-making. I knew full well that the consequences might cast a shadow over the rest of my life, but I can not regret what we did. I was not clear-headed, my reason was long since burned to ashes in her passion. Given the same choice again, I'd have no need of my doomed rationality. I gave myself to her, a deranged offering. Eventually, we fell asleep. While we dreamed we were locked in one another's arms. The woollen quilt made us sweat. We slept deep and sound. I wished that we might sleep like that forever.

One thing puzzles me. If I was sleeping, how could I wish for anything? But I never usually ask myself stupid questions like this.

The sun rose.

I had been lying there for too long. I still had many things to do.


1 2

I WANTED TO KNOW how many days I had been in Maqu. I thought it would be easy enough to work out. I tried to count on my fingers but I didn't get very far. My sense of time relied too much on clocks. I had left in a hurry and forgotten my watch which showed the date. I remembered clearly that I had spent May Day in Lhasa, then set off on May 2. The journey lasted two days, so I arrived on May 3.

I tend to hypothesise on the basis of existing coincidences or things. Where time's concerned I'm fond of the number seven; for repeated experience, I prefer the number six. I assumed that half of the entire time I was to spend in Maqu had already passed, let's say four days. Then today should be the fifth day. To tell the truth I don't much care for the number five, a truly gloomy numeral. But then I couldn't do anything about that.

The morning was overcast. The clouds were high and slow-moving, it was unlikely to clear. I dismissed the idea of moving out of her room. The *second* thing I had to do today was visit the sacred trees. I had decided on the first thing yesterday. The old mute's home was in the south-western corner of the village.

I needed to be certain about something. I stood at the gate looking northward. If I was right, he should be half way up the mountain. I stood there for a long time, looking hard. I must admit that something had gone wrong with my powers of premonition. He didn't appear.

I thought that after bumping into me the other day, by now he would surely have returned to his usual daily rhythms, and he'd be climbing the mountain this morning.

It seems that this word 'would' describes a vain desire.

I didn't want to waste any time. I took my bearings, set off on a short cut, and, in the time it takes to smoke a cigarette, arrived at his dwelling.

His rooms were extremely squat and lacked the usual walls surrounding Tibetan houses. He had a hunched back. Maybe it was the low ceilings that gave him his back.

The door wasn't bolted. I didn't knock. I didn't want to give him any warning. Breaking in suddenly, I might discover something unusual. I pushed the door open and walked in so quietly that nobody would've noticed my entrance. As soon as I was inside I realised my mistake. The room had no windows and I could hardly see anything. Anyone in the room would be able to see me clearly while I, having just come out of the light could see nothing.

All I knew was that my head was touching the ceiling. I lowered it. I could heard a blood-curdling sound, like a ferocious dog growling at the sight of food. I was panicky, my skin electrified. But I couldn't back down; to back down at this stage would be ridiculous. I decided not to move. My eyes would soon adjust to the light.

I was right. After a minute or two, I was able to make things out in the room. He wasn't there. An old dog was lying on his mattress. A toothless dog but a dog nonetheless. The memory of its past prowess was clearly deeply engraved in its mind. It produced a most ferocious bark in order to scare me off. Quite effective. Its eyes were full of hostility. I couldn't understand why. It had no reason to hate me.

I didn't care. I wasn't afraid of ferocious dogs with big teeth — I was trained in wrestling and boxing and dogs aren't so tough. As for a decrepit, old, toothless dog, its somewhat affected barking simply amused me. The way it was lying seemed peculiar, however. Close up,

I discovered that it had only one foreleg. So here was a cripple receiving its disability pension. The reason I've concentrated on describing the dog was because there was nothing else worth mentioning in the room. Besides, there is another reason why the dog merits some attention — its ears had been cut off at the roots.

I had been bed-ridden for two days and was all but bored to death. I'd hoped to stumble on something interesting. I even wished that the dog would leap up at me and give me an excuse to beat it up. Judging by its fierce looks, one step more forward would be enough to get it going. So I took two or three steps forward. Oddly enough, it completely lost its murderous look and stopped barking. As I moved closer, the dog show itself more pitiable than anything else. A miserable creature. I lost all interest in it.

I wanted to uncover something extraordinary in the house of this Chinese-speaking, gun-toting, fake-mute old man. I turned the place over with some care. Apart from an iron stove, an aluminium water bottle, and a pile of pine cut for firewood, there was a pair of old-fashioned, couldn't-be-more-worn-out leather shoes, a square Tibetan table, a Tangut-style sack for *tsampa* and two wooden bowls. The wall was bare and pictureless. The only place to hide anything in this room was under the mattress stand.

I knelt down on one knee and looked under the mattress, my face right on the ground. I had found something, though I couldn't tell what. It wasn't a pair of shoes, that was for sure. As I got closer to the mattress, the dog rolled on its back and began trembling with fear.

I slid my foot went underneath and hooked out whatever it was without a great effort. It was an old army officer's cap. A large blue-sky-white-sun emblem* was set in the middle of the cap. It gave me a real start, and I hurriedly kicked it back under the mattress, my heart pounding. At this very moment the door was pushed open, and sunlight poured in. Needless to say, he was back.

13

LIKE ME, HE COULD NOT SEE at once that anyone was in his room. He first turned and closed the door. As he did so the dog barked joyfully, which gave me a start. I still remembered clearly how he had aimed the pistol at me. I didn't want to unnerve him, and decided to speak first, giving him a little time to adjust to the situation.

---

* Of the Guomingdang (Kuomintang or KMT), anti-communist, Nationalist army from the pre-1949 civil war.

'I've been here for a while, waiting for you.'

I thought he'd be startled to find somebody in his room, but he wasn't. It was as if he hadn't heard me.

'Why didn't you climb the mountain?'

He walked up to the mattress and scratched the dog's itchy belly.

The dog was pleased and stretched out on its back, straining to spread its back legs wider. I could see it was a bitch which appeared never to have bred puppies. Her three pairs of teats were as dried up as they are on a male dog. Old bitches that haven't had puppies are rare, that's to say I've never seen one before. Once again I broke the silence.

'Don't you remember me?' I asked in a low voice.

He wouldn't respond. I thought he was being overcautious. I lowered my voice once more, 'You really can't remember me?'

He was intent on scratching the dog, his face turned away from me. But I noticed from its gestures that the bitch was on heat. I didn't dare acknowledge what I was thinking.

There was no way I could make any connection between the officer's cap, the Mauser and this wizened old hunchback. It was particularly difficult to imagine how he had lived during the past thirty years and more.

I summoned the courage to touch him with my hand. He looked up — a complete imbecile. He could not have been putting it on. I'd stake my life on it. No one could fake such an idiotic expression. I started to doubt my own memory. I could no longer explain what had happened on the mountain only a couple of days ago. He appeared to be as dim as the short woman. Could he and his gun have been an hallucination? Was I suffering from hallucinations? I looked under the mattress. The cap was undoubtedly there. What did it all mean?

Perhaps there was another explanation. He was mad, as the people in the village said. Mad? Gone mad in just two days?

I worked out some history in my head. The 'liberation' of Tibet took place in 1950, that is to say, he must've come to Maqu about thirty-six years ago. But why hide himself here? Didn't he realise that leprosy is highly infectious? If he did, then surely he was on the run from something deadly. Going a step further, we can guess that he must've committed some serious crime. (If not, the risk wouldn't be worth taking.) If this reasoning were sound, he might have been a big wheel in the Nationalist army or party. Perhaps this 'VIP' had disappeared mysteriously at about the time Tibet was liberated. He'd been hiding here for thirty-six years, which meant he was now very old.

As I worked this out, my heart began pounding. If he really was such a person, then I was now in his hands and could be in great danger. Somehow he did not seem to mean me any harm. I was standing behind him, and he was not at all on his guard. The look of an idiot.

I was convinced that he was either insane or a first-rate actor — a demon and a vicious murderer.

I thought I should get out of there, no point in waiting for the axe to fall. Perhaps there was still a slim chance of making a getaway. Since he won't talk to me, I thought, why shouldn't I try my luck? As I fled from the room, I cast a final glance back at the old man and the bitch. I was shocked by what I saw. His fore and middle fingers were buried deep in the animal's vagina. Its eyes were closed with pleasure.

I escaped easily from the cave-house.

I didn't understand what there was for him to fear in his own home — even if he were mad, he had not lost his power of speech. He ought to have said something. If he *was* mad you'd expect him to have lost control. He wouldn't have retained the fear of exposing himself. Now he wouldn't even acknowledge to me. Why should he be so resistant?

The fierce sunlight reminded me that I had returned to the world where I had spent more than thirty years. I walked west from his house towards a spot where there were some trees. I didn't want to think about him. I tried to forget everything about him.

Thanks to the sacred trees I managed to do so for half a day.

## 14

IT TOOK ABOUT AN HOUR to walk to the trees from the village.

I could see two people in front of me, who were in turn quite a long way from each other. I was walking along a track. It was only wide enough for one person. Here the rocky plateau was level. You didn't have to follow the path but everyone did. It was worn down by people's footsteps every day. I didn't want to cut a new path. I usually prefer to tread a path which others have opened up.

As I went higher and higher, the climb made me breathless. I stopped to get my breath back and looked back at Maqu. It seemed lifeless — deserted ruins. Maqu village lay on the verge of a vast plateau strewn with rocks and boulders set there by landslides. At a distance even the houses looked like boulders. There was very little soil and so very little green of plant-life. The plateau looked as if it had just been formed after some recent cataclysm. However, the two great trees waiting behind me reminded me that the last landslide must have been a thousand years before.

Two more people followed up behind us. Because it was morning and they were facing the sun, I could tell they were women. They walked the same way, one a long way ahead of the other.

I went on. It was no longer far to the sacred trees.

The roots of the two trees were intertwined, and the trunks were very thick, the thickest I had ever seen. I didn't know the names of the trees. In the blazing sun they offered a unique expanse of cool shade. Their leaves were dazzlingly green, yet those that grew on the top branches seemed so far away, so far removed. A pleasant tapping sound reached my ear.

A number of people were moving slowly around the trees in an anti-clockwise direction. I hurriedly got out my camera and started shooting pictures from various angles. They didn't seem to notice what I was doing at all. I remembered that in Lhasa, people moved clockwise when circumambulating to turn prayer-wheels. I didn't understand why they did it differently here. What's more, in Lhasa, both men and women go scripture-turning, but here there were only women. I recorded these activities on the Fujicolour I'd brought with me. Six or so women walked into my frame.

After I'd finished taking pictures from a distance, I strolled into the shade under the trees. Unexpectedly, I discovered a man sitting in the gap between the two trees. To my amazement, it was *him*! And it was he who was making the pleasant tapping sound.

Another difference here was that they did not use beads while scripture-turning, nor did they chant the Six Word Scripture aloud. They walked with their eyes almost closed, their footsteps mechanical and regular. None of them were less than forty-five, none were young any longer. Just as I was all but convinced that she was not amongst them, she appeared from behind me and joined the moving circle.

She did not look at me. Like the others, she kept her eyes shut, letting her legs move mechanically. With everybody behaving with such piety, I was ashamed to look on. I tried not to turn my head, but I couldn't help watching this solemn ritual out of the corner of my eye.

He was cutting a piece of stone with a hammer, an unfinished sculpture. A head in relief. I had not expect him to be a sculptor of Buddhas. There were no streamers nor *hadas* around the trees, only plenty of rounded boulders and a number of heads, carved in relief and spaced evenly around the trees. Despite my scanty knowledge of Buddhism, I could tell they were not representations of Sakyamuni,

Songtsan Gambo, or Tsonghapa. They did not even resemble the
Buddhas of Happiness with their various vivid expressions. But whoever they were, he had created holy figures to be venerated alongside
the holy trees.

I'd been thoroughly sunburnt in walking to this place and was
stinging all over. I should have stayed under the shade of the tree, but
strangely I followed them for a few circuits and the burning disappeared almost without my noticing.

It seemed to me that each of the women had set herself a definite
number of circuits to complete. I watched until those who had come
earlier had left and then until the later-comers had gone, when the sun
told me that it was time for lunch. I became the last of the scripture-
turners. She too had left. She left without even glancing at either him
or me. I felt cool and fresh, as calm as a lakeful of blue water. If he
hadn't gestured at me, I might have carried on turning round the
trees.

I did not understand his language but I understood his gestures all
right. He wanted me to take some photos of him. Of course I would. I
indicated that he should carry on with his chiselling, and I took pictures of him from two different angles. Then I took a full length picture of him from the front.

I could feel his goodwill, his feeling of friendship for me. We walked
back together, without communication of any kind. Then I felt a deep
tremor of my heart, a great unease I couldn't comprehend. I didn't
know how or why, but I knew something, something serious was going to happen. We parted before entering the village. I gave him a tin
of pork (the same type as we had eaten at her place the night before).
He accepted gladly and said he would give me one of his relief carvings
of the Buddha. This was completely unexpected. I trembled with excitement and anticipation.

15

I COULDN'T SAY WHY, but I was very upset at the prospect of
parting. I went to the basketball ground for the second time. Although
I hadn't yet decided to leave Maqu the next day, I felt intuitively that
this would be my last chance to be with them. They may share the
same planet as we do, but our worlds were so different. I wanted to
walk amongst them, to let my eyes dwell a little longer on each of their
faces, to see the men playing their match, and the rest assemble as en-
thusiastic and willing supporters. I was no longer worried about being

noticed. I drifted slowly amongst the crowd. I saw that many young and middle-aged women had children, and all about the same age.

That night I asked her, 'I've heard, perhaps, the infection ... I mean you people here, your sickness, it's contagious?'

She said, 'I don't know. Other people are afraid of us.'

'The disease is hereditary, so I've heard. If an infected person gives birth, the child will be a leper.'

This was the first time we had mentioned the name of the disease.

'Everyone says that. But what can you do?'

'I've noticed several women with children. Couldn't they live without? If her children are born diseased, what does that say for a mother's love? Isn't it too much to bear?'

'What else can they do? They have to have more and more children.'

'They may not understand. But what about you?! You've had an education. You're being irresponsible.'

'I may not want to, but I have to give birth if I'm carrying. Perhaps I'm pregnant again now, this time by you. If so, it won't be long before I have another child.'

'Just don't get pregnant. Don't!'

I wasn't aware that I'd become hysterical, my voice loud and shrill.

'That isn't just the woman's look-out, as you should know.'

'Well, well — why not — why not use contraceptives?'

'I don't know what you're talking about. What did you say?'

I forgot where I was. How was I to explain all these new words and concepts? I became more and more unreasonable.

'Well then,' I said, 'in that case, men and women shouldn't sleep together here ...'

'What else is there to do? You've seen it all here. Apart from watching the men playing basketball and sleeping with them, what can the women do? None of the younger women go to turn scripture. There's only me going along with the old ladies. The men have nothing to do and neither do the women. If we can't do the other what else have we got?'

I tried to remind her that they ought to think of the children. At once I realised how hollow it would sound. I kept my mouth shut.

Later I remembered to tell her that the short guy wanted to give me a carving of the Buddha's head. She gave a gentle smile.

'He likes you. People take to you.'

Her words made me mad. I'm not a three year old. I don't like to be spoken to like this. Suddenly I noticed a change in her. In anger she had used a string of questions, three in quick succession. It might not seem important to anyone else, but to me the change was significant. I wasn't sure whether I should tell her about my observation and discovery. I hesitated.

She said, 'You know that he likes you.'

I nodded solemnly.

She said, 'Didn't you realise that he is a Loba Tibetan?'

I certainly didn't. I replied deliberately, in a calm, unruffled tone, 'No I didn't.'

'They don't like Lobas, they don't allow me to have anything to do with the Lobas. He has not been with me for a long time.'

I didn't feel able to ask who 'they' were. There might be a reason for her not explaining. Maybe it wasn't easy to explain. I remembered how, at the sports ground, she had told me with pride that the child was his — and how cold she had been with him that time in her room. Simply because others ('they') didn't allow them to be together, she had abandoned him. This made me furious. I hated and despised her for it. At the time, as I considered this, I felt no jealousy.

'You're making me very angry.'

'I don't understand what you say half the time,' she said.

'I hate you for this. You infuriate me. I despise you! Now do you understand.'

'So despise me,' she said.

Her response left me speechless.

The most disappointing of disappointments came later. After making love, I was breathless, exhausted. I had used up every last ounce of my strength.

But she told me, 'You only look strong. You're not up to him. He came here, made love the whole night and never huffed and puffed like that.'

Could I tell her I was suffering from altitude sickness? I just can't trot out things like that, feeble excuses for one's own incompetence.

16

BEFORE I FELL ASLEEP, I felt again that deep tremor of the heart. I started to think of it as the result of my indulgent passion. I was overtired. She had already drifted off into a relaxed sleep. Her full breast and thighs were touching me. I loved them. I didn't care that her nipples were wasted away. I could see that half her fingers and toes were touched by corruption. She was a warm and tender woman, and that was what mattered. There was something else I knew — she loved me. For a moment, I even thought of staying behind, to be by her side.

I consoled myself with the thought that the tremor was not an ill-omen, I hoped (very, very much) that I could persuade myself. Only then would I be able to fall asleep. Impossible. Impossible. Im ... possible ... not possible. Unconsciously, I overcame the groundless fears that were causing my insomnia. I was confident that once I had had a refreshing sleep, the world would be bathed in bright sunshine when I awoke.

My tremulous unease melted into the void with the brilliance of the sun. The morning promised another bright day.

After visiting the sacred trees the day before, I had clean forgotten about the old mute. The first idea that came to me as I opened my eyes was to go over what had happened in his house.

I went through the details one by one.

The KMT army officer cap. His masturbating the bitch. His idiotic look.

And that day in the street when we pretended not to see each other, brushing shoulders and passing by. I was sure I was close to the heart of the matter.

Half an hour later I was walking along the little track made by the old mute. I deliberately put on my bright red down jacket, and set off up the mountain at a leisurely pace. I climbed, then stopped to look back. As the sun rose, it got quite warm and I began to feel hot.

Half way up the mountain I sat down to rest. I deliberately chose a prominent boulder to sit on. From here the pale beige boulder-strewn plateau stretched out as far as the eyes could see. You could see the boulders which had rolled into the river, the two larger buildings now looking like matchboxes, and the dark green river steadily flowing on. The craggy mountains opposite were less high than the one behind me but more beautiful. They were already speckled with a pleasing yellow colour.

I lowered my gaze and saw a tiny figure moving quickly through the village below. I knew he was coming. So I'd finally done it. He'd already left the village and was moving towards the foot of the mountain. To make him sweat a bit, I got up and ran upward towards the top of the mountain.

Looking back, I was pleased to see him running desperately up behind me. I sat down to wait behind a huge rock, my back against the cool stone. I'd forgotten that he was an old man of over seventy.

He was closer now. I could hear his panting.

I stood up from behind the rock and stood calmly in front of him. At the sight of me he collapsed, and sank down onto the ground.

The sweat dripped off him like rainwater and he looked terrified. Pity welled up inside me, but I knew he was not really worthy of compassion. There were ghosts in his cupboard. He had chosen to climb up after me like that. He might have chosen another way of life altogether and then he wouldn't have needed to live in fear.

I bent over to have a look at him. His true age was probably eighty. The marks of old age were all over his face, neck and hands. He was still in the grips of his idiocy, his eyes clouded, the light of his youth had all but gone out of them. He was finished. He was breathing hard.

I was shocked by the transformation. Four days before he had been so strong, so aggressive and threatening. Just four days ago! Seeing that he'd somehow survived the past thirty years' of suffering, I couldn't imagine what might have destroyed him in four days.

Perhaps he'd been demented from the beginning (this place was a fine breeding ground for madness). Perhaps it was the arrival of a Chinese speaker that had prompted him to speak about what he'd been suppressing all this time. Perhaps after this one outburst he would never again be his old self. Anything was possible.

The fact that he had chosen to live in a leper-colony was unthinkable in itself, but then to seal his own lips and become a deaf-mute! Once a deaf-mute opens his mouth he is no longer what he was. It's as simple as that. I had no way of knowing whether he had contracted leprosy. He had no obvious symptoms. But I could see that he was a exemplary madman. He had collapsed completely.

I was no longer sure what to think. Perhaps he had been the most evil of criminals. Perhaps he was harmless. In any case he must have had some dark secret to hide for him to have buried himself in Maqu. I had no desire to know who he was or what he'd done. I just could not understand why he had chosen to live like this.

To my surprise, he opened his mouth to speak again.

'I'm a deaf-mute. The people here all take me for a deaf-mute. I was afraid that I'd long forgotten how to speak Chinese. Now that I'm talking to you, I realise I must have retained it. Tell me, how old do I look to you?'

'How old are you?'

'Give me your immediate impression. Don't go easy on me. Don't say anything just to make me feel better. Tell me the truth. You won't offend me, you know.'

'I think you're eighty. Did you hear? Eighty.'

'My father was rich. It was me who didn't want to carry on at school. Nobody here knows that I've had some education. My father was an Indian merchant.'

'And your mother? Your mum?'

'I stopped speaking all together. Then later nobody spoke to me. They took me for a deaf-mute. What does it matter what they call you? I've lived all these years without a name. They took me for a fool when I climbed the mountain.'

'They didn't know *why* you climbed the mountain.'

'I know for sure that you'd never believe that I have a gun.'

'I do know you've got a gun, a Mauser which takes twenty cartridges.'

His eyes stared straight ahead. He was no longer able to repeat what he had said four days ago. I anticipated what he was going to say next.

'Do you want a biscuit?'

After thinking for a while, he answered, 'Biscuits. What do mean by biscuits?'

I took two pieces of hardtack from my rucksack and put them into his hands. He examined them over and over again, then looked up at me.

'I'm sure you wouldn't believe that I've got a gun,' he said.

'A twenty cartridge Mauser. I believe you.'

He was despondent. He knocked the hardtack against the rock, smashing it to pieces. This time he wouldn't look up.

He said in a lower voice, 'I know for sure that you'd never believe that I have a gun.'

I tried to sound natural in my response, but ended up saying something laced with irony. 'Of course I wouldn't.'

'A twenty cartridge Mauser,' he retorted with pride.

'I still don't believe you,' I said.

He said, 'We'll see it soon enough. I keep it where the rain can't get at it. There's not a speck of rust on it. Nobody knows about it. From the very first day arrived, I started to climb the mountain. I blazed this trail.'

At this point I had a minor realisation. I'd heard every word he said once before. Whatever else, happened, I wasn't going allow the melodrama of four days ago to play itself out again. I had no belief in my own part. And I didn't want to hear his last line.

'It's a pity there are only six bullets left,' he said. 'Not bad after all these decades.' Six left after the last time. This time there'd be five.

I'd been worrying unnecessarily. He never got up off the ground again. It seemed the climbing had exhausted him. He was simply too old.

I guessed that he wouldn't recover quickly and I went ahead down the mountain.

## 17

PERHAPS IT WAS GUILT. I was afraid of being shot in the back. I went down hill at a fair clip. This generated a kind of hallucination in me. I felt as if the whole slope was sliding downwards with me. I knew it was dizziness. I knew I wasn't fully recovered. I shouldn't have been climbing up and racing down at such great speed.

When I looked back, the old deaf-mute was no longer in sight. Nonetheless I took the precaution of taking cover behind a huge boulder. Nervous exhaustion left me shivering all the time. I didn't like the sensation, and the deep irrational unease which accompanied it. The world swam before my eyes. The plateau of boulders detached itself from the mountain and slipped away. I hated these sensations. I would have preferred to give way gradually to my tiredness. I continued down hill, without seeing his shadow.

All the way down I kept telling myself not to panic, to remain steady-footed. But my pace quickened step by step. I was really frightened.

I didn't go back to her place. I remembered what I had wanted to do the other day. I remembered her saying that he was a Loba. No wonder his accent was different. I was sure I could find where he lived. There were only two dozen odd houses in the village, and I'd been there long enough to know my way about. There shouldn't have been any problem.

Last night she had said: You know he likes you.

At the time I nodded. In truth, I wasn't so sure. I could see he was friendly towards me. But couldn't he see how I was with her? Wouldn't he think that I had taken his woman from him? I wasn't familiar with the customs here about, but there isn't a man anywhere who'd be completely unruffled in such circumstances. Why should he be an exception? When she was boasting about how good he was, I know that I didn't feel so comfortable.

I could see clearly that she did not consider herself the property of any one person. She was free, and answered to herself alone. And he didn't seem to object.

But I was not that broad-minded. Even in my imagination I couldn't stand the idea of her belonging to other man. I wasn't her man; I was just a tenant — a male lodger — that was all. But I was emotional, I was eaten up with jealousy. She had born him a child. This fact was unbearable. In order to assert my claims, I wanted her to bear me a child, and more particularly, a male child. I believed that mine would be much better than his. With this in mind, I almost gave up the idea of going to see him.

But I couldn't. His stone sculpture was too tempting. Besides, I had already given him a present. To receive his present in return was within the rule of human conduct. Although I knew well that the two presents were not of equal value, I had no reason to employ the principles of exchange in order to try and achieve mental equilibrium. I wasn't going to think too much, I just had to find his house.

It wasn't so simple for me to find somebody in Maqu.

In the first place, I didn't speak their language, and then the villagers did not have the custom of paying visits on one another. Each household kept its door closed, making it difficult for you to knock at any door. I wandered around in vain. In the end I decided to go back and ask her.

I realised now that I was slightly afraid of her. Our conversation the previous night before we went to sleep had put a distance between us. After all, we were from two different worlds which neither communicated nor interfered with one another. Two people making love in a tight embrace are prey to a host of profitless fantasies — Is leprosy contagious or can it be prevented? Who belongs to whom? Then there's the needless feeling of love itself, the desire to offer oneself to love, etc., etc.

I was nothing more than a Lhasa resident who wrote novels, inspired from time to time with excessively romantic notions. I'd read a few books and gained some fragmentary understanding of human nature. Then I became a true romantic, allowing my imagination to run wild, like my old friend the 'heavenly horse roaming the clouds'. Nobody could be more useless than I was. At regular intervals I became fervent and impassioned as I had done the night before, droning on about human experience in philosophical terms, giving lectures on ways of living. Then I'd cool off and get back to what I had to do, the usual business, my tail between my legs.

I'd shout and make a big fuss, then scarper. What problems would I have solved? Contraception? The prevention of hereditary contagion? In actual fact, I might well be leaving some trouble behind me. I had no power to change the life of Maqu, yet here I was dishing out the remedies of 'civilisation'. The likely results were difficult to anticipate. Thinking back on it, what I said to her must have cut her to the quick.

Just a minute. He was a Loba. She said he was a Loba. Lobas didn't live in stone houses. If he still followed Loba custom, he should be living in a wooden house.

There were two wooden houses in the village. That much I had learned, but hadn't really taken in. A Loba should live in one of these houses.

The two houses stood in the same alley, not far from each other. Standing in the front of the houses, I saw that one had its door wide open. A big dog was lying there on its stomach, the kind of dog that intimidates visitors. I had no wish to disturb him, so I went and knocked at the closed door.

Someone called an answer and the door was pushed open from the inside. The woman that emerged from the house was very short, pretty and young, in typical Loba dress. I was stumped again. She was certainly not a leper, and she was surprised at my visit. She had fairer skin than the others. She hadn't been outdoors very much. I had to speak to her in Chinese.

I asked if her husband was at home.

She shook her head. I felt that she understood me, that she shook her head to say that he wasn't in, not that she couldn't understand

I asked her where he'd gone.

She at once pointed to the west. Then he must still be at the western end of the village carving Buddhas. Her finger pointed, and her other made a gestures to indicate height, so I understood she meant the sacred trees.

I asked whether he was her husband.

She nodded, full of pride.

Then I saw a boy behind her back, about as tall as her hip and thin as a monkey. The child looked like him, except that he was a bundle of bones. The eyes were too big for a child so small. He was trying hide behind his mother but couldn't help peeping out at me. Squalls of a baby's crying came from inside the house. At once, she left me and the boy to go and see to the baby. The boy was timid and followed her at her heels. I followed too.

I don't like to describe the inside of the house, it would be too cruel. But I will add something which is equally heart-rending. I saw six children in the room, each one smaller than the last, all by him and this woman.

I couldn't bear to look to see which of them had the symptoms of leprosy. I was choked. I did notice the can I had given him yesterday, which he'd put in a place out of the children's reach, as if it were an object of veneration.

I couldn't stay any longer. I noticed there were no sculptures in the house. I decided to return to the sacred trees.

It was nearly midday. The big dog barked after me.

# 18

STANDING AT THE WESTERN EDGE of the village, I saw several people coming in my direction. It was the old ladies. I didn't set off in their direction. I didn't want to get in the way of whatever was going on in the village. The little track was only wide enough for one person. If I walked towards them, someone would have to take another path, and that would never do.

I still made no move westwards, even after they'd reached the village. I stood at the edge of the village on my own. Not until noon did I see him coming towards me holding a block of stone in his hands. It must have been very heavy. He walked a little and then stopped every now and then. As I watched him, my eyes grew moist with emotion.

He saw me, and the friendly smile appeared on his face. Now I was certain that he liked me and I liked him all the more.

It was the Buddha I'd seen him working on yesterday. It had extremely large eyes which were almost expressionist. The nose was just a short narrow band. There was no mouth and a small pointed chin. The strangest looking thing was its forehead. The broad brows were vividly carved with the image of a mountain.

He placed it in my hands with great seriousness and then suddenly knelt down before me. I hastened to put the sculpture down on the ground and tried to help him up. Then I realised that he was worshipping the stone figure. This must be his god, his idol. Following his example, I knelt behind him. At last, he stood and walked away without looking back. For a moment I didn't move, I remembered my one Tibetan word and shouted after him, 'Tuchechi!' (Thank you!) He turned to show that he had heard me. But in my heart I was already saying, 'Good-bye. Good-bye.'

# 19

DEAR READER, BEFORE THIS TRAGIC STORY reaches its conclusion, I must warn you that my ending is contrived. Along with many other story-tellers, I'm concerned that some of you might take it for the truth. After all, my stay in Peaceful Repose Convalescent Home won't last forever. Eventually I'll be back amongst you all. I'm a tall, bearded, male citizen called Ma Yuan. Some of you might spot me in the crowd. I've no wish to be taken for a monster, a man who had an affair with a leprous woman. What particularly worries me is that public places might be closed to me, or that I might even be sent back and isolated in a place like Maqu. Hence the ending which follows shortly.

I happen to possess a valuable relief carving, a Loba artefact. I'm not going to tell you its history or provenance.

I've been to many distant parts of Tibet. Since, as the geologists say, Tibet is part of a 'young' mountainous formation, spectacular rocky plateaux are everywhere. They are awe-inspiring and seem to have a life of their own.

My wife is a journalist. In the course of an interview at a conference, she got to know a female doctor who had worked for over a year in a hospital for lepers. My wife told me all about the things that went on in the hospital and which she'd heard from the doctor. My wife has no secrets from me.

By chance, I read a book written by a Frenchman entitled *Kisses for a Leper*. I adored the sensational title. And then I stumbled across another book by an Englishman on life in a leper colony.

Not long ago, in the spring, I went to the southern part of Tibet. There, the Yalutsumpu river flowed steadily eastwards, its waters crystal clear, a few gulls skimming across its surface. Behind me were the tall, imposing mountains. Nearby, a young Tibetan shepherdess intoxicated me with her folk singing. I experienced a silent communion with the mountains. Across miles of rocky plateau, we spoke to one another without words.

I returned to Lhasa by truck. The driver was a friend of mine who'd been almost everywhere in Tibet. For some time he didn't speak. When I asked why, he said that he'd just passed through a village of lepers a few miles to the north. He also told me that he'd slept with one of them, a plumpish woman with an infant child.

I bumped into all these people. I'm a writer. Finders keepers. I have to admit it — I'm a lucky guy.

I also have to tell you that the following ending is a whitewash, for my benefit. I don't have a choice about it. My repeated explanations may take the shine off my masterpiece, but I'll just have to put up with it. As I've said, there's no other option. I just have to swallow it, unlucky bastard that I am. Who forced me to choose this damned subject? Who forced me to go into this damned profession? No one. It was me. So it bloody-well serves me right.

Still, I'll let you have the fabricated ending. I'll tell it to you under my breath. Here lies all my sorrow and satisfaction.

# 20

THAT VERY NIGHT something happened.

I was packing. I wrapped my sleeping bag around the carving and stuffed it into my rucksack. She was helping me. The child no longer thought of me as an outsider. He was sitting on my shoulders as we worked, his two hands grasping my hair tightly. I was using my torch for light.

She said it was too heavy. I said no problem, I could carry it.

She said that I'd never come back.

She said once more that he liked me, as she had the night before.

I said that I'd seen his woman and their six children. She said he had other kids in the village.

'He's very good,' she said.

I didn't want to hear her say that.

After a while she spoke again.

She said that early in the morning, before dawn, the birds would start singing on the roof. She said I'd wake up early and be on my way. Her voice was very calm.

I forced myself not to respond. I turned away without saying a word. It seemed that she didn't expect me to say anything.

She said that she'd seen the old deaf-mute returning from the mountain at dusk. He walked back and forth. She thought that he wasn't acting like he normally did.

'How is he different?' I asked.

She said, 'He was walking slowly. Normally he walks very fast. You saw that. This evening he was walking very slowly.'

'Has he only just come back from the mountain?'

'Yes, he's just come back. I saw him on the mountain this afternoon. He used to go up the mountain in the mornings.'

'I'm leaving,' I said.

She said, 'You can leave in the morning.'

'OK, in the morning.'

141

She said, 'Anyway, you're leaving. You can go in the morning. The others will still be asleep. I'll be asleep too. So leave tomorrow morning.'

I said, 'I want to take a picture of you. All right?'

'I'm not sure about that,' she said.

She raised a hand and wiped her own cheeks. She did it slowly. I saw tears streaming down. Suddenly I realised why she didn't want to have her photo taken. She knew that she wasn't good-looking. After all, she was a woman. I paused to think. Perhaps, before her sickness, she had been a beautiful young girl. She must have been very beautiful.

'I'm not sure I understand about pictures,' she said.

It was at this moment that I heard the gunshot. I knew it had finally happened. As I reached the door, she said, in a whisper, 'Leave in the morning. In the morning I'll be sleeping.' I gave my promise with a grim nod of the head.

## 21

THE GUNSHOT MADE EVERYTHING CLEAR.

The crescent moon had risen to the zenith, candid, pale. Maqu was bathed in clear moonlight. The road was smooth and flat. I ran through the village. My footsteps startled the stray dogs, each echoed the others barking. Soon all the dogs were howling in chorus.

Somehow, it seemed, the gunshot had not disturbed the villagers. So much the better. I ran to the old deaf-mute's place. The door was wide open. He was dragging the bitch out of the house. He had just shot her dead. Why was he heaving her out?

He dragged her with one hand by a hind leg and threw her into open field the way one throws away rubbish. His movements conveyed his inward revulsion. The gun wasn't in his hand.

I had my torch. I thought that I should find the gun first to try and avoid making matters worse. I reached the room one step ahead of him and flashed the torch. I couldn't see the gun either on the ground or on the mattress. I did see the army officer's cap with its blue-sky-and-white-sun emblem trampled under foot. No doubt that was his doing.

He stood right beside me, his eyes following the torch light. I could hear his heavy breathing. I didn't believe that he'd try and do anything to me. I had no grounds for such confidence, of course.

I figured he might have left the gun outside. Following the little circle of light I made my way step by step outside. The moonlight was like limpid water, the rocky plateau seemed more vast and desolate than ever.

The dead dog was lying like a heap of rags. There was no sign that she had ever been full of life. It was so simple to end a life.

I couldn't think of anywhere that a gun might be hidden. For the past few minutes my mind had been obsessed by the gun and there had been no room for other thoughts. This gave him plenty of time to act. As if in a dream, I heard another shot. Dimly I understood that he had had the gun with him, and that I had given him enough time to kill himself without hurry.

I decided not to go back into his house again.

I decided to leave that very night.

By the time I returned to her room, she was already asleep (or pretending to sleep). Quietly, I took my rucksack, and then used the torch to have a last look around the place. Finally I switched off the torch, and put it down beside the three cans of food I had left for them.

I had wanted to kiss her but I ended up kissing the child. With the rucksack on my back, I walked out of the door, and closed it behind me. Then I went out of the front door, and closed that behind me.

Lastly, I left the village.

## 2 2

THE RUCKSACK WAS VERY HEAVY, the road long. I breathed heavily as I walked and saw a light far in the distance.

I wouldn't let myself rest. I was dead tired but I wouldn't put down the rucksack. I didn't stop once. I knew that if I did, I would never be able to get going again.

The little light winked before me like the fireflies we used to catch when we were young. I walked and walked and began to daydream. I dreamed of my kindergarten sweetheart. We took a nap together in a big bed, sharing the blanket. I peed the bed. She started to cry and afterwards I couldn't remember whether I started crying too. I knew I was tired. It was only when I was tired that I wet the bed or started dreaming. And because of that firefly; because I'd already reached the little light in front of me.

I remember knocking on the door and opening it. I don't remember the two road maintenance men moving to one mattress and leaving me the other. I was so tired that I couldn't keep my eyes open. Dazed and exhausted, I slept until the morning of the day after.

I was woken by a thunderous rumbling but went back to sleep until the sun was high in the sky. I continued to dream after my eyes had opened. I wondered how I'd come to be lying in this strange place. I saw two men standing at the door, talking as they looked out at something.

'What's happened?' I asked.

The stocky one told me that the night before there had been a landslide. Half a mountain to the north had collapsed. I leapt up, ran to the door and saw huge boulders everywhere. God knows how, but they had now come to a stop. I never saw Maqu village again. The slide of mud and stone must surely have buried the two great trees under the boulders.

The thin man turned to switch on the radio, I was looking north absent-mindedly. '... We are now broadcasting live from the Beijing Worker's Stadium — the May Fourth Invitational Football Cup sponsored by *China Youth* magazine. Taking part in the cup we have some of the world's strongest teams: Italy, West Germany, Uruguay ...'

Just a minute, something wasn't right. What was it? You guessed it: time. I knew something wouldn't be right. 'Excuse me, could you tell me what date it is today?'

The stocky one answered, 'Youth Day, May the fourth.'

Mechanically, I repeated his words, 'May the fourth.'

# ONE KIND OF REALITY

YU HUA

## 1

THERE WAS NO DIFFERENCE between this morning and other mornings. It was raining. Since it had been raining on and off for over a week the two brothers, Shangang and Shanfeng, had the impression that fine weather was a million miles away, as far away as the days of childhood.

Day had just dawned when they heard their mother grumbling that her bones were going mouldy or something. Her whinging sounded like the constant dripping of the rain. They were still in bed, listening to their mother's footsteps as she walked towards the kitchen.

She broke a couple of chopsticks in two and said to her two daughters-in-law, 'During the night I'm always hearing the sound of chopsticks breaking inside me.' The two daughters-in-law didn't answer, just carried on making breakfast. She went on, 'I know it's my bones cracking one by one.'

The two brothers got up and came out of their bedrooms, muttering, 'Not again,' as though they were fed up with the endless rain and their mother's simultaneous outpouring of grumbles.

Now, as usual, they were sitting round the table eating breakfast, which was rice porridge and noodles.

The old lady was a vegetarian, so on the edge of the table there was a saucer of vegetables, which she'd pickled herself. She wasn't going on about her bones going mouldy anymore, but began to speak again, 'It's as if there's moss growing in my guts.'

The two brothers thought of the moss with worms crawling over it, that grows on the sides of wells and on the corners of tumble-down walls, with its glistening greenness. Their wives didn't appear to have heard what their mother-in-law said. The expression on their faces was as thick as mud.

Shangang's four year old son, Pipi, wasn't at the table with the grown-ups, but was eating breakfast sitting on a small plastic stool. He wouldn't eat his noodles so his mother had put some sugar on his rice porridge.

Just then he'd crept up next to his grandmother, and pinched some of her pickled vegetables. More and more tears welled up in her eyes, as she went on relentlessly, 'You've got the rest of your life to eat all you want, you have, and me, I've hardly any time left at all.' His father hauled him back to his little plastic stool. He wasn't at all pleased with this, and banged a spoon on the edge of his dish, yelling, 'Not enough. I can't finish it.'

He yelled and yelled, louder and louder, but the grown-ups didn't pay any attention to him, so he decided to cry. And then his cousin, lying in his aunt's arms, started up just as shrilly. He watched his aunt taking his cousin to one side to change his nappy. He walked over and stood at her side. His cousin was crying in little fits, his body squirming, and that funny thing you wee'ed with shaking about. Very proud of himself, he said to his aunt, 'He's a boy.' But his aunt didn't take any notice, and when she'd finished changing the nappy she went back to her seat. He stood there without moving. His cousin wasn't crying any more, and was looking at him with eyes like marbles. He walked away, a bit dejected. He didn't go back to the little plastic stool, but went over to the window. He was too small. He had to strain his neck to reach up to the windowpane and watch the raindrops outside beating on the glass, twisting and turning like worms as they slid downwards.

Breakfast was over. Shangang watched as his wife wiped the table. Shanfeng watched as his wife went into the bedroom with the baby in her arms, leaving the door open, and then came straight out again and into the kitchen. Shanfeng looked round at his sister-in-law's hand as she wiped the table. On the back of her hand were veins that sometimes stood out and sometimes didn't. Shanfeng watched for a while then looked up and over towards the criss-crossing drops of water on the window, and said to his brother, 'It feels like it's been raining a hundred years.'

'Yeah, it feels that long.'

Their mother was still going on relentlessly. She was sitting in her own room now, so her voice seemed much quieter than before. She began to cough, a very exaggerated cough, followed by the sound of spitting, tense and springy. They knew she would be spitting into the palm of her hand and looking to see if there were any traces of blood. They could imagine the scene.

Not long afterwards, their wives came out of the bedrooms, each with two umbrellas. It was time to go to work. The two brothers stood up and when they had taken their umbrellas the four of them went out together, out of the lane where their house was. Then the two brothers went westwards, and their wives turned east. The two brothers walked together, but as though they didn't know each other. Without a word they went as far as the gate of the middle school, where Shanfeng turned on to the bridge and Shangang carried on. Their wives walked together for only a very short time. As soon as they came out of the lane they bumped into their respective colleagues, as they always did, and, after quick greetings, they went off with the people they worked with.

A long while after they'd gone Pipi was still standing in the same place, listening to the rain. He'd been able to hear four kinds of raindrops, the sound of raindrops on the roof was like his father's fingers drumming on his head, the raindrops falling on leaves sounded as though they were leaping down. The other two sounds were from the cement in front of the house and the pond at the back of the house — compared with the clear tight sound of rain on the pond, the sound of rain on cement was of course much heavier.

The child tunnelled his way beneath the table, then step by step, he walked over to his grandmother's door, which was half open, and saw her sitting on the edge of the bed as though she was dead. The child said, 'There are four kinds of rain now.' His grandmother heard this and gave a resounding belch. The child could smell the foul air. Recently his grandmother's belches had been getting more and more foul. So he turned away immediately, and headed for his cousin.

His cousin was lying in the cradle, his eyes gazing at the ceiling, smiles all over his face. The child said to his cousin, 'There are four kinds of rain now.'

His cousin had obviously heard him, and his two little legs began to kick about playfully and his eyes started to wander about. But they didn't fall on him. With both hands he stroked his cousin's face, which felt as soft and gentle as cotton wool. He couldn't help pressing harder, and with a magnificent 'wa' his cousin began to cry.

At the sound of the crying he felt an inexplicable pleasure. For a while he watched his cousin with delight, then he slapped him on the face. It was how he'd seen his father hit his mother. When he was slapped, his cousin suddenly went quiet. His mouth fell open for a moment, and then, just like a gale blowing open a window, the crying burst out. The sound was loud and wonderful to hear, and it excited the child. It wasn't long before the cries became weaker and weaker, so he gave him another slap on the face. In self-defence his cousin had grabbed the back of his hand and there were two scratches, bleeding, which he hadn't noticed. He was only concerned that after the last slap his cousin had carried on crying, but although it was a little louder, it wasn't even half as exciting as a moment before. So he hit him a bit harder. It was no different, the crying only lasted a little longer. He abandoned this method and stretched out his hand to grasp his cousin's throat. His cousin's hands began to grip on to the back of his. When he let go, the crying sound which he so longed to hear rang out again. So he kept on and on grasping his cousin's throat and then releasing it, enjoying, time after time, the sudden violent cries. Then when he released his hand his cousin didn't give out that exhilarating cry, and there was merely his open mouth quivering as it belched out air. He began to lose interest and walked off.

He went back to stand beneath the window, but there were no more raindrops drumming on the glass now, only criss-crossing traces of water, like little pathways. The child began to picture buses racing along these roads and crashing. And then he saw leaves floating on the window, and thousands of little gold lights glistening on the glass which enchanted him. He immediately pushed the window open, wanting to let the leaves come and float inside, and the little lights leap in and dance all around him. The light burst in just as he'd wanted, not drop by drop like the rain, but in one great whole. He noticed the sky was clear now, and the gleam of sunlight was shining on him. He could see the leaves clearly, the elm tree outside the house leaning over, its leaves sparkling green, and slowly the beads of rain dripped off, the leaves shuddering at each drop. It was so beautiful it made the child smile.

Then the child appeared again at his cousin's cradle, and told him, 'The sun's come out.' The cousin had forgotten all about what had just happened, and was smiling at him. He said, 'Do you want to go and see the sun?' His cousin stretched up his legs, and began to cry out 'ai ai'. 'But can you walk?' His cousin stopped his little cries, and began to look at him with his eyes like marbles, putting out his arms as though he wanted to be picked up. 'I know, you want me to carry you.' As he spoke he struggled to pick him up out of the cradle, and held him up just as he held the little plastic stool. He felt like he was holding a big lump of meat in his arms. His cousin began to 'ai ai' again. 'You're really happy, aren't you?' he said. Then he struggled to carry him outside.

In the distance someone was letting off firecrackers, while next door they were lighting the stove in the yard, and the thick smoke came rolling over the wall towards them. His cousin was delighted to see the smoke and cried out 'wa wa'. He wasn't interested in the sun. Another reason he wasn't interested in the sun was because a few sparrows had just flown down from the roof and stopped on the branches, which were now swaying up and down in time with their chirping.

The child began to feel more and more weighed down by the bundle in his arms, so he loosened his grip. As the bundle fell he could hear two sounds, a heavy thudding then a crisper, brighter sound, and then no sound at all. He felt much lighter and freer now, and he watched the sparrows hopping about the branches. As the branches shook the leaves fluttered like a fan. He'd been standing there for while when he began to feel thirsty, so he turned around and went back into the house.

He didn't find water immediately. He had gone straight to the glass standing on the bedside table, but it was empty. So he walked into the kitchen where there were two enamel mugs with lids on the table. He had no way of knowing whether or not there was any water in them as he couldn't reach high enough. So he walked out again and came back carrying the little plastic stool. It was just as he was carrying the stool that he suddenly remembered his cousin, and how he'd carried him outside a while ago, and now he was here by himself. He thought it was strange, but it didn't distract him from what he was doing. He climbed on to the stool, and as he pulled the two mugs over he could feel that they weren't empty, and he took a couple of sips of the water from each mug. Then he remembered the sparrows and went back outside. On the elms outside there were no birds hopping about the branches. They'd flown away. He could see the concrete starting to whiten as it dried, and then he caught sight of his cousin, lying on his back on the ground with his arms and legs in the air. He went over to his side, squatted down and pushed him a few times, but his cousin didn't move, and then he saw the little pool of blood on the concrete near his head. He leaned over to have a look, and found that the blood was coming out from his head on to the concrete where it looked like a flower slowly opening out. Then he saw some ants racing over from nowhere, and stopping when they reached the blood. Only one ant went around the blood and climbed up on to his cousin's hair, along several strands congealed with blood, and straight into his head through the place where the blood was coming out. He stood up, bewildered, and looked all around him, then went back into the house.

He saw his grandmother's door half open as before, and went over to it. She was still sitting on the bed. He told her, 'My little brother's

149

gone to sleep.' His grandmother looked round at him, and he saw that her eyes were swollen with tears. That was boring, so he went into the kitchen and sat down on his little stool. His right hand began to hurt where it had been scratched. He had to think for a long time before he remembered that he'd been scratched by his cousin when he was beside the cradle, and then he remembered how he'd come to carry his cousin outside, and how he'd let go. The thinking made him tired, so he stopped thinking anymore. He lent his head against the wall and fell fast asleep.

It was much later that she got up and heard the chopsticks breaking inside her again. The noises burst out through her flabby skin and then it went unusually quiet. She heard the noises quite clearly despite being a little deaf. Her eyes began to swell with tears again, because she felt she hadn't long to live — her bones were breaking every day. She felt that not only would she be unable to stand or sit but soon she wouldn't be able to lie down either. By that time she wouldn't have a whole bone left in her body, just a pile of higgledy-piggledy bits of broken bone splintered together any old way. Her foot bones might be pushing out of her stomach, and her arm bones might be sticking into her guts, overgrown with moss.

She walked out of the bedroom, and didn't hear any more cracking, despite being overwrought with worry. The glare of the sunlight streaming in through the open window blurred her vision so that all she could see was a shining brightness. She didn't know what she could see, and walked to the door. The sun was shining down on her, turning her hands a frightful yellowish colour. She saw something yellow lying in front of her. She didn't know what that was either. So she crossed the threshold and slowly walked over to it. She still hadn't made the yellow thing out to be her grandson when she noticed the pool of blood. It gave her a shock and she rushed back to her bedroom.

2

THE CHILD'S MOTHER CAME HOME from work earlier than usual. She was a bookkeeper in a factory producing children's bikes. Some time before it was time to leave work, for no particular reason, she'd started worrying that something had happened to her child. She hadn't been able to sit still and told her boss that she had to go home to look after her son. She grew more and more anxious on the way home. When she opened the gate to the yard, she realised why she'd been so worried.

She saw her son and his shadow lying together in the sun. As her anxieties became fact she went blank. She stood at the door for a while. She'd seen the dried blood on the ground by her son's head. In the sunlight the blood didn't look real, and her son lying there on the ground didn't seem real either. She walked over to his side and called his name a few times to see what would happen, but he didn't respond. She seemed a little relieved, as though that might not be her son lying there after all. She straightened up and raised her head to the sky, which was shining too strongly and made her feel dizzy. It took some effort to walk back to the house and go inside, where she felt cold and miserable. The bedroom door was still open, so she went in. She stood in front of the wardrobe, pulled open a drawer and looked for something amongst a pile of woollen shirts. She searched for a while but didn't find what she was looking for. Then she opened the wardrobe door, where the coats belonging to her and her husband, Shanfeng, were hanging, but still couldn't find what she was looking for. She went and pulled open all the drawers in the desk, took one glimpse and walked away. She sat down on a chair, her eyes scanning the room. Her glance moved from the wardrobe, then slid off the glass top on the round table, gliding over to the three seater sofa, then it leapt from the sofa on to the rest of the room. Only then did she notice the cradle. She was stunned, and leapt to her feet. The cradle was empty, her son wasn't there. Suddenly she recalled the child lying on the ground outside, and pelted out like a madwoman. When she was beside him she didn't know what to do. Then she remembered Shanfeng, turned and went out.

She was walking as fast as she could down the lane, as though someone was coming to greet her. But she didn't make a response, just stormed past everything as she rushed to the end of the lane. When she got there, she stopped and stood still. The broad street lay there before her, she didn't know which way to go, she was flustered and out of breath.

Shanfeng came into sight, talking with someone as he walked towards her. Now she knew which way to go. By the time she'd made up her mind, Shanfeng had seen her, and she'd burst out crying. In no time she felt Shanfeng's grip on her arm and heard her husband ask, 'What's happened?' She opened her mouth but nothing came out. She heard her husband ask again, 'What on earth's happened?' But she still she couldn't get any words out of her wide open mouth. 'Has something happened to the child?' He began to roar. Somehow she managed to nod her head. Shanfeng pushed her aside and ran to the house. She turned and walked back. There were so many people around and so much noise. She walked very slowly, and within moments saw her husband come running up with the child in his arms, then brush straight past her. She turned again. She wanted to speed up and catch her husband, she knew he was bound to be heading for the hospital. But she couldn't go any faster. She wasn't crying any more. When she reached the end of the lane again she didn't know which way to go, and had to ask someone coming towards her, who pointed her to the west, and then she remembered where the hospital was. She started walking westwards very slowly along the pavement, her body like a leaf being blown in the wind. When she'd walked as far as the department store she began to regain her senses a little. She knew the hospital wasn't far now. Then she saw her husband walking back towards her with the child in his arms. Shanfeng's impassive expression told her everything, and she burst out crying, sobbing violently. Shanfeng walked up to her and gritting his teeth, he said, 'You can cry at home.' She didn't dare cry any more. She followed Shanfeng home hanging onto his shirt.

When Shangang came home his wife was already in the kitchen. He went into their bedroom and sat down on the sofa. He had no pressing business, and was waiting for his lunch. Then Pipi appeared. He'd woken up when his mother had gone into the kitchen. He felt cold after his sleep and told his mother so. She was busy with the lunch and told him to go and put on something else. So he'd appeared at his father's side, moaning all the way. Shangang didn't have much patience for the way his son was behaving.

'What's all this about?' he asked.

'I'm cold,' Pipi answered.

Shangang didn't say anything, ran his eyes over the boy and looked towards the window. He saw the window was still closed, and went over to open it.

'I'm cold,' said Pipi again.

Shangang didn't pay any attention to his son and stood by the window. He felt very comfortable with the sun on him.

Shanfeng walked in holding the child, with his wife behind him. Shangang could see from their faces that something had happened. The two brothers looked at each other, without saying a word. Shangang listened as they dragged their feet into the house and the door closed with a creak. Shangang was sure something had happened.

Then Pipi said 'I'm cold,' again.

Shangang walked out of the bedroom and sat down at the dining table. His wife was coming out of the kitchen with the lunch, and Pipi was already sitting on the little plastic stool. He could hear Shanfeng roaring in his room. His wife sat down. She asked Shangang, 'Shall we go and call them?'

'No,' he answered.

The old lady came out with a saucer of pickles in her hand. They never needed to call her. She always appeared at the table promptly.

There was another sound in Shanfeng's room on top of the roaring. Shangang knew what it was. He swallowed his food, but his eyes were gazing outside, through the open door. Before long he heard his mother grumbling. He looked round to see her face piled high with wrinkles and frowns as she stared at the bowl of rice, and he heard her say, 'I've seen blood.' He turned back again and carried on gazing at the sunlight outside.

Shanfeng had carried the child into his room, laid him in the cradle, and kicked the bedroom door shut with all his strength. Then seeing his wife sitting on the edge of the bed, he said, 'You can cry now.'

His wife was gazing at him absently, as though she hadn't heard what he'd said. It was as though those staring eyes had died, although she was sitting quite steadily.

Shanfeng said again, 'You can cry if you want.'

But she merely shifted her gaze a little.

Shanfeng stepped forward and demanded, 'Why don't you cry?'

Only then did she shift slightly, and looked up wearily at Shanfeng's hair.

Shanfeng continued, 'Go on, cry, I want to hear you cry.'

Two teardrops fell from the empty caverns of her eyes, and dropped slowly down.

'That's better,' said Shanfeng, 'but it would be better still with some sound.'

But she was just wept silently.

And then Shanfeng hit the roof. He grabbed hold and yanked his wife's hair, roaring, 'Why don't you cry a bit louder?'

Her tears stopped suddenly, and she looked at her husband in fright.

'Tell me, who was it who took him outside?' Shanfeng began to roar again.

Bewildered, she shook her head repeatedly.

'So he walked out by himself, did he?'

This time she didn't shake her head, and didn't nod either.

'So you know absolutely nothing about it?' Shanfeng had stopped roaring, and was speaking through gritted teeth.

She thought for ages before nodding.

'You mean that when you got home the child was already there on the ground?'

She nodded again.

'And you came running out to find me?'

Her tears started up again.

Shanfeng thundered, 'Why didn't you take him straight to the hospital, instead of leaving him to die?'

She began to shake her head wildly in confusion, then watched as her husband's fist swung in the air. In an instant it had landed smack on her face. She fell back on to the bed.

Shanfeng bent over and dragged her up by the hair, then landed another fist on her face. It knocked her to the ground, yet she still didn't utter a sound.

Shanfeng pulled her to her feet again. She put her hands up to her face to try and protect herself. But Shanfeng aimed at her solar plexus and she felt everything go black. With a breathless sob she sank to the ground.

When Shanfeng went to haul her up again he found her particularly heavy, as though her body was sinking down through water. So Shanfeng held her up against the wall by pressing his bent knees against her stomach. Then grabbed her hair, and beat her head violently against the wall three times. 'Why wasn't it you who died?' he roared. When he'd finished, he let go, and her body slid along the wall to the ground.

Then Shanfeng opened the bedroom door and went out. Shangang had finished his lunch by then, but he was still sitting at the table. His wife had just cleared away their bowls and chopsticks, leaving clean ones out for Shanfeng and his wife. Shangang saw Shanfeng emerge with a murderous look on his face and go up to his mother.

His mother was still sitting there rattling on, moaning about how she'd seen blood. Her bowl of rice hadn't been touched.

Shanfeng asked his mother, 'Who was it took my son outside?'

His mother looked up at her son, and, her face wrinkled in a frown, said, 'I saw blood.'

'I'm asking you,' shouted Shanfeng, 'who it was took my son outside?'

She still took no interest in what her son was asking, but was hoping her son would show an interest in her having seen blood, or that he might show some concern for her appetite. So she answered again, 'I saw blood.'

Then Shanfeng grabbed his mother's shoulders and began to shake her, 'Who was it?'

Shangang, who was sitting nearby, opened his mouth, and said calmly, 'Don't do that.'

Shanfeng let go of his mother's shoulders, turned to Shangang and roared, 'My son's dead!'

Shangang was horrified and couldn't say anything in response.

Shanfeng turned back and demanded from his mother, 'Who was it?'

This time his mother's tears welled up as she began to mutter, 'You've broken my bones with your shaking.' She said to Shangang, 'Come here and listen, my body's filled with the sound of bones breaking.'

Shangang nodded and said, 'I've heard.' But he didn't move from his seat.

Shanfeng roared as if for the last time, 'Who was it took my son outside?'

And then Pipi, who'd been sitting on the little plastic stool, answered in a voice even louder than Shanfeng's, 'I took him outside.' The first time Shanfeng asked his mother this question Pipi hadn't shown any interest. Then Shanfeng's manner caught his attention. He'd had some trouble trying to make out what Shanfeng was yelling about. Once he'd understood, there was no stopping him roaring his answer and then turning to his father, really pleased with himself.

Shanfeng let go of his mother immediately, and went over to Pipi. He looked so fierce and violent that Shangang stood up.

Pipi was still sitting on his little stool. He thought Shanfeng's blood red eyes were wonderful.

Shanfeng stood in front of Shangang and shouted, 'Let me by.'

Shangang said very, very calmly, 'He's only a child.'

'I don't care.'

'Well I do,' Shangang answered, still very calm.

Shanfeng punched Shangang right in the face. His head rolled a little but he didn't fall down.

'Don't do that,' said Shangang.

'Let me by,' roared Shanfeng.

'He's only a child,' said Shangang.

'I don't care. He'll pay for this with his life.' When he'd finished this speech Shanfeng punched Shangang once again, and his head rolled a little like before.

The old lady was stunned at all this, and cried out over and over, 'You're scaring me to death.' But she didn't move from her seat, because Shanfeng's fist was still some way away from her. Shangang's wife came running out from the kitchen, and yelled at Shangang:

'What's going on?'

Shangang said to her, 'Get the child out of here.'

But Pipi didn't want to go, he was really enjoying Shanfeng's punches. It thrilled him that his father hadn't fallen over. So when his mother began to pull him away, he began to cry with fury.

At this point Shanfeng turned to hit Pipi. Shangang blocked his fist and grabbed hold of Shanfeng's arm, not letting him any closer to Pipi.

Shanfeng went for Shangang's stomach with his knee. Shangang huddled over in pain, unable to stifle his groans. But he still kept his grip on Shanfeng's arm, and only when he'd seen his wife take the child into the bedroom and shut the door did he let go. He moved back a few steps and sat down on the stool.

Shanfeng went up to the door and kicked it violently, screaming, 'Bring him out.'

Shangang watched Shanfeng kick the door like a madman, heard his wife yelling out his name from the bedroom, and the child crying. He sat still. He sensed his mother getting up from beside him and walking away, muttering to herself as if her mouth were stuffed with cotton wool.

Shanfeng kicked furiously for a while, then stopped. He stared at the door for a long time, before turning again. He looked at Shangang, and went over and sat on another stool, his eyes still watching the door, as though his gaze was nailed there. Shangang sat and watched him.

And then when Shangang felt Shanfeng's breathing had calmed down, he got up and walked over to the bedroom door. He felt Shanfeng's gaze boring into his back. He knocked on the door. 'It's me. Open the door.' He thought he heard Shanfeng getting up, but Shanfeng was still sitting not making a sound. He was relieved, and went on knocking.

The door was opened cautiously, and he saw his wife's troubled face. He said to her gently, 'It's all right.' But it didn't stop her shutting the door quickly behind him.

She glanced up at him. 'He's really beaten you up,' she said.

Shangang smiled. 'It'll be gone in a few days.'

As he spoke, Shangang went over to his son who was still tearful, and stroked his head. 'Don't cry.' Then he went over to the mirror on the wardrobe and saw the swollen face of a stranger. He looked back at his wife, 'Is this me?'

His wife didn't answer, she was watching him in horror.

He said to her, 'Get out all our savings.'

She hesitated for a moment, then did as he said.

He stayed by the mirror. He noticed that his forehead was unscathed, and his chin was the same as always, but the rest of his face had let him down.

His wife handed over their savings, and as he took them he asked, 'How much is there?'

'Three thousand *yuan*,' she answered.

'No more?' he asked, doubting.

'But we need to keep back a little,' she explained.

'Bring it all out,' he said firmly.

So she had to go and get the other two thousand. Shangang took the money and went out.

Shanfeng was still sitting in the same place, and when Shangang opened the door and walked out, his gaze left the door and attached itself to Shangang's stomach. Now Shangang was walking over to him, his focus began to shorten. Shangang stopped in front of him, and his eyes rose up level with Shangang's chest. He saw Shangang's hand stretched in front of him, tightly gasping a dozen or so savings books.

'There's five thousand *yuan* here,' said Shangang. 'Let's call that the end of the matter.'

'No way.' Shanfeng's voice had become hoarse. He answered categorically.

'This is all the money we have,' Shangang said again.

'Fuck off,' said Shanfeng. Shangang's torso blocked his line of vision, he couldn't see the door.

Shangang stood silently in front of him for a long time, watching Shanfeng, taking in the dull, stupid look about him. At last he turned and went back to the bedroom. He gave his wife the money.

'Doesn't he want it?' she asked, surprised.

He didn't reply. He simply went over to his son, and tapped him on the head, saying, 'Come with me.'

The child first looked at his mother then stood up, and asked his father, 'Where are we going?'

157

She realised what he was doing, and blocked his way. 'You can't do this. He'll beat him to death.'

Shangang pushed her aside with one hand, and dragged his son out with the other. He heard her calling after him, 'Please, I'm begging you.'

Shangang went up to Shanfeng and shoved his son in front of him. 'I'm giving you my son.'

Shanfeng looked up at Pipi and Shangang for a while. It seemed he was about to stand up, but he just shifted his body slightly. Then his gaze veered round and settled outside the door in the yard. He saw the pool of blood. He noticed that the blood was giving off a light, just like the glinting of sunlight.

Pipi stood there, clearly bored, and looked up at his father. But there was no expression on his father's face. It was the same as Shanfeng's. So he looked around, and noticed his mother standing behind him. He didn't know how long she'd been there.

Shanfeng stood up and said to Shangang, 'I want him to lick that blood clean.'

'And then?' asked Shangang.

Shanfeng hesitated a moment before saying, 'And then it's finished.'

'All right,' Shangang nodded.

Then the child's mother said to Shanfeng, 'Let me do the licking. He didn't know what he was doing.'

Shanfeng ignored her, and led the child out by the hand. She followed them out. Shangang hesitated and then went back into the bedroom, but moved over to the window.

Shangang saw his wife go up to the pool of blood and lean down to lick it up. She looked like a real glutton. Shangang saw Shanfeng go up to his wife and kick her one in the backside. She fell to her side, then got back on her knees and vomited uncontrollably, her throat uttering that sound that makes your hair stand on end. Then he saw Shanfeng pressing Pipi's head down, so that he ended up on all fours. He heard Shanfeng's voice which had almost the same quality as his wife's retching, 'Lick.'

Pipi crawled forward, gazing at the blood glistening in the sunlight. It made him think of a particular kind of fresh jam. He stuck out his tongue and gave a lick to test it, and a completely new taste filled his mouth. So he started licking with pleasure, and felt the cement underneath the blood very rough. In a few minutes his tongue was numb. Then trickles of blood began to appear on his tongue, and he found his own blood even tastier. Although he didn't know it was his own.

Then Shangang saw his sister-in-law appear looking bruised, battered and exhausted. 'I'll bite you to death,' she screamed as she bent down over Pipi. At that very moment Shanfeng lashed out with his foot and landed a kick right in Pipi's crotch. Pipi's body shot into the air, and then fell head first on to the cement with a dull thud. Shangang saw his son struggle for a moment, then lie sprawled out, unmoving, as though he was paralysed.

3

WHEN THE OLD WOMAN heard the 'thud', she was quite taken aback. The sound had bored its way out from inside her stomach. It was as though it had burst out after having been closed up inside her for so long, the sound full of all that moaning. At once she made up her mind that her intestines were rotting, and that the corruption must already be long-established. She heard the sound of two 'thuds', only this time much clearer, like the sound of bubbles bursting out into the air. If she thought about it like that, her intestines must already be completely decayed. She couldn't conceive of the colour that things turn to after they'd decayed, but she imagine their shape — a thick liquid giving off bubbles as it swilled around inside. She even smelt that odour of corruption, belching from her mouth. Before long she felt that the entire room was filled with the stench of decay, as though even the room itself was rotting. And she knew why she didn't feel like eating.

She tried to stand, and immediately felt the corruption in her abdomen sink down into her thighs. She decided that eating would really much too dangerous because her stomach was not a bottomless pit. There would come a day when all the nooks and crannies in her body would be packed, and it would simply burst. She'd explode like a bomb. Her flesh would be plastered on to the wall, like a banner, and her bones — already more or less shattered — would be heaped up like a little pile of firewood.

She could imagine her brain rolling along the ground like a football into a corner and stopping for good.

Tears welled up in her eyes again. She felt that even they were giving off a smell of decay, and when the tears rolled down her cheeks they were much heavier than usual. As she walked over towards the door her body seemed as heavy as a sandbag. Then she saw Shangang carrying Pipi inside, holding him like he would a toy. Shangang didn't come up to her, he avoided her and turned into his room. As he did so she saw the traces of blood on Pipi's head. This was the second time today that she'd seen blood. This time it was not as bright as before, this time it looked dull. She felt she was going to be sick.

Shangang had watched his son fly up into the air like a bit of rag, and fall swiftly to the ground. Then he didn't see anything at all, he saw wild grasses grow before his eyes, and a well of a glistening green.

When it happened, Shangang's wife had raised her head. She didn't see her son being kicked by Shanfeng, but instantly her convulsed stomach let loose. When she looked up, all she saw was her son with his limbs lying limp after his struggle, just like her guts. The sight of him baffled her, and she stared blankly. The blood on his head was slowly seeping out, like red ink.

'Shangang,' she screamed, as she turned away. Shangang was standing behind the window. He didn't move. He closed his eyes as though he were already sleeping. She turned back, and addressed Shanfeng who was standing there motionless, 'My husband's scared stupid.' Then she said to her son, 'Your father's scared stupid.' And she went on muttering to herself, 'What should I do?'

At about this point, the wild grass and the well disappeared and the scene of a few moments before presented itself to him. Once more Shangang saw his son flying upwards like a rag and dropping back down. Then he saw his wife standing there looking at him, and he thought, 'What you staring at me like that for?' He saw Shanfeng looking this way and that, and then, as though there was nothing else to do, walk back inside. Shangang's wife followed, weighed down with hurt. Their son hadn't got up yet. He was still lying on the ground. He thought he should go out and take a look at his son, so he did.

As Shanfeng entered the room, the footsteps of his wife behind him made him crazy. He looked back at her and said, 'Don't follow me.' Then he met Shangang in the doorway. Shangang was smiling at him, but the meaning of the smile eluded him. Shangang brushed past him like a gust of wind. Shanfeng realised his wife was still there behind him, and roared, 'Don't follow me.'

Shangang went straight up to his wife. She said to him blankly, 'You're scared stupid.'

He shook his head. 'No I'm not.' Then he went up to his son. He leaned over and saw that his son's head was still bleeding. He pressed his finger on the wound, but it kept bleeding, trickling out over his finger, and he shook his head, thinking there was nothing he could do anymore. He opened the palm of his hand and brought it close to his son's mouth. He felt a very slight breathing, but it was getting weaker all the time. Soon there was nothing. He moved his hand down to find his son's pulse, but couldn't find it. Then he saw that there were ants crawling towards him. The ants were of no interest to him. So he stood up and addressed his wife, 'He's dead.'

His wife nodded when she heard this and said, 'I know.' Then she asked, 'What do we do now?'

'Bury him,' answered Shangang.

His wife was staring at Shanfeng who was still standing by the door, and said to Shangang, 'Is that all?'

'What else is there?' asked Shangang. He knew that Shanfeng was looking straight at him, and turned to stare back, but Shanfeng had already turned to go in. Then Shangang, as though he had thought of something, turned back to his son, and took him in his arms. His son was heavy. He went inside.

As he walked in he saw his mother coming out of her bedroom, and heard her saying something, but by this time he was already in his own room. He put his son down on the bed and pulled a blanket up to cover him. Then he turned round and said to his wife who was coming in, 'See, he's sleeping.'

Again his wife asked him,' Is that the end of it?'

He looked at her with bewilderment as though he didn't know what she meant.

'You're scared silly,' she said.

'No I'm not.'

'You're a coward.'

'I'm not,' he carried on arguing.

'Then get out there.'

'Where?'

'Go and give Shanfeng what he deserves,' she said between clenched teeth.

He started to smile, went up to his wife and patted her on the shoulder, saying, 'Don't get angry.'

His wife smiled coldly and said, 'I'm not getting angry, I just want you to go after him.'

Shanfeng appeared at the door and said, 'No need to look.' In his hand were two cleavers. He said to his brother, 'Now it's our turn,' and handed him one of the knives.

Shangang didn't take it. He was just staring at Shanfeng's face, and thought it looked unusually pale. He said, 'You look terrible.'

'Don't talk rubbish,' said Shanfeng.

Shangang saw his wife go to take the cleaver, and pass it to him. He put his hands in his pockets and said, 'I don't need it.'

'You're a coward,' said his wife.

'No I'm not.'

'Then take the cleaver.'

'I don't need it.'

His wife stared at him for a long time, then nodded to show that she understood. She put the knife back into Shanfeng's hand. 'Listen,' she said to Shangang, 'I'd rather you were dead than have to see you living like this.'

He shook his head as if to say there was nothing he could do about it. Again, he said to Shanfeng, 'You look awful.'

Shanfeng turned away and went into the kitchen. When he emerged the cleavers were no longer in his hands. He turned to his wife who was standing in the corner, racked with fear, and said, 'Let's eat.' Then he went into the kitchen and sat down at the table. His wife walked over.

Shanfeng didn't start to eat as soon as he sat down. His eyes were still on Shangang. He saw Shangang's right hand reach into his pocket for something, as though he was looking for his keys. Then Shangang turned and walked outside. His brother started to eat. He put the food into his mouth and chewed; it felt like chewing on mud. His wife, sitting next to him, was still trembling. This really infuriated him. 'What are you trembling for?' When he'd finished he swallowed the mouthful. Then he looked up at his wife who hadn't budged and said, 'Why aren't you eating?'

'I don't feel like it,' she answered.

'If you're not going to eat, then get out of here.' He got angrier and angrier and kept stuffing food into his mouth. He heard his wife stand up and go into the bedroom. She sat down on a chair next to the wall. He began chewing again. This time it made him feel sick, but he was still able to swallow.

He couldn't eat any more. It had left him gasping for breath, and the sweat was dripping off his brow. He wiped away the beads of sweat with his hand, and they felt to him like little balls of ice. He saw Shangang's wife coming out of the bedroom. She stood at the door staring darkly at him for a while then went over to him. From the way she walked he thought she was floating over. She floated up to him, then drifted down on to a stool. She was looking at him with a drifting glance just as she had walked. He couldn't stand the way she was staring at him so he told her to fuck off.

162

She put her elbows on the table, and resting her chin in her two hands observed him closely.

'Fuck off and leave me alone,' he yelled.

But she stayed there without moving.

Suddenly, he swept all the dishes from the table on to the floor, stood up, picked up the stool and hurled it violently to the ground.

She waited for the noise to subside and then said quietly, 'Why don't you give me a kick and finish me off?'

He flew into a rage. He walked up behind her, and raising his fist, he shouted, 'You're asking for it.'

Shangang had just come back. He'd brought a big bag of things with him, and following him there was a small brown dog.

When Shanfeng saw him come in, he lowered his fist, and said to Shangang, 'Tell her to fuck off.'

Shangang put the things on the table, went up to his wife and said, 'Go back to the bedroom.'

She looked up, and asked with some curiosity, 'Why don't you hit him?'

Shangang helped her to her feet. 'You should go and lie down.'

She started towards the bedroom, but stopped when she got to the door, looked back and said to Shangang, 'At least hit him.'

Shangang didn't say anything. He began to put the things out on the table. There was a bundle of meat and bones. He heard his wife say once more, 'At least hit him.' Then he knew she was in the bedroom.

At this point Shanfeng sat down on another stool, pointed to the floor, and said to Shangang, 'Clear it up.'

Shangang nodded and said, 'Let's wait a minute.'

'I want you to clear it up now,' said Shanfeng, bursting with anger.

So Shangang went into the kitchen, fetched a dustpan and brush and swept up the broken pieces. Then he picked up the broken stool. He took the rubbish into the yard. When he came back in Shanfeng pointed at the dog which was just coming into the room, and asked Shangang, 'Where's it from?'

'I found it in the street. It followed me all the way here,' answered Shangang.

'Get it out of here,' said Shanfeng.

'All right,' said Shangang. He went towards the dog, bent over to call it, then picked it up and went into the bedroom. When he came out he closed the door tightly. 'Anything else?'

Shanfeng didn't respond. He wasn't about to sit there any longer and got up to go into his own room.

His wife was still sitting in the corner, her eyes on the cradle. Her son was lying there quietly as though he was sleeping. She was watching her son's stomach, and she thought she saw it rising and falling. She thought he was still breathing. Then she heard her husband's footsteps. She raised her head and without knowing why, stood up.

'What are you standing up for?' said Shanfeng as he glanced into the cradle, where the sight of his son sprawled there aroused his predatory instincts. And these thoughts made him sick, so he went to lie down on the bed.

His wife sat down again. Shanfeng was exhausted, and lay on the bed looking out of the window. Beyond the window, he felt, everything was chaos and it was all nothing. His eyes turned back into the room and looked about. He saw his wife, still sitting in the corner, as though she'd been there for years. The sight disgusted him. He sat up and said, 'What are you sitting there for?'

She looked at him fearfully, as if she didn't understand.

He spoke again. 'Don't just sit there.'

She got up immediately, without any idea of what to do next.

He was furious, and yelled at her, 'Don't just fucking sit there.'

At once, she left her corner, and went over to the clothes stand. There was a chair there, but she didn't dare sit down. She was watching her husband carefully, even though he wasn't looking in her direction. By this time Shanfeng was lying down, and his eyes seemed to be closed. She hesitated before sitting down cautiously. Then Shanfeng started up again, 'Stop staring at me.'

She looked away from him at once, and her eyes wandered restlessly all over the room, worried that if she wasn't careful her gaze would stray back to the bed. Then she fixed her gaze on the mirror in front of the wardrobe. The mirror was shimmering, its angle catching the rays of light. She daren't go to look into the cradle, afraid that her eyes would leap from there to the bed. Then she heard that aggressive tone again, 'Stop staring at me.'

Suddenly she stood up, and this time she didn't hesitate or falter. Her gaze went through the door and she followed it out of the room. When she reached the hall she caught sight of Shangang's back disappearing into the bedroom. He looked very substantial from behind, but then disappeared in a flash through the doorway. She looked all around her, then went out into the yard. The light in the yard set her head spinning. She felt dizzy and sat down on the doorstep. Then she saw the two blood stains. She noticed how fresh the blood looked in the sunlight, as though it were still flowing.

Shangang didn't wash the bones. He put them in a pan and then, without adding any other ingredients, took them into the kitchen, poured on a little water, and put the pan on the gas stove to cook. Then he came out of the kitchen and went back into his own room.

Shangang's wife was sitting on the edge of the bed beside her son without looking at him. She was staring out of the window just as Shanfeng had. Outside there were leaves, and her gaze was resting on one of these leaves.

Shangang walked up to the bed, where his son was lying with his head tilted to the right, the wound barely noticeable. It had stopped bleeding, and there was only a small stain on the pillowcase, which looked like part of the printed pattern. He stared at it for a while and then went up and moved his son's head over on the other side, so that the wound was hidden, and the pattern was covered, this piteous pattern.

The little dog nuzzled its way out from under the bed, ran up to his feet, and began playing with his trouser legs. His gaze wandered out of the window and onto a leaf, but not the same one as his wife was staring at. 'Why don't you hit him?' he heard his wife saying. Her voice was quivering like the leaf.

'I just want you to hit him,' she repeated.

4

THE OLD LADY HAD LOCKED the door and climbed gingerly into her bed. She stuffed her quilt under her pillow, so that when she lay down her upper body would be raised up high. She did this to prevent her rotten gut from creeping up into her chest. She had decided not to eat any more, because it would be really dangerous to do so. She was quite clear that by now there was hardly any space left in her body. So, to stop her rotten gut from swilling about all over the place inside her, she didn't move once she was lying down. She couldn't hear any noises at all and was pleased about that. She was no longer loaded down with worries but was actually rather satisfied with her own intelligence. She stared at the light on the ceiling from morning to evening, watching as it expanded and grew smaller. As far as she was concerned now only the light was living, everything else was dead.

Next day at the crack of dawn, as Shanfeng awoke he felt a terrible ache in his head. The pain made him feel as though it was going to burst. He sat up and the pain seemed to ease a little, but his head still seemed to be in danger of swelling and bursting and he knew he had to do something about it. He got out of bed, went over to the chest of drawers and took out a white cloth from the top drawer. After he'd wrapped it round his head, he felt much more secure. Then he began to get dressed.

As he was putting on his clothes he noticed the black armband on his sleeve. Then he remembered that yesterday afternoon Shangang had come in carrying an armband. At the time he was still lying on the bed. Although the pain in his head was unbearable, he remembered Shangang considerately helping him put on the armband. He remembered roaring at Shangang with absolute fury, so furious that he'd forgotten what he was roaring about. Later, Shangang had gone out and borrowed a wheelbarrow, which he'd left outside the yard gate. He hadn't seen Shangang carrying Pipi outside, he'd only seen him come in and pick his son up from the cradle. He'd followed after them. He trailed along after the wheelbarrow, and he remembered that his wife and sister-in-law had also accompanied the barrow. Just then he felt the pain in his head. He remembered swearing and cursing all the way, but all he'd been cursing was the sunlight, which all but knocked him off balance. He'd walked the length of the street and then walked back again. He seemed to have bumped into a lot of people he knew in the street, yet he hadn't recognised anyone. It was odd the way they'd closed in around him, and their voices seemed like a flock of sparrows chattering together. He noticed Shangang answering their questions. Shangang looked as though nothing had happened, but he was very serious all the same. It was dusk by the time they got back home. By then the two children were already inside the urns. He remembered seeing two chimneys towering upwards in the distance. Then he'd walked for a long time, across a bridge, into an expansive park land filled with bright, green pines and cypresses. A group of people emerged, weeping and wailing. It made him sick. Then he was standing in a large hall, where there were only the four of them. Since they were the only ones there the hall seemed particularly large, almost the size of a town square. He stood for a long time before hearing some very familiar music, which made him sleepy. By the time the music had finished he was no longer drowsy, and at that moment Shangang turned, looked at him, and said something. Something he'd understood, something about the two children. He heard Shangang saying, '… due to two unfortunate accidents.' It was a farce. Much later, long after night had fallen, he returned to where he was now. He lay down on his bed, and as he closed his eyes he felt a swarm of bees flying into his head, buzzing wildly inside, where they stayed the whole night. Only after he'd woken did they vanish. But his head was in terrible pain.

He was already dressed, and was standing by the bed when he saw Shangang walk in, and promptly sat back down on the bed. He saw Shangang smiling at him tenderly, Shangang taking a chair and sitting down close to him.

Shangang had gone into the kitchen immediately after getting up. The two women were already busy making breakfast. They were silent as usual, as though nothing had happened, or as though everything that had happened was already long past, no longer on their minds. Shangang went into the kitchen and took the lid off his pan. The bones had boiled down to a thick soup and their powerful aroma rushed out from under the lid. Satisfied, he went out of the kitchen with the little dog sticking close to his heels. The smell pouring out of yesterday's pan had it yapping non-stop, and this yapping seemed to give Shangang some peace of mind. Now the dog was glued to him, which further eased his anxieties.

Shangang emerged from the kitchen, sat down at the dining table, put the dog on to his lap, and said to it, 'I'll be asking you for some help in a minute.' Then he screwed up his eyes and looked out of the window, wondering whether or not to let Shanfeng have his breakfast first. The little dog was very still on Shangang's lap. He thought about it for some time and then decided not to let him have breakfast. 'What's the use of having breakfast?' he said to himself. Then he stood up, put the dog down on the floor, and went over towards Shanfeng's bedroom, with the little dog following on behind.

Shanfeng's door wasn't locked, so Shangang pushed it open and went in. The dog followed him. He saw Shanfeng looking pale and tired as he stood by the bed, his head wrapped in a white cloth. Shanfeng saw his brother come in and fell back down on the bed, as though his body had just been dropped down onto its rear end. Shangang pulled up a chair and sat down. The moment he'd opened the door and come in, Shangang sensed that everything was going to go smoothly. He was thinking, 'Shanfeng's finished.'

To Shanfeng, he said, 'I gave you my son. Now who are you going to give me?'

Shanfeng looked at him blankly for a long time, then, frowning, he asked, 'What do you mean?'

'Simple,' said Shangang, 'give me your wife.'

167

Shanfeng remembered that his own son was dead, and that Pipi was dead too. He felt there was something peculiar about these two deaths. But he really couldn't make out what it was. He was so exhausted. He knew that whatever it was, it connected the deaths of the two children.

So Shanfeng said, 'But my son died too.'

'That's different,' said Shangang decisively.

Shanfeng was confused. He knew that his son's death was a different matter, unconnected with Pipi's death. Pipi, he remembered, had died after he kicked him. But why had he done it? And again, he couldn't work it out. He didn't want to go on thinking like this. It would only make him even more confused. He thought Shangang had just asked him something, and he asked, 'What did you just say?'

'Give me your wife,' answered Shangang.

Shanfeng rested his head wearily on the bedstead and asked, 'What are you going to do to her?'

'I think I'll tie her up under the tree,' Shangang pointed to the tree outside the window, 'for an hour.'

Shanfeng drew back his head and stared outside for a while. He felt that the glistening of the leaves in the sunlight was unbearable. He turned back to Shangang, 'And afterwards?'

'There's no afterwards,' said Shangang.

'All right,' said Shanfeng. He wanted to nod, but he hadn't any strength. Then he added, 'But tie me up instead.'

Shangang smiled. He knew it would be like this. He asked Shanfeng, 'Would you like some breakfast first?'

'I don't feel like eating,' said Shanfeng.

'Then let's not waste any time,' said Shangang as he stood up. Shanfeng stood up as well. His body weighed heavily as though it was filled with silt. He said to Shangang, 'I think I'm about to die.' Shangang looked back at him and said, 'That makes a certain amount of sense.'

The two of them walked out of the room, then Shangang went into his bedroom, and came back with two ropes in his hand. He gave them to Shanfeng, asking, 'Do you think they'll do?'

Shanfeng took them, found them heavy, and answered, 'Aren't they too heavy?'

'They won't be heavy when they're tied around you,' said Shangang.

'Maybe not.' Shanfeng was now able to nod in agreement.

Then the two of them went out into the yard. The sunlight was dazzling, and Shanfeng felt heaven and earth spinning around him. He said to Shangang, 'I'm losing my balance.'

Shangang pointed to the tree in front of them and said, 'Then go and sit down in the shade under the tree.'

'But it's so far away,' said Shanfeng.

'It's very close. Only two or three metres away.' Shangang supported Shanfeng as he spoke, and helped him over to the tree. Then he pushed him downwards and Shanfeng collapsed, his bottom half falling against the tree trunk.

'That's much better,' he said.

'It'll be even more comfortable in a moment.'

'Really?' Shanfeng was straining to look up at Shangang.

'In a moment you'll be laughing away,' said Shangang.

Shanfeng smiled wearily. 'Will you help me sit up, then?'

'Of course I will,' answered Shangang.

Then Shanfeng felt the rope winding around his chest, tighter and tighter, pulling him against the tree trunk. He was finding it hard to breathe and said, 'It's too tight.'

'You'll get used to it,' said Shangang as he finished tying up Shanfeng's upper body.

Shanfeng felt like he had been wrapped up. He said to Shangang, 'It feels like I'm wearing too many clothes.'

Shangang had already gone inside. A moment later he came out again carrying a wooden board and the pan from the kitchen. He went back to Shanfeng. The little dog followed him and was circling round and round Shanfeng.

'Would you feel my forehead for me?' asked Shanfeng.

Shangang put his hand out to feel it.

'It's hot, isn't it?' asked Shanfeng.

'Yes,' answered Shangang, 'forty centigrade.'

'That's for sure,' Shanfeng was quick to agree.

Shangang was kneeling down now, placing the wooden board under Shanfeng's legs. Then, with another rope, he tied the board on to them.

'What are you doing?' asked Shanfeng.

'Giving you a massage,' replied Shangang.

'You should be massaging my temples.'

'All right.' Shangang had just finished tying up the two legs securely. He stood up and gave Shanfeng a quick massage on the temples with his thumbs, and asked, 'How's that?'

'Much better. More.'

Shangang stepped forward, then bent over and began to give him a proper massage.

Shanfeng felt Shangang's thumbs twisting into his temples, and felt very contented. Then he noticed the two red stains stretched out on the cement in front of him. He asked Shangang, 'What's that?'

Shangang answered, 'Stains from Pipi's blood.'

'And the other one?' It seemed he thought that one of the stains was not Pipi's blood.

'That's Pipi's too,' said Shangang.

Shanfeng thought he might have got it wrong, so he didn't say anything more. After a while he said, 'You know, Shangang... ?'

'Know what?'

'... I was really scared yesterday, after kicking Pipi, and killing him, I was really scared.'

'You're not scared of anything,' said Shangang.

'No,' Shanfeng shook his head, 'I was truly frightened, particularly when I handed you the cleaver.'

Shangang stopped massaging, and gave his brother's face an affectionate pat, saying, 'You're not scared of anything.'

Hearing this, a smile crept on to Shanfeng's face and he said, 'You don't believe me.'

As he said this Shangang knelt down and started taking off Shanfeng's socks.

'What are you doing?' Shanfeng asked him.

'Taking off your socks for you,' answered Shangang.

'What on earth for?'

This time Shangang gave no reply. After he'd removed Shanfeng's socks, he took the lid off the pot, and smeared the stewed bones on to the soles of his feet. The little dog smelt it and came running over.

'What are you putting on my feet?' Shanfeng asked.

'Cooling ointment,' said Shangang.

'You're doing it wrong again,' laughed Shanfeng. 'You should be rubbing it into my temples.'

'All right.' Shangang brushed the little dog away with his hand, scooped out of the pot what looked like two handfuls of mud and smeared them on to Shanfeng's temples. Then he put the lid back on the pot. Shanfeng's face looked grossly made up.

'You look like a playboy,' said Shangang.

Shanfeng felt something sliding slowly down his face. 'This isn't cooling ointment, is it?' he said. Then he tried to stretch out his legs, but they were tied to the wooden board and he couldn't move them. He said, 'I'm so tired.'

'Have a little sleep,' said Shangang. 'It's half seven now, and I'll come and untie you at half eight.'

Just then the two women appeared at the door. Shangang noticed them looking on calmly. Then he heard a scream high and loud enough to whistle through your bones and get your hair standing on end. He saw his sister-in-law rush up and grab his clothes. He heard her yelling at him, 'What are trying to do?' 'It's nothing to do with you,' he answered.

She was dumb struck for a moment, then shouted, 'Let him go.'

Shangang chuckled, and said, 'You'll have to let go of me first.'

As soon as she'd loosened her grip, he pushed her away with such force that she fell to the ground. Then Shangang looked at his wife, who was still standing there, and smiled at her. He saw that she was smiling back. When he turned his head back, the little dog had started to make its way over to Shanfeng's feet.

Shanfeng saw his wife come rushing out of the house. He noticed how her body seemed to glisten and shine as though it was covered in lights, how it swayed and rocked like a boat. He thought he heard her yelling something, and then saw Shangang push her to the ground. His wife looked so funny as she fell over. Then he felt some stiffness in his neck and tried to move his head a little. He noticed once more the two blood stains as he had a moment before. He saw how close together they were, how they both glistened in the sunlight, how a few drops of blood from each place had run out from the pools and joined together. It was then that he remembered, remembered that the other stain wasn't Pipi's but his son's, remembered that it was Pipi who had dropped his son and killed him. He found the answer to his question, why he had killed Pipi by kicking him. He realised that Shangang was tricking him, and he shouted, 'Let me go!' But Shangang didn't answer, and shouted again, 'Let me go.'

However it was also just at this moment that a strange feeling began to rise slowly up through his feet, creeping upwards more and more quickly, until, in no time, it had reached the pit of stomach. He called out a third time but Shangang didn't appear, and he couldn't help bowing his head and starting to laugh for all he was worth. He wanted to pull in his legs, but he couldn't bend them. All he could do was move them up and down. Although his body felt as if it was twisting up in convulsions, he hadn't moved. His head was shaking enough to make you dizzy just looking at him. Shanfeng's laughter was like two pieces of aluminium rattling together.

Shangang seemed to be in fine form. To Shanfeng, he said, 'You look so happy.' Then he turned back to his wife and said, 'I'm a little envious, seeing him so happy.' His wife wasn't looking at him; her eyes were fixed on the little dog, which was greedily licking the soles of Shanfeng's bare feet. He thought that his wife looked just as greedy as the little dog. Then he went to have another look at his sister-in-law who was still sitting on the ground, utterly confused by Shanfeng's strange laughter. She was staring at him blankly as he laughed like a madman. She wasn't quite all there anymore, since she couldn't make head nor tail of what was going on.

Shanfeng no longer had the strength to move his legs or shake his head. All his strength was going into his neck and throat, straining with the crazy laughter. The tickling of the dog as it licked the soles of his feet had him laughing so much he barely had any chance to breathe.

Shangang was looking on attentively the whole time, and now asked him, 'What on earth can be so funny?'

Shanfeng answered him with more laughter, which was now coming out in hiccoughs. It sounded as though the laughter was being shaken out of his mouth in ones and twos. At every shake he was able to draw in a little gasp of air. The hiccoughs sounded like a whistle in a sports ground, with a strong piercing rhythm.

Shangang said to his wife who was standing by the door, 'I've never seen anyone look so happy.' His wife was still eagerly watching the little dog. He went on, 'He's so happy he doesn't even need to breathe.' Then he leant over and said to Shanfeng, 'What is it that's so funny?' Now the strong rhythm in the laughter had stopped and the sound had become disjointed. Shangang stood and addressed his sister-in-law, 'He won't tell me.' Shanfeng's wife was still sitting on the ground, and from the look on her face you'd imagine she was far away.

Then the little dog drew its tongue back into its mouth, arched its back and gave a good few shakes. He sat back as though pleased with the work he'd done. His eyes looked towards the two feet, then at Shangang.

Shangang saw that Shanfeng's head had drooped, but that he was still breathing. Shangang said, 'You can tell me now … what was it that was so funny?' But Shanfeng didn't respond, he was struggling to breathe. He seemed to be gasping for his last breath. Shangang walked over to the pot, took the lid off, scooped out another handful, and smeared it over Shanfeng's feet. The dog immediately rushed up and carried on licking.

Shanfeng didn't laugh out loud any more, the 'mmm mmm' coming from his drooping head sounded like the wind blowing through
the lane in the middle of the night. The sound grew longer and longer,
until it hardly paused at all. Not long afterwards, Shanfeng's head
suddenly bolted up straight, and his laughter became a mad explosive
convulsion. This lasted nearly a minute, then stopped with a wheeze.
Shanfeng's head dropped down, and hung there on his chest. The dog
carried on licking away at his feet to it's heart's content.

Shangang went up, stretched his hand out under Shanfeng's chin.
He found the head particularly heavy. As he lifted it he saw a face con-
torted and strained. He stared at it for a while before letting it go, so
that it swung back down to hang against Shanfeng's chest. Shangang
glanced at his watch. Only forty minutes had passed. He turned and
went inside. He stopped on the doorstep, and heard his wife asking, 'Is
he dead?'

'Yes,' he answered.

Inside the room he sat down at the dining table. Breakfast was like a
guard of honour awaiting his arrival. As usual it consisted of rice porridge and cold noodles. His wife walked in. She was watching him,
but she didn't sit down beside him, and she didn't say anything. From
the look on her face you couldn't have said that anything had happened. She went into the bedroom.

Shangang looked out through the open door to where Shanfeng's
body was sitting. He looked as though he'd just nodded off. A dark
shadow slid towards Shanfeng and his sister-in-law appeared in his line
of vision. Shangang saw her standing beside the body for a long while
before leaning closer. She seemed to be talking with Shanfeng. After a
while he saw her get up and look all around as though she didn't know
what to do next. Her gaze ventured in through the doorway and struck
his face. She stared at him like that for a while and then moved towards him. She walked right up to him, furrowing her brow as she
watched him, as though she was looking at something disagreeable.
Finally she spoke, 'You've murdered my husband.'

Shangang found her voice as penetrating as Shanfeng's laughter. He
didn't answer.

'You've killed my husband,' she said again.

'No I haven't.' This time Shangang answered.

'You've murdered my husband.' She grit her teeth as she spoke.

'No I haven't,' said Shangang, 'all I did was tie him up, I did not
kill him.'

'Yes you did!' she screamed, her nerves jangling.

Shangang went on, 'I didn't do anything. It was the dog.'

'I'm going to denounce you.' She began to cry.

'That would be a false accusation,' said Shangang, 'and it is an offence to make a false accusation.' He smiled.

She seemed unable to decide what to do next. She looked at Shangang with puzzlement. After a long time she said quietly, 'I'm going to denounce you.' She turned and walked out of the door.

Shangang watched her every step as she left. She stood for a moment at Shanfeng's side, then raised her hand to wipe the tears from her eyes. Shangang thought, '*Now* she's crying.' She went out through the courtyard gate.

Shangang's wife emerged from the bedroom. She was holding a bulging black bag. She put the bag down on the table and said to Shangang, 'There's a set of clean clothes and all our cash in here.'

Shangang seemed not to understand what she meant. He looked at her blankly.

So she added, 'You've got to run.'

Shangang nodded in agreement. He glanced at his watch. There was still one minute left before half eight. He said, 'I'll get up in one minute.' He carried on watching Shanfeng sitting there beneath the tree, still looking as if he'd just nodded off. He noticed his wife sitting opposite him.

He didn't look at his watch before standing up, he just felt that a minute had passed. He walked out of the yard. By this time the little dog had licked Shanfeng's feet clean and had moved on to his temples. Shangang walked up to them and gently kicked the little dog aside, then squatted down. First he undid the rope binding Shanfeng's legs, then the rope around his body. After that he stood up and left. He hadn't taken more than a few steps when he heard a heavy thud behind him. He looked round to see Shanfeng's body had fallen over on to the ground. He walked back and propped Shanfeng up once more against the tree. Finally he walked out of the yard.

He went out into the lane, which was dark and gloomy, as if it was going to rain. But when he looked up he saw the dazzling sun. That seemed strange to him. He kept on walking straight ahead, aware that other people were passing him on either side, like the blades of a slowly turning electric fan, flicking past him, one by one.

When he had walked as far as the fish stall he stopped. Inside there were a few people smoking and chatting. He said to them, 'The stench is unbearable.' But no one took a blind bit of notice, so he said it again. This time someone opened their mouth, 'Then what are you

standing there for?' Shangang didn't move. They began to laugh. He
frowned and said, 'The stench is unbearable.' He stood there for some
time after speaking. Then he lost interest and carried on walking
straight ahead.

When he came to the end of the lane he started dithering. He
couldn't decide which way to turn. The main road lay before him,
complete confusion. He saw people and bicycles and buses and trac-
tors and handcarts all jammed together like a crowd scrambling to buy
tickets for the cinema. Then he noticed a cobbler sitting at the base of
a lamppost repairing shoes, and he went over to him. He stared at him
in silence for a while, then lifted his leather-soled shoe and asked him
what he thought of the leather. The cobbler gave it a quick glance and
answered, 'Nothing special.' The answer clearly didn't satisfy him, and
he informed the cobbler it was in fact no lesser stuff than cattle hide.
The cobbler told him that it was not cattle hide, but pigskin with a
good shine on it. This was a great disappointment to him, so he
marched off.

He was now heading west, walking on the pavement, scared of the
bicycles, buses and everything else on the road. Even in the middle of
the pavement he walked with great caution, so as to avoid being
knocked over by other people, in case, like his brother, he'd never be
able to get up again. He hadn't been walking for long when he came
to a public toilet, and since he was just needing a piss he went in.
Inside there were a few men standing by the shit-hole pissing away
contentedly. He squeezed his way in, took his thing out and aimed for
the hole. He stood like that for a long time, but all he could hear was
the sound of the other people pissing. He couldn't understand why
nothing would come out. More people kept coming and going on either side of him, yet he was still standing there. Finally he woke up
and told himself, 'I didn't come in for a piss after all.' He went back
out, still walking on the pavement. But he'd forgotten to put his thing
away, so there it was, out in the open, shaking along to the rhythm of
his stride, so smug. He kept on walking along. At first no one noticed.
It was only after he passed the cinema that it was spotted by some
young people coming towards him. He saw them suddenly curl up like
prawns and begin laughing out loud, just like Shanfeng. When he was
past them he heard them shouting in voices broken up with laughter,
'Get a look at that!' But he didn't catch on and kept walking. Finally
he began to notice that everyone changed their expression the instant
they saw him, collapsing with laughter and falling about all over the
place. A few women ran off as fast as they could as though they'd just

seen a mugger. He thought it all very amusing, and started laughing himself.

He walked along like this until he came to a stop at a building site. He looked the shell of the building up and down for quite a while before walking in. It felt damp inside, but he liked the place. Inside there were many rooms, all without doors. He looked into the rooms one after the other, then decided to go into one. It was a fairly dark room. He went and sat down in a corner. He leant back against the wall, felt he could take a rest now in peace and quiet. He was exhausted. So he closed his eyes and fell asleep.

Three hours later he was woken with a shove. He saw several armed guards standing in front of him. One of them said, 'Would you please put that thing away.'

5

ONE MONTH LATER Shangang was tied up in an open-topped truck surrounded by a group of armed guards, guns on their shoulders, as though they were protecting him. He saw people everywhere, gathering together like sparrows, straining get a look at him. And when he lowered his head to look at *them*, he had the impression that their faces had all been painted on. Just then the two guards' vans in front let out a sound like the north-west wind and began to move forward, but the truck just gave out a couple of farts and wouldn't budge. By this point Shangang knew what was going to happen. He'd been waiting for this ever since he was woken up on the building site. Now the time had come. He turned to one of the guards and said, 'Could you make it quick.'

The guard's eyes were fixed straight ahead, and he didn't answer. So Shangang looked around, turned to face another guard and said, 'Shoot me now.' The guard was indifferent.

Shangang saw a river of bicycles flowing along in front of him. The truck shook a few times, then he felt the wind rushing past his ears, and saw the dense flow of bicycles part to both sides in an orderly fashion. The leaves of the trees leaning out over the road slapped him in the face a few times. Not long afterwards a stretch of rough grass came into his line of vision and he knew he would soon be standing in the middle of this green field. At the same time as the green expanse came into view so also did a crowd of people standing there like wild grass. And he also noticed an ambulance, parked near the green strip. Both sides of the road were cluttered with bicycles, leaning every which way all over the place. He had a sense that the ambulance had come for him. He thought that perhaps if one shot left him only half dead, the ambulance would take him to the hospital to save his life. As he thought about this, the truck juddered again, and his ribcage was thrust hard against the rails on the truck. He didn't feel any pain. Then he felt someone tugging at him, and he turned around. He saw some of the guards jumping down from the truck, and he too jumped when he was pushed. He found himself kneeling on the ground, then he was hauled back on to his feet. He had the impression that he was being moved forward by the people around him, that the top half of his body — tied round with ropes — was losing consciousness. His legs were swaying for no apparent reason. He seemed to be seeing many, many things, but at the same time there was nothing in front of him. As he walked forward he became absent, vacant. Moments later hands gripped him. He could no longer move forward. He came to a stop.

He stood there with a look of bewilderment. The long grass at his feet was poking its way into his trouser legs, and he felt it tickling. He looked down, but he couldn't see anything. He could only raise his head again, a comical expression spreading over his face. Gradually he became aware of a clamour of voices, and the noise revealed the crowd all around, standing there like tall grass. And then, as though waking from a dream, he remembered once more where he was. He knew that in no time his head would be blown apart, blown to bits.

Now he remembered, remembered that long, long ago he used to come here quite often. Nearly every time a criminal was executed he would rush to the front row to watch. But this was the first time he'd stood in this place, and it felt extraordinary to be standing here now. His eyes searched for the other places where he used to stand before, but he couldn't see them. Suddenly he needed a piss, so he said to one of the guards, 'I want to have a piss.'

'All right,' the guard answered.

'Could you help me get it out?' he said.

'Just piss in your trousers,' said the guard.

It seemed that everyone was laughing at him on all sides. He couldn't understand why they seemed to be having such a good time. He moved his legs apart, and his face creased up slightly.

After a while the guard asked, 'Finished?'

'It won't come out,' he said painfully.

'Then forget it,' the guard said.

177

He nodded assent, then looked into the distance. His glance floated away, on over the hair of a short person, past the ears of a tall one, to the paved road laid out like an artery. He felt someone kick him behind the knee, and he slumped to kneeling position on the ground. He could no longer see the blood-coloured road.

A guard standing behind him raised his automatic rifle, and took aim. Then the 'bang' rang out.

Shangang's body somersaulted at the sound of the shot. Terrified, he stood up, and staring at the people all around him, asked, 'Am I dead?'

No one answered him, everyone was laughing out loud, and the sound saturated the air like thunder and rain. Then he lost his senses and began to sob and wail uncontrollably, since he didn't know if he was dead or alive. His ear had been shot off, and the blood was pouring out. He asked again, 'Am I dead?'

This time someone answered, 'You're not dead yet.'

Shangang was surprised and happy, and he yelled as loud as he could, 'Get me to a hospital quickly.' Then he felt a foot behind his knee, and he was kneeling on the ground again. He still hadn't worked it all out, when the second gun appeared.

The second gun pressed against the nape of Shangang's neck. This time there was no somersault, only his head hitting the ground heavily. His rear end was the bit of him standing proud. He still wasn't dead, and his rear end wouldn't stop shivering, as though he was freezing with cold.

The guard took a step forward, put the gun barrel to Shangang's head, and fired a third shot. It was as though someone had kicked him in the stomach. His body flipped over on to its back. His two bound hands were buried underneath, but his legs began twitching. Finally, they too lay still and limp on the ground.

## 6

EARLY THAT MORNING Shangang's wife had seen someone walk in, with only half a head. Dawn was just breaking. She remembered having locked the door securely, but the way he came in convinced her that the door must still have been open. Although he had only half a head, she still knew at a glance that it was none other than Shangang.

'I've been released,' he said.

His voice sounded hoarse, and she asked, 'Have you got a cold?'

'Maybe,' he answered.

She remembered that there were some fast-acting cold capsules in the drawer, and asked him if he wanted one.

He shook his head, and said he didn't have a cold. He was all right, it was just that he didn't know where the other half of his head was.

She asked if the other half of his head hadn't been blown off by a bullet.

He said that he couldn't remember, and sat down on a chair. Once he'd sat down, he said he was hungry. Could she give him some money to go and buy some breakfast. She took out some ration tickets and a one *yuan* note and gave them to him. He took the money, stood up and went out. He didn't shut the door as he went, so she got up to close it after him. She discovered that the door had been tightly shut after all. She didn't think it at all strange, and undressed to go to bed.

There was the sound of solitary footsteps, the sound of someone walking towards the end of the lane. It was about this time that she woke up, just as dawn was breaking, and she saw that the room was beginning to get lighter. Everything was quiet. She could hear the sound very clearly, as though it were someone walking out of her dreams — she had this distinct impression that the sound of the footsteps was walking out of her dreams, then out of the room, and had now all but left the lane.

She began to get dressed, and the sound of the footsteps faded away. She went over to the window, and when she opened the curtains the sunlight came flooding in, still fresh and flushed with the dawn. Soon afterwards it turned the yellowish colour of a hepatitis sufferer. She folded up the bedding, sat at the dressing table, looked at her face in the mirror, found it dull and lifeless. So she got up and went out of the bedroom. In the other room she saw Shanfeng's wife was already eating breakfast. She went into the kitchen to make her own. She lit the gas, then moved one side where she brushed her teeth and washed her face.

Five minutes later she brought her breakfast out and sat down opposite her sister-in-law, silently beginning to eat. Her sister-in-law stood up and went into the kitchen. She'd finished. She could hear the noise of her washing up in the kitchen. Soon she appeared again and went into the bedroom. Finally she emerged, locked the door behind her and went out.

Shangang's wife carried on eating her breakfast. She found it difficult. She had no appetite. Her eyes stared out of the window towards the tree, which now looked as if it was made of plastic. She kept on staring. Then she remembered something, turned her gaze back into the room and began to look around. She remembered that she hadn't seen her mother-in-law for several days. Her gaze alighted on the lock to her mother-in-law's door. But after a while it shifted again, back to the tree outside.

On the morning of the sixth day after Shanfeng's death, the old lady also passed away quite suddenly. That morning when she'd woken she felt unusually excited. She could even feel the excitement flowing inside her. At the same time she could feel her body itself dying bit by bit. She sensed quite distinctly that her heel was the first to go, then both feet, followed by her legs. She felt her feet as if they frozen to death, like ice or snow, silent and breathless. Death hesitated for a moment in her lower stomach, then rushed like the tide up to her waist, and having gushed up that far, it began to spread out indiscriminately. She felt her hands leaving her far behind, and her head like it was being bitten by a little dog. In the end all that remained was her heart, but death had already surrounded her heart, as though countless ants were crawling on to it from every direction. There was a stinging in her heart. When she opened her eyes she saw endless rays of light streaming towards her through the curtains. She couldn't help smiling, and then the smile fixed on her face as on a photograph.

Obviously, Shanfeng's wife knew that something had happened that morning. She got out of bed very early, and was now already going out of the lane, towards the main street. The sun was just beginning to yellow. She knew exactly where she wanted to go. She was heading for the Tianning Temple, because beside the temple was the detention centre. That morning Shangang was to be taken out from there.

As she walked along the road she could hear them talking about Shangang. It seemed that many, many people were walking the same way she was. In this town it was over a year since anyone had been executed, so today was something special.

For over a month she'd been going the law court to inquire about Shangang's case. She told them she was Shangang's wife (even though one month before she was the one who made the original complaint as Shanfeng's wife — no one seemed to notice). She had been doing this right up until the day before yesterday before they told her what would happen today. She was satisfied, she told them, she wished to offer Shangang's body to the country. When the people in the law court heard this they weren't exactly delighted, but they agreed nonetheless. She knew the doctors *would* be delighted. As she walked along the street, she began to imagine how the doctors would carve him up, and the corners of her mouth began to rise into a smile.

7

IN THE MIDDLE OF THE ROOM where the dissection was soon to take place, there hung a thousand watt electric lamp. The lamp was on and it flooded the room with light. Beneath the light were two table-tennis tables, already old and shabby. Under the tables was a dirt floor. A group of doctors from Shanghai and Hangzhou were standing at the door chatting, waiting for the ambulance to arrive. Then their work would begin.

For the moment they looked relaxed and carefree. Not far away there was a pool, with water plants floating on the surface, surrounded by willows. By the side of the pool was a strip of glistening golden rape. In surroundings like these the conversation is, quite naturally, relaxed and carefree.

The ambulance drove down the dirt track, raising a pall of dust behind it. It drove right up to the doctors. They turned round to look. As the back door opened, someone jumped down, turned and pulled two legs out of the ambulance, followed by the body. Another man grabbed hold of Shangang's arms and jumped down too. The two of them carried Shangang inside as if he were a sack.

The doctors carried on chatting by the door, as though they were more interested in their conversation — which was about prices — than they were in Shangang. The two men came out again. These two often went to the hospital to sell their own blood for ready cash. But they couldn't get away just yet; they still had things to do. In a while they'd have to dig a trench and bury Shangang. By then he'd be nothing more than fat, muscle, hair, teeth and anything else the doctors didn't want. They went over to sit by the side of the pool. They were pleased with their day's work, since in a short while they'd be paid, out of someone else's pocket into theirs.

The doctors stood a little longer at the door, then drifted in one by one, each with his or her own bag. They started to get changed, putting on their robes, their caps and masks, and last of all their surgical gloves. Then they began to prepare their instruments.

Shangang was lying on his back on the table-tennis tables, already stripped of his clothes by the two men. His naked body, lying under the thousand watt bulb, glistened as though it was covered in paint.

The first doctor walked over, without any surgical apparatus, because he was going to be left with Shangang's skeleton. He'd have to wait while the others skinned Shangang and emptied the rest of his body. So he seemed quite casual in his approach. He looked Shangang all over, then put out his hand to pinch his arm and calf. He turned to the others and said, 'He's tough.'

A doctor in her thirties from Shanghai, wearing high heels, was the second to go over to Shangang. The ground was uneven, so that as she walked over her bottom swung rather more than normal. She positioned herself to Shangang's right. She didn't pinch his arm, but moved her hand over the skin on his chest, then turned and said to the first doctor, 'Not bad.'

Next she picked up her scalpel, and inserted the blade into his sternum below the neck. The knife moved down in a straight line, at which other doctor gasped in admiration. She said, 'I learnt how to draw a line without a ruler during geometry at middle school.' The long knife was cutting the body open like a melon, and the fat inside shone a golden colour. All over the fat tissue there were little red spots. The female doctor picked up a long scalpel shaped like a double-edged sword and inserted it under the skin, and began working it back and forth to free the skin. In no time, the skin was cut away from Shangang's body and lay like a piece of cloth just covering it. Again she took up the scalpel and began to remove more skin on his arms. She ran the knife from the top of his shoulders to the back of his hand. Afterwards she went to work on his legs, from a muscle near his abdomen down to the tops of his feet. When this was done she inserted the long scalpel and worked it back and forth. She rested a few moments, then said to the doctor beside her, 'Could you turn him over please.' The doctor turned Shangang over. Then she drew another straight line down Shangang's back, and again moved the long scalpel back and forth. By this time Shangang looked as though he were covered head to foot in bolts of cloth. She put down the long scalpel and took up the shorter one to cut apart the pieces of skin where they joined. Finally Shangang's skin was gathered together, piece by piece, like bits of scrap are bundled up. After the skin on his back had been lifted away, they turned Shangang over again, and soon Shangang's front was skinned clean as well.

Without the skin around it, the gold coloured fat started to slacken. At first it was like cotton, rising up in bumps, then it began to drift, and ooze like soft mud. The doctors seemed to see rape flowers in the sun as they had done a moment before at the door.

The female doctor carried Shangang's skin to the corner of the table-tennis table, and began to cut it into strips. Then, using the long knife, she scraped the fat off, as though she were brushing clothes. The noise was like the wheel of a car turning in the sand.

Several days later Shangang's skin was used to patch up a victim of extensive burns. But in three days the grafts still hadn't taken, so his skin was thrown into the rubbish, and finally into the hospital cesspit.

The doctors who'd been standing by approached. There were two who didn't squeeze in on the right but came over on the left. However, since they couldn't reach from that side, they climbed up on to the table-tennis tables where they squatted as they carved Shangang up. The thoracic surgeon sliced through the cartilage where the sinews of his chest met and cut open the chest at both sides to reveal his lungs. As soon as the doctor hovering over the abdomen had cut away the fat tissue and the muscle, the intestines, liver, and kidneys he needed came clearly into sight. The ophthalmologist had just taken out one of Shangang's eyeballs. The stomatologist had destroyed Shangang's face and mouth with his scalpel. Both upper and lower jawbones were exposed. But he noticed that the upper jaw had been damaged by a bullet. It disappointed him no end, and he mumbled, 'If only they'd done this to his eyes instead.' If the bullet had entered a fraction higher, the upper jaw would have been left unscathed, but the eyes would have been messed up. The doctor who was removing Shangang's other eye smiled when he heard this, and suggested to the stomatologist that the executioner may have had an ophthalmologist for a father. He was so smug about it. As he was lifting out the second eyeball, he saw the stomatologist struggling as he sawed away at the lower jaw, and said to him, 'So long, sawbones.' The eye doctor was the first to leave. He had to get back to Hangzhou that afternoon, and carry out a corneal transplant on a patient that very evening. Then the woman doctor finished cutting the skin, folded it up like pieces of laundry, and left.

The thoracic surgeon had removed the lungs, and had happily cut Shangang's pulmonary artery and pulmonary vein, the aorta, and all the blood vessels and nerves leading from the heart. As he cut he felt particularly contented, because when he was performing operations on living people he had to be so careful and hold back so that he always felt constrained. Now he was operating extravagantly, with great pleasure. He said to the doctor standing beside him, 'I feel like money's no object.' The doctor standing beside him thought it a pretty speech.

The urologist had been pacing anxiously up and down. He hadn't squeezed himself in and so was waiting in the wings. He had the word 'urine' written on his mask. It really got at this doctor to see them all at the table-tennis tables. He couldn't control the anxiety rising inside him in waves, and kept on telling off the doctor who was dealing with Shangang's abdomen, 'Don't go messing up my balls.'

Shangang's chest was emptied first, followed by his abdominal cavity. A year later Shangang's intestines, liver and lungs — preserved in formaldehyde — would be gawped at by onlookers in a physiognomy exhibition somewhere. His heart and kidneys were used as transplants. The heart transplant was unsuccessful. The patient died on the operating table. However, the kidney transplant was a great success. The patient has been living for over a year now, and from the looks of things, will probably keep going for quite some time. But he's still full of complaints — that the kidney transplant was too expensive, that he'd spent thirty thousand *yuan* on it.

Now there were only three doctors left in the room. When the urologist discovered that his balls were all right after all, he calmly set about removing them. The stomatologist was still sawing at the lower jaw, but the end was in sight. The doctor who was to remove the skeleton was still pacing up and down to one side. The urologist told him, 'You can start now.' But all he said was, 'No hurry.'

The stomatologist and the urologist left together, carrying respectively the lower jaw and the testicles. They would also be doing transplants. The stomatologist would saw away a living patient's lower jaw and refit it with Shangang's. He had absolute confidence in this kind of transplant.

Shangang would have been most proud of his balls. The urologist transplanted them on to a young man who'd had his own crushed in a road accident. Not long afterwards the young man was actually married, and his wife got pregnant straight away. Nine months later she gave birth to a very healthy little boy. Shanfeng's wife would never have anticipated this in a thousand years. Her revenge had twisted back on her, and helped to ensure that Shangang would have his descendants.

The final doctor waited until the others had gone out carrying the lower jaw and the testicles before setting to work. He started at Shangang's feet, cutting the muscle and sinews from the bone. Neatly, he piled everything he cut away on one side. His work was slow, but he had plenty patience to cope with it. When he had worked his way up to the thigh he pinched the thick muscle between his fingers and said to Shangang, 'You may be tough, but by the time I've hung your skeleton up in the lab, you won't even have what it takes to keep the wind out.'

# GLOSSARY OF CHINESE CHARACTERS AND FINDING LIST

| MAGAZINES | ABBREVIATION | | |
|---|---|---|---|
| *Beijing Literature* | BL | 北京文学 | |
| *Harvest* | H | 收获 | |
| *The Purple Mountain* | PM | 钟山 | |
| *Shanghai Literature* | SL | 上海文学 | |

| | | | |
|---|---|---|---|
| A Cheng | *The King of Chess* | 阿城 | 棋王 |
| Avant-Garde Fiction | | 先锋小说 | |
| Bei Cun | | 北村 | |
| Can Xue | 'Mountain Cabin' | 残雪 | 山上的小屋 |
| ———— | *The Muddy Street* | | 黄泥街 |
| Chen Cun | | 陈村 | |
| Chen Jiangong | 'Curly' | 陈建功 | 鬈毛 |
| Chi Li | | 池莉 | |
| Duo Duo | | 多多 | |
| Fang Fang | | 方方 | |
| Ge Fei | *The Lost Boat* H 1987.6 | 格非 | 迷舟 |
| Han Shaogong | *Da Da Da* | 韩少功 | 爸爸爸 |
| Hong Feng | *Going to the Funeral* | 洪峰 | 奔丧 |
| ———— | *Not Far from the Pole* | | 极地之侧 |
| ———— | 'The Prairie Song' | | 勃尔支金荒原牧歌 |
| Li Hangyu | 'In a Little Corner of the World' in *Zuihou yige Yulao'er* | 李杭育 | 人间一隅 |
| ———— | *Zuihou yige Yulao'er*, Beijing: Renmin Wenxue Chubanshe, 1985 | | 最后一个渔佬儿 |

| Liu Xihong | *You Can't Change Me* | 刘西鸿 | 你不可改变我 |
|---|---|---|---|
| Liu Zaifu | | 刘再复 | |
| Liu Zhenyun | | 刘震云 | |
| Ma Yuan | *Fabrication* H 1986.5 | 马原 | 虚构 |
| _____ | 'Mistakes' H 1987.1 | | 错误 |
| _____ | *On the Level Up or Down* | | 上下都很平坦 |
| _____ | *The Temptation of the Gangdisi* | | 冈底斯的诱惑 |
| Mo Yan | *Five Dreams* | 莫言 | 五梦记 |
| _____ | *Red Locust* | | 红蝗 |
| | *Red Sorgum* | | 红高粱 |
| New Realist Fiction | | 新现实小说 | |
| *The Purple Mountain (PM)* | | 种山 | |
| Reportage | | 报告文学 | |
| *River Elegy* | | 河殇 | |
| Roots-Seeking Fiction | | 寻根小说 | |
| *Shanghai Literature (SL)* | | 上海文学 | |
| Stray Youth Fiction | | 失落代小说 | |
| Su Tong | *The Escape of 1934* | 苏童 | 一九三四年的 逃亡 |
| Sun Ganlu | | 孙甘露 | |
| Trashi Dawa | | 札西达娃 | |
| Wang Shuo | *Leader of the Pack* | 王朔 | 顽主 |
| _____ | *Half Fire, Half Sea Water* | | 一半是火焰 一半是海水 |
| _____ | *Playing Heartbeat* | | 玩的是心跳 |
| _____ | *Whatever You Do, Don't Take Me Seriously* | | 千万别把我当人 |
| Wen Yuhong | 'The Mad City' PM 1988.6 | 温雨虹 | 疯狂的城市 |
| Wu Bin | *City Monologue* | 吴滨 | 城市独白 |
| Xu Xing | 'Variations Without a Theme' | 徐星 | 无主题变奏 |
| Yang Zhengguang | 'The Dry Ravine' SL 1988.4 | 杨争光 | 干沟 |

| | | | |
|---|---|---|---|
| Wu Bin | *City Monologue* | 吴滨 | 城市独白 |
| Xu Xing | 'Variations Without a Theme' | 徐星 | 无主题变奏 |
| Yang Zhengguang | 'The Dry Ravine' *SL* 1988.4 | 杨争光 | 干沟 |
| Yao Fei | | 姚霏 | |
| Ye Shuming | | 叶曙明 | |
| Ye Zhaoyan | *The Story of the Date Tree* | 叶兆言 | 枣树的故事 |
| Yu Hua | '1986' | 余华 | 一九八六年 |
| ———— | *One Kind of Reality* *BL* 1988.1 | | 现实一种 |
| Yue Ling | | 乐陵 | |
| Zhao Botao | | 赵伯涛 | |
| Zheng Wanlong | 'Yellow Smoke' | 郑万隆 | 黄烟 |
| Zheng Yi | | 郑义 | |